# Promises
## on a Ring of Stone

# Promises
## on a Ring of Stone

*"A Novel"*

J. R. Campbell

iUniverse, Inc.
New York Lincoln Shanghai

**Promises on a Ring of Stone**

Copyright © 2006 by Richard J. Campbell

All rights reserved. No part of this book may be used or reproduced by any means, graphic, electronic, or mechanical, including photocopying, recording, taping or by any information storage retrieval system without the written permission of the publisher except in the case of brief quotations embodied in critical articles and reviews.

iUniverse books may be ordered through booksellers or by contacting:

iUniverse
2021 Pine Lake Road, Suite 100
Lincoln, NE 68512
www.iuniverse.com
1-800-Authors (1-800-288-4677)

This is a work of fiction. All of the characters, names, incidents, organizations and dialogue in this novel are either the products of the author's imagination or are used fictitiously.

ISBN-13: 978-0-595-39202-5 (pbk)
ISBN-13: 978-0-595-83593-5 (ebk)
ISBN-10: 0-595-39202-4 (pbk)
ISBN-10: 0-595-83593-7 (ebk)

Printed in the United States of America

# CHAPTER 1

David stood and watched as Brendan angrily jerked his car into gear and sped off down the driveway, the jeep's oversized tires churning up a spray of pea-sized gravel as it disappeared into the dark summer night. He remained outside the house, unable to bring himself to go in. He was staring off to the east, in the direction of the Tovey's house, straining to search the twilight skies for a column of smoke that marked for all the scene of his guilt. Even now, Brendan's shouted words of denial and advice were fading, swallowed up by the rustle of leaves and branches now swaying all around. Indeed, the wind was changing over the island, shifting to blow in from over the warm restless waters of the Caribbean. The fresh salt scent of the sea air began to burn the singed insides of his nose; he turned to walk inside.

The wind rose up as he stepped across the age-worn threshold, slamming the door shut loudly behind him. The sound echoed strangely through the vast emptiness of the kitchen, causing him to take note of his surroundings. The housekeeper had been given the night off, leaving him alone in the old house. This was the oldest part of Buxton Hall, having survived more or less unchanged for the last one hundred and thirty years. From the hardwood cupboards on the white plaster walls, to the long oak table at which he'd been served breakfast every morning for the last few weeks, most of the kitchen's furnishings were held over from that time. All of a sudden he stopped his slow passage through the room, struck by a curious appreciation of that fact for perhaps the first time. He stood still in the darkness, listening to the silence, sensing behind the veil of nighttime's shadows the presence of lives long past. As he dwelled in the detached solitude of those moments, he had no doubt at all that Hannah once had stood where he was standing now.

David continued through the narrow hallway that led out from the kitchen to the main part of the house until he had reached the study, the guilt he felt inside gnawing at him with every step. He switched on an antique brass table lamp and decided to take some of Brendan's loudly proffered advice, finding for himself a bottle of well-aged scotch whiskey from the amply stocked liquor cabinet. With bottle in hand, he slumped down into the consoling luxury of a tall-backed leather chair. As he raised his hand to wipe beads of sweat from his forehead, he immediately experienced pain: he must have burned his face and hands. But he didn't care about any physical scars he may have suffered; his heart instead was heavy with regret. Rhonda Tovey was dead, of that he was sure, no matter what Brendan had to say. And the blame for that death, he knew, fell squarely at his feet.

He would sit brooding in the underlit room for hours, reflecting on questions about himself and the type of person he had become. Why had he really gone there tonight? Was the acquisition of a foolish little story really worth a woman's life?

However, the dread feelings of remorse quickly began to fade, replaced by more compelling thoughts of self-preservation. If the old woman was dead, then his complicity could mean prison, or worse…They still hanged people for murder on Grand Kirkmuir; that unfortunate vestige of the island's British Colonial past was still very much alive.

The question now was what to do? Catch the next flight back to Miami was his first thought. But sooner or later they would find him, and his hasty departure from the island would only serve to convince a jury of twelve good citizens of his guilt. He let out a sigh and shook his head; the irony here was not missed. He had lived most of his adult life trying always to do what he thought was right, and attempting to see that others did no less. But his efforts in this current little crusade had backfired. Now *he* was the one in desperate need of help.

Reaching again for the bottle, he caught sight of his own reflection in the polished mahogany of the end table beside him. The cheerless image he saw there befit his downcast mood. His dark brown hair was a wild mess, and his tired eyes now were not far from closed as he struggled to remain alert. He raised the glass to his lips with a trembling hand and quickly threw down half its contents.

As his head sank back into the chair, his eyes began to wander the rich wood-paneled walls of the room around him, coming inevitably to rest upon the dominating portrait of Hannah Taylor. This was still very much her house, and she knew it well. Her proud face sneered down at him from above the mantel. She seemed to be laughing at him, taunting him from across the years with the thin red line of her smile, accusing him in his tortured thoughts of committing the ultimate crime. Finally, he shook himself loose of the grip of his morbid deliberations and began to reconsider his situation. No matter how badly he felt about what happened, it had indeed happened. He could not go to bed safe in the confidence that all would be made well in the morning. It was time to look towards the future and protecting his own skin. Only Brendan knew that he'd be hiding back there, and he couldn't say anything without implicating himself…So, why worry?

But worry he did. His thoughts began to drift back to events of barely hours past, recalling reluctantly the vivid details of every disastrous moment…The fire starting, his frantic efforts to put out the flames, the shouts and screams of women seeking to escape the burning room. The Chapel was quickly engulfed in flames. Who would have thought that a fire could spread so quickly?

He had watched in pained helplessness as the ceiling began to collapse, trapping the old woman instantly behind a torrent of heat and flames. He had tried to reach her without success. Brendan pulled him out before he himself became a victim. He now sat alone with his thoughts and a half-filled bottle of rye for comfort, punishing himself with the rueful knowledge of what he had done. Just how had he let himself get into this mess? The truth, he knew, was rooted in the frustrations of his own misguided ambitions. His thoughts began to slip backwards in time, past events passed and recent happenings, back to his arrival on the island; it had all started off so well…

David Llewellyn made a fair enough living as a writer of modern interest stories, and in his continuing efforts as a science-fiction author, he had likewise achieved a modicum of success. He had flown down to Grand Kirkmuir intent on resting up after having completed a demanding series of articles on the myriad frustrations of the urban poor. A friend in New York City, the celebrated theatrical Producer, Francis Gordon Hurrell, offered him the use of his summer house in the Islands but David had not expected anything as grandiose as this. What had been described to him as a 'quaint seaside cottage', turned out to be more like a residence fit for a visiting head of state.

Before him stood a white, three-storey mansion with curved flights of stairs rising up to an open, flowered terrace that ran the length of the front of the house. No sooner than he had stepped out of the airport taxi did the house servants appear. His suitcases were whisked off, and he was presented with a cold glass of freshly brewed iced-tea on a polished silver tray that glinted in the bright sun. Not too surprisingly, he took an instant liking to the place. He walked into the cool comfort of an open marble-tiled foyer, and immediately noticed the faint but delicately sweet fragrance of Country Lavender; he looked around for flowers but saw none. From there, he was shown into the large formal living room where he saw for the first time the magnificent, life-sized painting of a beautiful red-haired woman. He would soon learn who she was.

But first the housekeeper, Jeanna Hendrie, sat him down on a huge but firm leather settee, informing him of amongst other things, the 'house rules'. She was a small-framed black woman with a friendly but direct attitude that beamed from her dark eyes. In accordance with her instructions, he was to be permitted use of Mr. Hurrell's limousine, an older model black Mercedes Benz diesel sedan. The house itself had twelve rooms, all of which were his to enjoy, all that was except for a portion of the third floor which was kept locked. At the time it did not seem like much of a matter for further question or concern, since he was informed that these rooms were his host's private living quarters. Her instructions were acknowledged readily.

With the formalities pleasantly out of the way, David decided to ask the question which had been burning to come out. "So tell me," he turned and looked over towards the fireplace, "who's the woman in the portrait?"

"That *was* Miss Hannah," answered Jeanna without hesitation. Her steady voice was rich with the flavor of the islands. "Hannah Buxton-Taylor. She owned the house when Queen Victoria was alive."

"Queen Victoria?"

"Yes sir. Now, if you will excuse me, I have household matters to attend to. Please feel free to dial 'seven' on any telephone in the house if you be needing anything."

"Seven? I think I can remember that. Thank you."

Jeanna departed the room with a smile. Thus, properly apprised of his new status and squatter's rights, David walked closer to the fireplace. He found himself staring at the handsome woman in the portrait, at her luxuriant red-orange hair and her pale, almost translucent blue-white skin. The artist must surely have been a visionary in his time he thought, for the style of the work was not typical of the Victoriana he had seen. The pose and expression were natural, the background was solid but bright, and the brushwork on the canvas was imperceptible to his eye; all combined to create a likeness that seemed incredibly vibrant and alive.

"Hannah Taylor," he repeated the name, intrigued by its almost elegant simplicity. He thought of how lovely a woman she must have been in life, and sighed at the realization that she probably died a hundred years ago.

It would not take long for his curiosity to get the better of him. Back home in New York, the chilled temperatures of an unpleasant spring endured as it had been raining for several days straight. On the island however, the warm, cloudless skies spoke of nothing short of tropical perfection; he was eager to get out. He went up to his room to dig out a pair of sandals and shorts from his luggage and headed out to enjoy the sun on the short walk into town. But first, he had to get his bearings straight; he stopped to look around. Behind him, in the near distance, was a low mountain range that as near as he could reckon ran the entire sunrise-to-sunset length of the island. Before him lay the island's coastline, and the warm blue welcome of the sea. He set off cheerfully down the road, ready to explore this new land.

Along the way, he discovered the island's beautiful beaches. He'd been told they were nothing short of spectacular and wondered how they could've been kept secret for so long. The town could wait to be explored. He made a short climb up a small, rocky hill behind him dotted with scraggly trees, and from there looked out across the clear, light blue waters onto a shallow, sandy bay. A few hundred yards out, he could see the darker-hued waters delineating the drop-off beyond the reef. He took in a deep breath of the fresh sea air and thought glad thoughts of Paradise: "It would be nice to build a house here one day."

Carefully, he made his way through stubborn thickets of bushes, down to the white sand beach and began to marvel at the brightly colored pieces of coral and seashells that had washed up on the shore. As he was picking through and examining the fragments, he was startled by the sound of a man's voice behind him.

"How you doing?"

David turned abruptly to see a gray-bearded, elderly black man sitting barefoot in the shade behind him; he appeared to be repairing a fishing net. On his head was a worn old sea captain's hat tipped slightly to one side. David wondered how he had not noticed him before.

"Uh…Hello," he replied. "I'm doing fine, thank you."

"Good. You must be new to the island."

"Yes," David replied, slightly amused by the man's lyrical West Indian accent. He made a conscious effort to listen to and understand the man's words. "Just got here today, as a matter of fact."

"Well, allow me to welcome you to Monmouth Bay. Me name's Billy Redditch."

He put down the net and leaned forward, extending a hand up in greeting.

"David Llewellyn," came the reply as he walked over to accept the handshake. "Pleased to meet you Mr. Redditch."

"Most folks 'round here call me Billy, or Red-eye. Red-eye Redditch," he smiled back. "You is from Canada?"

"Huh? No, I'm from Michigan originally. I've heard that before, that I sound Canadian I mean. Guess it must be the proximity to the border."

"Ah…Well, I hope you had a nice flight over here."

"It wasn't too bad. I had the one connection to make in Miami."

"So you must be staying at the Somerset?" asked Billy. "It's the best hotel in Monmouth."

"No, actually I'm staying up at Buxton Hall."

"Buxton Hall?" the old man sounded surprised.

"Yeah…The big white house on the other side of the road back there." He looked back the way he came. "It's a great old place, got a lot of atmosphere. Is there, er, something wrong?"

"No, no, man…I didn't mean that at all. I mean," Billy continued, "that's the home of the Red Witch."

"The 'red' what?"

"The Red Witch…You must've seen the portrait in the living room."

"Oh, the big picture over the fireplace. So you mean Hannah was the Red Witch?"

Billy nodded his head slowly.

"Okay," David decided to play along. "So tell me, why is she called the Red Witch?"

Redeye gladly obliged the request and related the legend with due sincerity. The 'Red Witch' was the nickname given to Hannah Buxton-Taylor, the most famous mistress of Buxton Hall. As proud a woman as she was beautiful, she had lived alone in the great house for many years, surrounded by all the worldly excesses her inherited wealth would afford her.

But having nearly every material possession that money could buy was not enough. Hannah was rumored to have been involved in demonic rituals, and said to be responsible for the brutal, unexplained murders of at least nineteen black children in the county. According to the local folklore, she would peel off her skin at night and venture out in all manner of physical forms to do her wicked, wicked deeds.

The circumstances of her own death were as mysterious and violent as her life had reportedly been. As one story had it, she was killed when people seeking to put an end to her ungodly ways, secretly poured holy water mixed with sea salt on her discarded skin before she put it back on. Another story had her death coming from poison by the hand of a jealous lover, whose lowly station in life would not permit him to even hope of marriage. He resolved a bitter end to his misery: if he could not have her, then no man would.

Whatever the truth was only Hannah knew for sure, and that truth she took with her to the grave.

"Yeesh!" exclaimed David at the tale. "I guess it's a good thing she's dead. She sounds too much like some of the women I've dated."

"It's all God's truth," assured Billy calmly.

"Now that seems kind of strange. Poison seems like, an odd way for a man to kill the woman he loves."

"That's how the story go," was his totally uncommitted reply.

David accepted and put great stock in the old man's sincerity, but dismissed most of the tale as not much more than island folklore cooked up for the tourists.

"So what else can you tell me about the island? What're you fishing for?"

"Jacks."

"Good eatin', huh?"

"Oh yessah," he laughed. "You cook them slow over an open fire and man, you'll think you're in heaven when you taste them!"

Billy went on to inform his newly found friend of the history of the area. Buxton Hall was one the oldest of the great plantation houses on the island. Its green and fertile lands stretched from the foot lands of the Azure Mountains, down to the tourist heaven of the coastline. The Buxton dynasty was founded some two centuries earlier by Samuel Claymore Buxton, Hannah Taylor's great-grandfather. He built the house with the wealth his financial successes in the shipping business had brought him. That same fortune served to make the former cabin boy and merchant seaman socially acceptable. Samuel married the much-admired Madeline Villiers, thus allying himself with one of the Caribbean's most affluent plantation families. Indeed, much of the wealth the Buxton family was later to amass was derived from land and agricultural holdings that were her father's wedding gift to them. After two fires and subsequent rebuildings, the current house was completed more than a century and a half ago, and lent its name to the county parish in which it was situated.

The day had grown hotter still while they talked. David offered to buy his companion a drink, that was, if Billy could recommend a good bar (meaning not one of the usual tourist hangouts). The offer was happily accepted. The two men then set off walking the hot half-mile or so into town, passing by tall sugar cane fields and what seemed like an army of foraging goats along the way. Billy explained that beef was very expensive on the island. And since not many of the ordinary people could afford refrigerators to keep milk and the like, the goats served many purposes.

Everyone they saw along the way had a smile or a quick story for Redeye. The friendliness they all seemed to show him did not fail to make an impression on the American. Once in town, the trappings and troubles of the Twentieth Century were readily apparent. Above their heads was a veritable cat's-cradle of electric and telephone wires, running haphazardly to the tops of the rambling two or three-story buildings on either side of the thoroughfare. The narrow main street though busy, was remarkably clean and free from debris, but the sidewalk was in urgent need of repair in places. Panels from wooden crates were pressed into emergency service to allow safe passage across the broken pavement.

Off in the lush green hills above the town, commanding no doubt a fine view of the harbor, sat a palatial white building with a red clay-tiled roof. Billy chimed in with a timely affirmation: the gracious building the American was admiring was none other than the Somerset House Hotel. They turned off the main road and continued down a steep hill towards the sea, eventually stopping outside the colorful exterior of what was very obviously a bar. A hand-painted sign hanging above their heads announced that this was the 'Coral Trees Cove'.

David followed the older man inside and discovered that the back of the building was opened up to the dockside, allowing in a noisy but panoramic slice of all that was going on out there. He was very pleased at how accepting the local folk were of him, becoming quickly the center of attention in an impromptu question and answer session. Almost everyone it seemed wanted to know what it was like to live in the States. As it turned out, Billy was the inn's proprietor, and they all enjoyed a good laugh when he revealed David's request to go to a 'good local bar'.

"I don't mean to be a proud or a boastful man," Billy explained with a smile, "but this is the best Pub for miles around."

But the laughs soon disappeared when David told of where he was staying; obviously, there was something more to this story than he knew. So being the investigative professional he was, he tactfully pressed to get some answers. However, people either just smiled politely in changing the subject, or excused themselves and went on about their business. Billy simply offered to fill his glass; all his drinks were on the house, at least for today.

"Bill, what is this stuff I'm drinking anyway?"

"Just beer and lemonade. We call it *Shandy*."

"Let me have another one, it really cuts a thirst."

David knew he would not be getting any more answers on the subject. Their silence, he was reasonably sure, had something to do with the legend of Hannah Taylor. He shrugged his shoulders, deciding it best to let the whole thing slide. Superstition and the power of myth apparently were still very much alive here. He remained at the bar until just after five in the afternoon, watching the brightly painted fishing boats as they sailed in and out on the endless swell of the waves.

# CHAPTER 2

David awakened late on a Sunday morning for him, and hurried downstairs in a borrowed bathrobe to have breakfast in the house's large kitchen. He was about to dig into a fresh, sweet-smelling pink grapefruit as his first course, when Jeanna first announced then brought in an unexpected visitor.

"I am sorry," the man began apologetically, taking note of David's bedtime attire. "I hope I'm not too early."

"Oh no, not at all." David hurriedly pushed himself up from the table and shook hands.

"I'm Brendan Costello. I was in the neighborhood and thought I'd drop by to welcome you to the island."

A tall, younger man stood before him, possessed of lean, rugged good looks and a serious cast to his glance; he wore his dark blond hair longer than what might be considered proper in the business world back home. He was dressed formally in a light gray suit, looking as if he had just come from or was about to go to church. Perhaps it was his years as a Journalist, but even as the man stood before him smiling, David couldn't help but notice what seemed like a hidden sense of purpose in his guest.

"Ah!" David exulted. "You're an American."

"I sure am," came an amused response, "from a drab little mill town in New Hampshire."

David laughed: "Please, sit down. My name's—"

"I know, David Llewellyn. Or do you prefer Edward Morris? That is the name you use for your books, right?"

"Right...How is it that you know so much about me?"

"This is a small island. News of strangers, especially white strangers, travels fast, my friend. Anyway," he continued in a New England-Irish brogue, "your host told me you'd be stayin' here, and asked me to come over and kind of acquaint you with things on the island."

"So you know Frank?"

"Yep, known Francis Hurrell for as long as I've been here."

"I see," came back a hesitant reply. He still wasn't sure how quite to take his visitor.

"How is he?" asked Brendan. "I haven't seen Francis in, must be a month now."

"Just fine, though he looks like he's losing a little weight. But he's still the same old Francis, challenges you on almost everything."

"Well, he's an extremely smart fella and a hard worker. Expects a lot of himself and the folks around him."

David readily agreed with the assessment of Francis' character: "Yes, I once heard someone refer to him as Francis 'Goddamn' Hurrell instead of Francis Gordon", he grinned. "So, you've read some of my work?"

"Read?...No, I wouldn't exactly say that. I'm not a great fan of that kind of stuff, but I have a friend who is."

"I'd like to meet this friend of yours," smiled David.

"I'm sure I can arrange something."

"Great! I'm always interested in finding out about the kind of people who buy my 'stuff'. It always helps to get some insights."

"Did I say she bought it?" He waited to observe then laugh at David's expression. "Man, I'm havin' a joke with you! I'm sure she bought it. Okay, let me tell you why I'm here..."

He went on to inform David of a formal dinner party that some people named Tovey were having, and that he was invited: "They live down the road at Hatherleigh. They'd be happy to have you."

"Hatherleigh? I don't remember seeing it on my map. Is that the next town over?"

"No," Brendan leaned back and shook his head. "That's the name of their house."

"Well, excuse the hell outta me. Do all the houses around here have names?"

"Only the nice, big expensive ones." He could see the antipathy continue to build in David's gray eyes. "Sure, these people are all rich, all very 'British' in their attitudes, and that despite the fact that a lot of 'em were born and raised right here. But that aside, they ain't too bad a bunch. You should come. There's not much else worthwhile going on. The Toveys are part of the island's old power structure, you know, 'the sun never sets on the Empire' kind of folks. You might even find them interestin'. And if nothing else," he continued, "there's all the free food and booze you can put away." He leaned forward with a charismatic smile. "So how about it?"

"It's sounding interesting. What's this party for?"

Brendan explained that the fete was to commemorate a naval battle embodied in the capture of the old fort at San Sebastian, some three hundred and fifty year earlier. The victory gave the British the island and control over the trade routes in that part of the Caribbean. It was a presage to the end of the Spanish hegemony and the rising fortunes of the British in the Americas. As such, the Governor-General would be coming over from the capital at Charlestowne for the festivities.

"The Governor-General? But I thought Grand Kirkmuir was an independent nation?"

"That it is. The position's mostly ceremonial now. As I understand it, he spends most of his time back in Charlestowne, dedicating buildings and stuff like that. He doesn't come over to this side of the island much, so they're making a big 'to do' of it."

"You said that this thing's pretty formal. Does that mean I have to wear a tux?" asked David.

"Ah, well you know the Brits. It's kind of 'expected'."

"Expected?" he repeated with the disdain evident in his voice. "How long did you say you've been living here?"

"Maybe four years now. If you're worried about rentin' a tux," he looked down at the slight paunch of David's seated figure, "you and I are er, almost the same size. I have a white dinner jacket you could borrow."

He thanked Brendan before noticing that his visitor had finished eating the slice of toast and made a belated invitation of his own. "Would you like to join me for breakfast?"

"No thanks. But I will have a cup of Jeanna's fine coffee!"

In the days that followed, David never found himself confronted with doing anything more strenuous than taking the hooks out of the fish he caught with Billy. Meanwhile, the indomitable Mr. Redditch was trying his best to teach his new American student the fine art of net fishing but without too much success.

In short, David was enjoying a true vacation, living a life so carefree and catered to that a pampered housecat might be envious.

Eventually Friday night arrived. A well-dressed Mr. Costello arrived at Buxton Hall in a desert yellow jeep with a roll bar, which not too unexpectedly caused David to remark about appearances.

"Now you don't want to be takin' this thing too seriously," replied Brendan. "Remember, we are Americans…'bloody Yanks' to most of these people. These guys would be very disappointed if we weren't at least a little unorthodox."

"And," added David in an affected British upper-class accent, "we wouldn't want to disappoint our public."

A shorter than expected drive out to Hatherleigh took them east along the Coast Road, allowing a fine evening view of the sea and sky along the way. After turning off the main road, they passed through a huge black wrought-iron gateway meant to impress, and continued up a long driveway towards a large, marble-columned house. David could not help but comment on how the house looked like one of the plantation mansions from the old Antebellum South back home.

The immediate area in front of the entrance was alive with the pomp and circumstance of the island's Colonial heritage, as chauffeured limousines and personal automobiles alike were busily discharging their mostly well to do occupants. The two Americans made their way in through a large, crowded foyer, passing police and military officials huddled near the entrance attired in smartly creased white dress uniforms. Brendan began to selectively introduce his countryman to those guests whom he believed wouldn't bore David with chatter of the inane.

David for his part took leave whenever he could to look around the brightly lit room, taking in everything around him to heart and mind. He hadn't been to many events as laden with the baggage of custom and state as this, but it was all just as he'd imagined it would be. The women especially caught his eye, dressed to the 'nines in some of the glitziest baubles and beads he'd ever seen. He helped himself to a glass of champagne as a waiter walked by. Normally, he wasn't much of one for the social sipping of wine of any sort, but having the weight of the glass in his hand made him feel just a little more comfortable.

A small band sat nestled in the midst of several potted palm trees played 'Forties style big band music in high-collared black tuxedos. Their snappy melodies however all but faded into the background, overcome by the sounds of a hundred voices. On every wall of the room were centuries old paintings of men and women whom David took to be undoubtedly the ancestors of their hosts this night. At the far end of the hall were multiple pairs of antique shining glass doors opened out to the expanse of the torch lit gardens beyond. High above their heads, in the center of the ballroom was a magnificent glimmering crystal chandelier; he could only guess at how much a thing like that would have cost.

His attention gradually drifted back to the people in the room. Whether black or white, they all looked remarkably the same to his uninformed eyes; he was really quite surprised by that fact. Here, surely, were the descendants of former slaves and slave owners, brought together to celebrate a victory in a war which meant little to the ancestors of one group, and helped make the fortunes of the other. After perhaps centuries of enmity and indifference, he surmised rather dryly, that money indeed made for the ultimate equalizer.

The philosophizing over for the moment, David began to follow the progress of a white-gloved waiter crossing the ballroom and was immediately struck by the sight of a beautiful young black woman who had appeared from the anonymity of the gardens. He turned to watch her walk across the room. She was wearing a low cut, blue-sequined dress that hugged the curves of the most perfect feminine figure he had ever seen. He grabbed Brendan's arm, anxiously inquiring who the woman was. But before a response came, their attention was drawn back to the entrance of the hall; the Governor-General had arrived to a flurry of attention.

He was a pink-faced old man who looked like he could be anyone's grandfather. To David's surprise, he was wearing a plain white-jacketed tuxedo: no medals or military ribbons adorned his chest. The band struck up the familiar theme of 'God Save the Queen'; the Governor-General stood promptly to attention.

David started slowly making his way through the crowd, towards the woman in the sparkling blue dress, irresistibly drawn to her like a butterfly to a bright desert bloom. He stopped a discrete distance away, respectfully awaiting the end of the anthem with one thought foremost in mind: he had to get to know her. He pretended to be studying one of the portraits on the wall above her head, while his gaze instead followed the intriguingly curved lines of her form. She was talking with an older, auburn-haired white woman. Although he was now close enough to hear both their voices, he could not make out any of what was said. Smiles and laughs passed freely between the two; he assumed that they must be good friends. He was utterly entranced by the sight of the younger woman, captivated by the way her silky black hair lay on her smooth, bare shoulders, drinking in with appreciative eyes the mellow brown color of her skin.

Suddenly, she turned her head in his direction, catching his eyes as they lingered on her person. Embarrassed, he turned away immediately, almost spilling his drink as he brushed against a man walking behind him; he began to apologize profusely for his clumsiness. When he turned back around, she was gone. He began to search the room for her.

"Where'd you wander off to?" came a voice from behind. It was Brendan.

"I have just seen one of the most gorgeous women in the world," was his animated response, "and as usual, I made a complete ass of myself."

"Gorgeous, huh…Not just beautiful?"

"Brendan, you had to see this girl. She was perfect."

"Oh-kay…And what did this 'vision of perfection' look like?"

David opened his mouth preparing to present the description in glowing terms, but stopped abruptly. The expression on his face fell from an enthusiastic glee, to a look of dry-mouthed dread. She was walking straight towards them.

"Hello Brendan," she smiled. "So you've finally shown up. I was beginning to think you weren't going to come." He put his arm around her waist; she delivered a formal kiss on the cheek. "So," she said turning to David, "is this your friend, the famous American writer?"

"Indeed it is. Allow me to introduce David Llewellyn."

She held out a hand; he meekly accepted.

"David, I'd like to introduce you to one of your readers, and one of the island's most special treasures: Constance Lorrha."

"Oh Constance is way too formal. Everyone calls me 'Connie'."

David shyly agreed; he could barely look her in the eye. Her playful expression made it clear that she had been keenly aware of his earlier attentions. Brendan then found a way to leave the two alone, saying something about talking with a woman about a piece she'd commissioned.

David stood entranced. He was now left alone with a woman whose every aspect easily matched his unspoken expectations, delighting in the delicately fragrant scent of her perfume. She smiled at him; she was much lovelier and a little younger than he had first thought. He wondered if he should apologize for leering at her earlier. But if she hadn't noticed, he'd make an even greater fool of himself by saying something. As he struggled within himself to come to a decision, she filled the void of awkward silence, bubbling forth into conversation with youthful exuberance:

"What brings a famous American author like you to our little out-of-the-way island?"

David was only too happy to follow her lead, telling her of his need to get away from the routine of 'deadlines and commitments' back home. As they spoke, his fascination with her grew; he stared at her wide-eyed, like a child covetous of a new toy. She appeared to thrive on his attentiveness, smiling and flirting with him in the ages old ritualistic dance of human courtship.

"You have an interesting last name yourself…Lorrha, what is that, Irish?"

"Yes, I believe so. I'm told our family was begun here by an itinerant Irishman, an ex-soldier who fought at Waterloo with the Duke of Wellington. Somehow he ended up here, married an ex-slave woman named Verity Tristham and, lo and behold, here I am. My family's part French, Spanish, even part Caribe Indian. We've a little bit of everything mixed in."

"A lot of ex's in there too."

Constance laughed out loud: "I like you, you're funny!"

He chose to take her remark as a compliment.

"You're practically an American, I mean with your mixed-up family tree. The way you speak, you don't sound like the *er*, the…"

"You mean like the other Black people."

"What I meant was—" He looked at her with that 'I blew it' expression on his face again.

"Hey, don't sweat it man. I'm not offended. I'm a Black woman and I'm proud of my heritage. But my accent's well, quasi-American. I went to an all-girls boarding school up near Stamford and after that, I attended college in the Washington, D.C. area."

"Connecticut?"

"Yup," she smiled back.

"How'd you like being at the boarding school?"

"Oh I loved it. Fainsbury was as much fun as an all-girls school could be." She rolled her eyes. "My dad's a former Member of Parliament here. He's into Banking now. He was supposed to be here tonight," she glanced back towards the entrance, "but I guess wife number two must be keeping him away. She and I don't get along too well. In fact, I'm sure it was her idea to send me to boarding school in America. After my real mother died, she just moved right on in."

She emphasized the last point with a wide sweeping motion of her arm. She paused, stating that she did not want to bore him with her family problems; the smiling face that looked back said that he was sincerely interested in what she had to say.

"You know, Mr. Llewellyn, I think I like you." She smiled again as she sipped champagne from her glass; he blushed slightly.

"Thank you," he replied, feeling very good about himself.

She took his arm and began to lead him around the room, as their discussion touched here and there on other family-type matters. Then David asked a question meant to clarify what it was that Brendan was working on for Ellen Wainwright.

"Oh, then you don't know…Brendan's a Sculptor. He's really good too. He's a 'New Realist'."

David shook his head; he didn't have a clue about what she was talking about.

"It's a more classical style of portrayal, not at all like that abstract, who-knows-what kind of thing you find at shopping malls in the U.S. It's really very lifelike. Brendan says that he draws his inspiration from Michelangelo Buonarroti."

"What?"

"Not what, who. Michelangelo…Brendan likes to refer to him by his full name: Michelangelo Buonarroti. With a name like that," she smiled, "I can see why he shortened it. Anyway, Brendan likes to quote him as saying something like 'the form is intrinsic in the stone, and the artist's hand simply liberates that form'…Great stuff, huh? You have got to come over to his studio."

David agreed to Connie's arranging a mid-week visit since, after all, he was on vacation. He happily admitted to having no obligations beyond having a good time and relaxing. He had noticed that she had a certain twinkle in her eyes whenever it came to anything involving Brendan, and decided that there was more to the relationship between the two than their formal kiss of earlier that night had led him to believe. He sighed quietly but after a few moments, he began to accept the reality of the situation; both Brendan and Constance seemed to be warm, beautiful people. Why shouldn't they be more than friends? After all, he reasoned, if he hadn't met Brendan then he wouldn't have met her. He decided to put all other thoughts out of his mind, and content himself for now with Connie's friendship and company.

"Why do use a pen-name to write your novels?" she asked. "David Llewellyn sounds very literary, very 'saleable' to me?"

"That's just the problem. It's too 'saleable'. As 'David Rhees Llewellyn', I'm pretty well known as a writer of 'human interest' stories. Now I know it's hardly practical or realistic, but I wanted my novels to be published on their own merits, and not because I'm looked on as a bankable asset. When I write my stories, I'm 'Eddie Morris'. My books get judged for what they are."

"Now that is *really* admirable."

It was at that moment that Brendan decided to rejoin them. It was now Constance's turn to excuse herself, leaving the two men alone once again with a smiled promise to return.

"Okay, I think it's time you met your hosts."

"Sure, lead on."

As they began to walk towards the entrance of the ballroom, David asked a question meant to find out more about the intriguing Ms. Lorrha. "Constance said something about looking for her father."

"Her father? Fat chance of that!" he exclaimed. "He's not too welcome here." Brendan explained that there was something of a history between the hostess of the party, Rhonda Tovey and Constance's father, Norman.

They were once good friends but almost twenty-five years earlier, the island suffered a considerable amount of damage from a hurricane. Property and agricultural losses were extensive. Rhonda's elder brother, Michael Edward, had inherited the Lloyd family estate and most of its holdings, but he was never considered a good businessman. He liked to gamble and carouse, using the income from the estate to finance his wanton life of leisure. It wasn't long before Michael had amassed some considerable debts, and took out a few loans to tide him over until the harvests came in. Then the hurricane hit and took care of most of that.

Unfortunately, a particularly large note came due at the same time. Norman Lorrha was the officer of the bank who made the decision to exercise its option on the note. Rhonda hoped to take advantage of their friendship, begging him to reconsider. But Norman refused, claiming that his obligations to the bank's depositors were unavoidable. As a result of that decision, the loan was called in and the Lloyd plantation and estate house were sold at auction.

"But that's not the end of it," continued Brendan. "Michael was a broken man after that. He took up drinkin' in a real heavy way and soon left the island for Cuba. He died there less than five years later, living in some cheap hotel with barely a cent left to his name. Rhonda hadn't heard from him for two years before he died. She claimed the body and had him buried back here in Monmouth. She openly blamed Norman Lorrha for his death."

"But why couldn't she have loaned him the money he needed to get him through? I mean, take a look at this place."

"Like I said, David. This whole side of the island barely survived. And who in their right mind would risk everything for an idler like Michael? More than likely, he would drag you down the pike with 'im."

"I see."

"Yup! But Rhonda's never seen it that way. All the heirlooms of the estate were auctioned. About all Rhonda could eventually buy back were some of the paintings you see on the walls, and most of an old silver collection they now have upstairs here."

They were now close to the ballroom's entrance. An older couple was engaged in conversation with a black man who David would later learn was the Governor-General's secretary. At their approach, the discussion broke up, the couple turned to greet them.

"Branden, glad you could come."

The welcome came from a frail, older man with a full head of neatly combed silver hair; he was introduced as Mr. William Tovey, retired. Then, following the graces of genteel etiquette, Mr. Tovey turned and courteously introduced his wife, Rhonda. David quickly recognized her as the same woman Constance had been talking with earlier in the evening. Up close, he could tell that her auburn hair was very obviously colored.

"Welcome to Hatherleigh, Mr. Llewellyn," she offered her hand in a stylized fashion. For a moment, David thought of curtsying but decided against it; she didn't seem like the kind of person who would appreciate his sense of humor.

"I have so been looking forward to meeting you," Rhonda continued. "We seldom have Americans visit this side of the island. You must promise to come and take tea with us one afternoon, this week."

"Take…tea? Sure, I think I'd like that," he replied. "This is a magnificent place you have here Mrs. Tovey."

"Thank you. But please, call me Rhonda."

"Rhonda it is." The Toveys stood smiling at him, arm in arm; they struck him as an unusual but nicely matched set of bookends. "I'm staying up at Buxton Hall. As I guess you know, Buxton's a great old house but this place is definitely something else!"

She was so pleased that he liked her home that she made a surprising suggestion. "Brendan, you're not a stranger to Hatherleigh. Why don't you take Mr. Llewellyn on a tour of the house."

"Sure," he agreed with a shrug. "I'll look forward to it."

Leaving the din of polite chatter behind them, they returned to the front hallway, climbing a dimly lit bank of polished wooden stairs up to the quieter regions of the house. David took the opportunity to bring up Constance's invitation to visit Brendan's workshop.

"…No trouble," replied Brendan. "Be happy to have you over."

"Great…Did you notice? The old fella called you 'Branden'."

"What?"

"William Tovey, our host. He called you 'Branden'."

"Ah…Well, he's getting a bit senile nowadays."

"These people crack me up! Did you hear her: inviting me to 'take tea'? When she said that, I almost asked her if she meant the stuff you drink."

Brendan barely broke a smile. David commented on how the Toveys must be trusting souls to allow them to roam so freely about their home. Brendan affirmed his opinion of the Toveys in response, saying simply that they were 'good people'.

They continued through the living quarters of the house passing at least half a dozen or so bedrooms, only two of which Brendan said were in use. Each room was more or less typical in size and furnishings, having a separate study area and luxurious bath; each room could easily have served as an apartment on its own. David couldn't help but remember how just recently he'd seen entire families living in less space, with the barest of amenities.

The second floor was also home to the prized collection of ancient silver pieces which Brendan had mentioned; a huge room with stylized black wrought iron bars on the outside of the windows was set aside for the purpose. David was impressed by the museum quality of many of the pieces, most of which seemed Celtic or early European in origin; he asked why the collection wasn't mentioned in his guidebook to the island.

"It's like I told you before David, the Toveys are old money and they enjoy their privacy. But I think they've allowed groups in on occasions."

David acknowledged their right to privacy, but decried the loss to public at large as they debated the pros and cons of the question. On their return to the ground floor, David expressed surprise to find that they'd traveled to the far side of the house.

"It's a big place," was Brendan's casual reply. "Well then, there's the tour. I'll collect my fee from the Toveys tomorrow. Think you're ready to move in?"

David declined with a loud, animated laugh. As they began to walk down a long darkened corridor, Brendan explained that work was being done on the electrical system to replace some of the house's old wiring. They stopped in front of a set of heavy-looking, high arching wooden doors set in a fluted, carved stone frame.

"What's in here," David asked, "Fort Knox?"

"No, but that's good," laughed Brendan. "This is the Chapel. It's a holdover from the original house built two hundred years ago."

David was impressed. But to his eyes, it seemed out of place considering the architectural style of the rest of the house. Standing on one side of the doorway was an unusual antique brass candelabrum shaped like a tree, complete with six new fat white candles.

"I see Mrs. Tovey chose my guide well. Can we go inside?"

"I think you're outta of luck there," he stepped forward and tried the door's handle. "No, they're doin' some big time work in there. Some of the roof beams have dry rot. Believe me, there's not much to see in there anyway."

David found Brendan's explanation a little strange to say the least, but said nothing. It seemed odd to him that they would lock the entrance to the Chapel, and yet leave the doors to their prized silver collection wide open. He gazed at the dark wooden doors; they certainly seemed sturdy enough. Why anyone with the obvious financial resources of the Toveys allow a 'conversation piece' like the Chapel to fall into such disrepair was beyond him. He looked around the hallway; there were no tarpaulins or signs of any work being done. But then, he reasoned that since the Toveys were hosting the celebration, the tools and materials were probably being kept inside the Chapel. And what possible reason could Brendan have to lie to him?

They were continuing on their way back to the party when David stopped abruptly again. He was staring at the bottom of a doorway.

"What's wrong?" asked Brendan.

"Hold it! I heard something behind that door."

"Well that's really not too surprising—"

David held up his hand motioning Brendan to be silent. He walked over cautiously and pressed his ear to the door. "I think someone's in there. Could be a burglar," he whispered.

Brendan stood where he was with arms folded: "Burglar," he laughed, "Or maybe a 'cat burglar'. I think I like that better. Do you want to go inside?"

David couldn't understand why Brendan would be taking the matter so lightly. "This is the perfect opportunity for someone to break in. The party's the perfect cover." While he stood listening, Brendan marched over and abruptly opened the door, causing David to tumble into the room ending up on his back. He sat up quickly, totally unprepared for what he saw.

Inside the room was a veritable garden: small trees and large wooden boxes were everywhere, filled to overflowing with wild grasses. But his undignified entry wasn't the worse part of it. He felt his eyes begin to tear, his nose begin to sniffle.

Something small abruptly jumped out of the undergrowth and charged right up to him, brushing up against his leg, climbing up onto his stomach. The next moment, a dozen pairs of colorful shining eyes and faces popped up and out from everywhere, all staring at him.

"Yes," continued Brendan. "Cats. Rhonda just loves cats. She has a parcel of 'em."

"Get 'em away from me...Scat!"

"Hey Davie, relax. This is *their* room. Be hospitable. They're all pretty friendly little critters."

He was on his feet in an instant, pushing by Brendan as he headed back to the door. "*Ah-choo*!" He started into a bout of rapid-fire sneezing.

"You've really got it bad, huh?"

"It's not that I don't like cats," he continued to speak from behind a hurriedly balled-up handkerchief, "but I've had this problem since I was a kid. If there's a cat within ten feet of me, I break out sneezing and can't stop."

"Maybe you should try some alfalfa tea. I heard it works wonders."

David looked at him incredulously.

"This is what Rhonda affectionately refers to as the 'Cheshire' room."

"Boy!" David exclaimed, glad to be getting out of there. "Aptly named I'm sure."

"Usually the little guys have the run of the house, but whenever company comes over, they get put up in here."

"I don't think I'll be taking Rhonda up on the tea-time invitation. Hey listen, why don't we just shut the door and head back to the party?"

"Tired of the tour, huh? Okay Davie," he looked at his watch, "it's about time for the fireworks show to begin. I hear it's gonna be really somethin'."

# CHAPTER 3

Although two days had since passed, the memories of the people David had met at the party were still very much alive in his thoughts. He was with Billy Redditch enjoying an afternoon on the beach near where they'd first met over cold bottles of the local beer. The two were contrasting the lifestyles of the island's elite, typified by the distinguished gathering at Hatherleigh, against the simpler existence that typified the lives of most of the folk in Monmouth Bay. The laid-back conversation soon progressed to broader themes, and quickly found David vigorously defending himself for being an American, and all that made him what he was.

"…Sure, we consume more of the Earth's resources, but look what we give back to the world in foreign aid! You tell me another country that does more."

Billy laughed. "Why you gettin' so upset, man? I'm not *talking* about how much the U.S. Government is handing out, I'm talking about what U.S. *Cor-por-rations* are doing. Man, they nothing but crooks, stuffing them pockets and stealing the whole world blind."

"…I wouldn't argue with you on that."

Suddenly, a woman's voice spoke up: "Won't argue with you about what?"

Both men were startled; they turned around to find Constance. She was perched just above them, sitting on the same fallen tree their backs were leaning against. She was wearing a pair of khaki shorts and an airy white cotton blouse, the buttons of which were opened up low enough to allow the air to flow through comfortably. David's wide eyes quickly took in as much as they could discretely.

"So guys, mind if I join you?"

"Gal," shouted Billy, "you shouldn't come sneakin' up behind people like that."

"I'm sorry, I didn't mean to scare you."

"You didn't scare us," assured David, standing up and brushing off the sand. "It's nice to see you again."

"Nice to see you too," she smiled back. "Mr. Redditch…" He touched his cap in response. "What're you fellas doing?"

"Just taking in some fresh sea air," replied David. "What brings you out this way?"

"Why, this is my favorite little cove. It's a great place to find driftwood."

"Driftwood?" asked David.

"That's what the gal said: drif'wood."

"Hey, do you fellas have anything besides beer in that?" Constance looked down at the cooler.

David reached in and pulled out a bottle of ginger ale, inquiring why she was looking for driftwood.

"Actually, it's for Brendan. He's planning to use it as decoration for the base of a sculpture he's working on. I'm collecting a few pieces so he'll have a choice."

"Sounds like it'll add a nice touch. Is that the piece he's doing for the woman at the party?"

"Yes, Mrs. Wainwright. She wanted something inspired by the Greek classics. It's a wonderful portrayal of Apollo in amorous pursuit of the nymph Daphne. I'll have Brendan show you the sketches when we visit his workshop."

The response came slowly: "I'd like that." He was mesmerized by the gleam of mischievous intent now sparkling in her eyes. "Yeah…I think I know the story. The gods took pity on her, and turned her into an olive tree or something."

Billy could not help but take note of the flirtatious interaction between the two and laughed aloud, tactfully restricting his comments to the spoken discussion: "And you say *my* stories they hard to believe. Turn the woman into a tree," he scoffed, shaking his head in amused disbelief.

"I'm going up to visit my friend Ellie in Bel Rios," Constance continued, "I haven't seen her in weeks. She invited me up to hear Mother Foster speak. She works tirelessly for social justice, and she's revered as a mystic and a healer by a lot of people around here."

"Some people think she's a crazy woman," added Billy.

"And what do you say, Connie?" asked David.

"I think she's one of those rare, special people who really make a difference in this world."

"Wow...That's a ringing endorsement if ever I heard one. And she heals people too? Where's Bel Rios?"

"Up in the Highlands," she replied. "It's not that far from here."

David quickly saw an opportunity to spend some time alone with her, and not so subtly pressed for and received an invitation to join Constance on the drive up into the hills. "The Highlands...I hear that's supposed to be some nice country."

"It's beautiful," she smiled. "But Bel Rios isn't exactly the kind of place tourists go."

"Hey, who are calling a tourist? You're forgetting I'm the guy who writes about life the way it is."

She carefully slid down off the tree and began pulling back her hair, clipping it in place with a gold barrette. "Okay...But I don't expect we'll be back much before midnight."

"That's fine. I didn't have anything else planned." The words had barely left his lips when he remembered friend Billy, and turned apologetically to him.

"Don't worry about me, man. You go on. You and the young lady go see the mountains. We can always finish our conversation later." He turned to the young lady and spoke to her with almost a warning in his voice. "You make sure to take good care of me friend."

With that they parted company. David followed Constance on the short, plodding walk over the hot white sands back to her little orange car. When they were far enough away, he asked her why Billy had seemed so concerned over his well being.

"I'm sure you've noticed that there's a lot of poverty on the island," she explained, "it's even worse up there. Used to be, the people up there could come down and get work in the cane fields, but with your country putting quotas on the sugar it imports, and the British abandoning our *special relationship* for the European Common Market, there just isn't that much work there anymore. A couple of tourists have been robbed by guys wielding machetes, but no one's been seriously hurt. They really don't mean any harm."

"Machetes...Not *seriously* hurt? That sounds very reassuring," he replied sarcastically.

"Oh, having second thoughts are we? Don't worry," she joked, "I'll protect you."

"Well thank you," he replied a little indignantly.

She laughed and took his arm, leading him the rest of the way to the car.

David sat back, accepting of his role as passenger as they drove up into the mountains, quietly taking in the scenery around him. It felt strange to be sitting on the left side of the car as a passenger, and stranger still driving on the left side of the road. Something in his brain kept signaling that this was all wrong, throwing off his senses, affecting how he sat, moved, and braced himself. It took a while to become accustomed to the change.

The further they went up into the hills, the thicker the foliage became, the lush tropical vegetation slowly reclaiming the intrusive man-made avenue. Gradually the theme became complete, the dense overhanging greenery of the forest triumphant, replacing even the calm blue of the skies above their heads. The road itself now seemed to wind or turn into blind curve every ten yards or so, causing Constance to lean incessantly on the horn of her little Volkswagen bug as she sought to warn any oncoming traffic.

"You don't look like you're having much fun over there," said David, giving voice to his observation.

"What do you mean?"

"Looks like a lot of work," he responded, holding onto the car door for dear life. His reference was to the effort it was taking, as she seemed to be constantly turning the steering wheel.

"Oh, you get used to it," came a half-grunted reply.

He looked at the fallen leaves strewn over the road, and made a comment that really didn't need to be made. "I guess it rains a lot up here: it looks slippery."

"Yes," she replied curtly, trying to concentrate on the road.

"So what do you want to do with your life?" he blurted out.

The question took Constance by surprise; she glanced his way with a quick smile. "What do you mean?"

"I mean, I remember you saying that you'd had a few years of college. Are you going back?"

"Eventually. I'd like to get into Journalism myself."

"Oh really?" His eyes opened wide. He turned in his seat to face her, a thousand unselfish thoughts of how he could help her flowing into his head.

"Well, I meant Broadcast Journalism…TV. I have a lead on a job in Charlestown that seems pretty promising."

"Writing?"

"No, silly. It's more of a reporting job for a television-news show."

"Ah…Now even that may require some formal writing skills, don't you think?"

"Maybe, but they told me it's not too important. They said that I'd get some help with that. I'll be the face in front of the cameras."

"Oh," he changed the tone of his voice. "I see…"

"Well don't say it like that," she laughed. "I'm not some floozy air-head, you know. Anyone can just read the news, but to deliver the lines with true *sincerity* and *understanding* takes real talent."

"So you're an actress too?"

"Sure honey and my talents don't stop there," she vamped.

As David turned three shades of red, she apologized through barely restrained laughter for the obvious embarrassment she had caused him. The conversation ended on that note for a few minutes, as David regrouped, reverting to the role of quiet passenger.

The tropical sun was passing into its afternoon descent, its bright rays filtering down through the trees just enough to cause David to divert his attention from the view outside the car. His eyes fell to gaze upon the smooth, shapely legs of the woman close beside him. He decided that she must have been in sports, or at least done some dancing in her time.

"I'm sorry the radio doesn't work. I love this old car, but maintaining it is getting a little too expensive. There's a mechanic in town who wants to buy it, and I just may sell. We've only got another few miles to go." Constance turned to her guest; he abruptly looked away. "David, you keep staring at me."

"I'm sorry," he blurted out. "It's just that…you are," he took a deep breath, "a very attractive woman."

"…Thank you." She turned away, a shy smile on her face.

"Connie, I meant what I said." He stared back at her, this time not caring if she saw.

"I'm sure you did."

She took her eyes off the road only long enough to see the puppy-dog expression in his eyes; she instantly decided it was time to change the subject. "My friend's name is Elouise Fletcher. We went to prep school together in Charlestowne."

He reacted slowly to her words, his thoughts preoccupied with reigning in the emotions in his heart. "But isn't that on the other side of the island?"

"Yes."

"Well, if the town is so poor…"

"You're going to ask how she could afford to go there, aren't you?"

"The thought did kinda occur."

"My father set up a scholarship to sponsor her. It's a long story, I'll tell it to you one day."

David's face lit up.

"Oh no, it's not what you're thinking. I can assure you there's not even a hint of scandal." She laughed. "You journalists are all alike."

"Yeah, poison-penned bloodhounds to the last!" he grinned.

"Okay 'hound dog', you'd better put on your 'nice guy' face. We're here, m'dear."

They had driven into a huge clearing in the forest. On either side of the road were small, brightly painted concrete block houses, most with corrugated tin roofs that stood out markedly from the tropical greenery. They didn't see too many people around; Constance guessed aloud that it was getting close to dinnertime. As they passed through what appeared to be the village center, they came upon a small group of people hanging around what passed for a grocery store. Constance pulled over and rolled down her window to verify her directions; she hadn't been there in a while.

A few children came over and peered inside the car with curious, friendly faces. A small boy, probably no more than four years old, tried to sell David a small, green red-throated lizard he pulled out of a pocket. But just behind them stood several, rougher looking young men; their expressions and every other aspect of their attitudes said that they were anything but sociable. One particular fellow in a tattered, bright orange t-shirt made a definite impression on David: he had a few fingers missing from his right hand. The skin on his forearm was similarly mangled. It looked as if his arm had been caught in a piece of machinery at one time; the almost pink scarred flesh contrasted very noticeably against the man's almost coal-black complexion. David smiled and tried to say hello to the group but they didn't respond. After what seemed like a minor eternity to David, Constance returned having gotten her directions straight and they were on their way again.

"Good!" he exclaimed.

"What's wrong?"

"I hope the folks around here aren't all like that. Those guys back there didn't look very friendly."

Constance really wanted to chide him with an 'I told you so', but resisted the temptation. She drove another quarter mile before she slowed the car and drove off the paved road, over a cow path that passed for a side road, down to a white-painted house with red wooden shutters over the window openings. The yard around them was a curious mixture of wild and tamed tropical greenery, and the semi-discarded leavings of modern civilization. They got out of the car and began to walk towards the house; a little brown and white dog on the porch began barking ferociously at their approach.

"…The welcome here just gets better and better."

"Oh David, stop it. Look, his tail is wagging. He's just happy to see us!"

"Yeah, right. Must be hungry."

The dog's barking brought out the house's occupants: two men and three women of varying ages. In moments, the scene was filled with warm smiles and embraces. Constance introduced David to Elouise as a friend visiting from America. She in turn introduced him to her parents, her elder sister and her brother Anton, a very powerfully built man. The two older women were wearing headscarves and colorful summer frocks, and stood flanking the Elouise's white-haired father.

"Lorri, I've got good and bad news," Elouise began, referring to Constance by her preferred prep school nickname.

"Oh? Well give me the bad news first," replied Constance.

"The meeting's been cancel. Mother Foster won't be here tonight. I'm sorry you had to drive all the way up here for nothing."

"Oh, you be quiet. I came here to see you and your family as much as anything else. And you promised me a home-cooked meal, remember?"

"That's so nice of you!" added Elouise's mother. "Okay, come on in. We been waiting for you to arrive to start dinner."

"You don't mind that I've brought a guest, do you?"

"Of course not! There's plenty o' room at the table."

They went inside and sat down to what was to David a sumptuously exotic meal of curried goat, rotis, yams, sweet potatoes, and a peculiar but pleasant drink made from carrot juice and beer. David took as quickly to the Fletchers as they did to him. They seemed like what he considered typical island folk: good people, hard working, ever-willing to share in a laugh.

As they were chatting exuberantly at the dinner table, David noticed a rather curious transformation beginning to take place in Constance. Ever since they'd met up with the Fletchers, her mannerisms and style of speaking had been gradually shifting from her very proper British-American prose, easing into the colorfully idiomatic speech of the Islands. It was contagious. He soon found even himself laughing the way they did, and peppering his conversation with terms like 'yeah man', almost as if he was subconsciously trying to gain their acceptance through imitation.

After dinner, they all moved to the living room. 'Pop Fletcher', as the patriarch of the clan was respectfully called, insisted that David sit in his chair, an old recliner which had seen years of faithful service. Everyone else pulled his or her seats up around an old *Grundig* wood cabinet radio-phonograph to tune in the news of the day. David hadn't seen anything like in it years, guessing it must have been made back sometime in the 'Fifties. Elouise explained that the hills surrounding the town caused poor television reception generally, so it made no sense to spend the money.

So there they were, six adults sitting together, actually talking with each other: a literal step backward in time. David was naturally the focus of conversation; apparently everyone on the island had an insatiable appetite when it came to hearing about life in America. He assured them it wasn't at all like the old Hollywood motion pictures they knew so well. But all things considered, everything was going along smoothly until David mentioned that he was staying at Buxton Hall. Again, the revelation was received with cryptic glances. Pangs of frustration began to set in as the conversation purposely drifted off in other directions. Eventually, he would have to get to the bottom of this little mystery.

The women very obviously wanted to talk by themselves. Almost as if on cue, Anton stood up and stretched, inviting David to join him and Pop outside for a beer. As soon as they got outside, the wooden shutters snapped close loudly on the windows. Pop elaborated in something of an explanation that the lights inside the house attracted moths and a host of other flying bugs that the women folk didn't like. The American suggested that they might try installing mesh screens; the old man took the advice with a smile.

"Here you go," said Anton handing David and his father a beer. "Rowentine's Lager," he pried off the bottle top and raised it to his lips. "Ahh, a cool sip o' paradise."

"You know, you could have a nice career back in the 'States doing beer commercials," observed David almost seriously.

Anton didn't have a clue about what David was talking about, answering the observation with a bellowed laugh.

It was getting late in the evening. Up and down the road, there was evidence that a few people were still active, as bobbing flashlights and lanterns marked their presence in the darkness like oversized fireflies meandering in the summer night. If Constance didn't have to work in the morning, David would've been content to stay and continue the exchange of thoughts with the Fletchers. But it was time to go.

"I guess I should use the bathroom first."

"One beer too many, huh?" inquired Constance. "It's a good thing I'm doing the driving."

He got up to go back inside the house but was quickly redirected to a wooden shack just behind the house. When he returned, he made a point of giving the Fletchers his address back in New York City, without really expecting to ever see or hear from them again. But he was glad to have made the imposition on Connie and coming along with her, since he enjoyed the time spent with the Fletchers. Theirs, he thought, though plainly a simpler view of life, out here beneath the clear mountain skies, held no less truth or relevance than his own attitudes.

They got in the car, and were almost back to the main road when a lantern suddenly flared on directly in front of them. Connie slammed on the brakes; a man went down in front of the car.

"Oh my God!" she screamed, scrambling to get out of the car. "I didn't see him, I couldn't stop! I wasn't going that fast."

David joined her as they ran around to check how badly the man was injured; he was laying face down. Almost the instant they reached him, two other men charged out of the undergrowth and tackled David. The man on the ground sprang up and raced over to the car shutting off the engine, turning out its headlights.

David shouted for Connie to get back to the house, but instead, she ran over to help him. The other man returned, pulled her away from his comrades and pushed her back against the car. He took something from his pocket, and then picked up the lantern and held it so she could see the light glint on a sharp metal blade. It was a knife. He ordered her not to scream, and warned David to be still.

"What do you want from us?" asked David, his arms locked up behind his back.

"We just want to borrow a little money," the man with the lantern said almost jokingly.

"Oh jeeze," David replied trying to maintain his cool. "Sorry guys, all I've got is American."

"No problem. Don't worry you'self," the man answered. "Yankee greenback will do just fine."

"David…Be careful," Constance warned. Her trembling voice said unmistakably that she was afraid.

"Gal, I told you to keep quiet—"

"Connie, relax. Everything's gonna be okay."

The man with the lantern laughed out: "Ha hah...Gal, listen to the man. Everything gonna be oh-kay," he mocked.

"Yeah," replied David, as coolly as he could. "Now, why don't we make a deal? You let the lady go, and I'll give you all the money I have, no questions asked. And I give you my word, I won't call the police."

"Your word, huh? Okay, I like a dealing man. Where's you money?"

"Let the lady go first."

The man then spoke to one of his confederates: "Joker, check him. Empty him pockets."

'Joker' complied, producing David's wallet. He handed it to the man with the lantern to check the contents. As he did so, the light revealed a damaged hand and forearm—the same scars David had seen earlier in front of the grocery store. He quickly stopped himself from saying anything, fearful that the revelation would cause the situation to get worse. The other men searched the rest of David's body, looking for a money belt or something. One of them indicated to the scarred man that David was 'clean', and then asked David what he was doing there.

"Why you come up here, man? You looking to score?"

"What? I don't understand."

"Man, you take me for a fool?...I'm talking 'bout herb! You people always come up here looking for herb. You want to buy some ganja, man?"

"No!" came back an agitated denial. "We just came here to visit some friends."

"Sure...So," the game of question and answer continued, "you like black women, huh?"

David didn't respond.

The other man holding him jerked back his head painfully by the hair. "Me friend ask you a question!"

"Leave him alone," pleaded Constance. "Take our money, take the car but leave us alone!"

"Shut you mouth gal!" The scarred man twisted her arm making her squeal. "If you make another sound, I cut 'im!"

"Leave her alone!"

Excited by the nearby commotion, the Fletcher's dog began to bark wildly back at the house.

"The man tell you to be quiet!" A forearm stranglehold was locked around David's throat.

"Girl, what you doin' with this white man?" demanded one of the men holding David. He couldn't understand her whimpered reply, so he prodded her with his foot: "I'm speakin' to you!"

"He's my *friend*!"

Her assertion was greeted with laughter.

"Friend?" The scarred man pulled her close, staring into her face. He'd been smoking marijuana himself; the distinctive odor was still strong on his breath. "Gal, you is a fool or what? All 'im want is some ass! What make you think 'im care shit 'bout you?"

A moment of tense silence followed. The scarred man backed Constance up and pushed her against her car, pinning her there with his body. He was sweating and smelled strongly of perspiration. He held up the lantern, and used his free hand to tug her head back.

"You know, you not a bad-looking girl…"

The words rang clear with ominous intent. David immediately began to struggle to get loose of his captors. He managed to knock one of the men holding him off balance then all three men fell across the car's hood in a heap. They slid off, bouncing to the ground.

In the next instant, pandemonium broke loose…The man holding Constance spun around and punched David square in the face. He fell to the ground.

"Hey! What the hell is going on here?" A loud voice shouted angrily from behind them. It was Anton. He charged towards them carrying a piece of wood in his hand. Constance screamed to him for help.

As David fought in a daze to get to his feet, he was thrown down to the ground again. A parting kick was landed to his side as all three of their attackers ran off in different directions. Anton gave chase.

Elouise arrived to find her friend kneeling over a nearly prostrate figure: "Lorrie!" she shouted. "Omigod! What happened? Are you okay?" She picked up the lantern the men had discarded in their rush to escape and brought it over.

David exhaled loudly, and then with Constance's aid he sat up against the car. "It's alright," he said checking his nose and mouth for blood. "I'm okay."

"Oh thank God!" wailed Constance in tears. "I was afraid they would kill you."

"Calm down, I'm fine. Those guys were just punks. I think I'd recognize one of them if I saw him again." He lifted his hand to Constance's face to wipe away a tear. "You were in more danger than I was…"

"What's wrong? Did they hurt you?" inquired Elouise concerned for her friend.

"What's happening here?" Pop and his wife ambled up to the car; the old man was holding a formidable double-barreled shotgun at the ready.

"I'm fine," assured Constance.

Anton returned out of breath, with a not too surprising announcement: "They got clean away...Hey man, you alright?"

"Yes," replied David. Four anxious pairs of hands helped him to his feet. With Anton and Constance on either side of him, they all began to walk back to the house.

"You were really brave," beamed Constance. "He stood up to those thugs," she repeated to Elouise and family.

"I was scared," admitted David. "I would've wet my pants if I hadn't gone to the outhouse."

Anton was the only one that laughed.

"Well I don't care," continued Constance. "You were great!"

"Please Connie, the next time I tell you to run," he smiled, "just do it..."

"But how could I do that," she kissed him gently on the cheek. "I said I would protect you."

Once back inside the house, David's injuries were examined and pronounced superficial, though his ribs might be sore for a while; the only really visible scar on his part was a swollen upper lip. Constance for her part suffered more from humiliation than anything else, and that was a feeling that was shared by all in the room. That such a thing could occur on his very doorstep enraged Pop Fletcher; he promised that the men would be quickly found and punished. David told Pop about the man with the flesh colored scar. Given the description, Pop knew pretty much who it was. Carlton Seely was the scarred man's name. Armed with that knowledge, it wouldn't be hard to find the other two.

Warm good-byes were exchanged again, but this time the visitors were escorted out to the main road. Fortunately, Connie's keys were on the floor of her car.

They began the long drive back to the security of the coastal lowlands and a more familiar civilization. Constance was now expressing feelings of indignation against their attackers: how dare they ruin what had been a very enjoyable visit! David for his part proved to be more understanding of the psyche of their assailants, citing and amplifying upon Connie's own assessment of their motivations just a few hours earlier. Predictably, she found no solace in this.

"David, I don't understand you. They beat you, they kicked you...How can you sit there and defend them?"

"Connie, I'm not defending anyone. Believe me, I've met some real killers in my time. Those guys were not. I'm just trying to get a handle on the feelings of resentment they had towards us. They're young, not unintelligent guys I guess, who've come to realize that the future just doesn't hold much promise for them."

"Oh what a crock!...And that justifies what they did to us?"

"Not at all. But I can understand why they would resent us. When I saw them this afternoon, the way they looked at you and me...I could *feel* the anger in their eyes. There I was: a white man, a foreigner, an American, intruding on their little corner of the universe. That solidified it for them: they knew then how little they had. They saw me as representing all the power in the world, possessing in their eyes, everything they probably can never have."

"Oh please," her eyes rolled as she looked to the heavens for divine guidance and patience.

"Connie, I didn't think I would have to explain it to you. You heard what they said: they looked at me as using you, just like any other trinket that money could buy. They weren't after the money. I had barely ten dollars in my wallet. They didn't utter a word...Don't you see? What they wanted was satisfaction. They got it from me by kicking and humiliating me. They would have gotten it from you...in another way."

Constance reacted instantly with an angry, short-lived stare. Yet all David saw in that moment was the poignantly vulnerable side of the woman, trapped in circumstances beyond her control. He decided it best to keep his peace; the point had been made.

For a good while after that, the only sound to break the car-bound silence was the annoying sound of the Volkswagen's horn as she approached countless blind turns. But Constance did not lean into the horn with the same enthusiasm as she had shown before. It was a little past midnight; he assumed she was getting tired. As not much more than an attempt to break the silence, David raised the enigmatic subject of Buxton Hall; what was it that he wasn't being told about the place?

Fatigue cast aside her caution and drew out the whole story. She revealed that around the time of Hannah Buxton-Taylor's notoriety, there were a number of unexplained disappearances of twenty or more young children in the area around Monmouth, young black children. Though the children's parents had complained mightily to the authorities, little was done. Feeling frustrated with the lack of official concern, a group of the parents decided to take matters into their own hands. A representative traveled across the island to Charlestowne to enlist the aid of a noted attorney, a man known for helping Blacks without charging unreasonable fees. The lawyer was Matthew Wellesley Lorrha by name, one of Constance's ancestors, and the mixed-race son of the so-called 'itinerant Irishman' himself. He agreed to help these former slaves because it was apparent that no one else would. The story he eventually uncovered was so fantastic, that it defied the ability of sane men to believe.

Speculation abounded that the proud, beautiful lady of society in whose home David was now a guest, was connected to the disappearances. But what Matthew Lorrha uncovered led him to believe that Hannah Buxton-Taylor herself was personally responsible for the deaths of the children. The former common-law wife of Hannah's Groundskeeper, a woman named Maureen Hancock, told the incredible story to Matthew Lorrha. She had lost her lover to Hannah. Matthew confronted Mrs. Buxton-Taylor directly with the disclosure, and she all but admitted her guilt to him in her arrogance.

But the authorities would hardly proceed on accusations made by a woman whose motives were likely fused by revenge. Matthew knew that he lacked the evidence to proceed, especially when these charges were leveled against one of the wealthiest women in the British Empire. It seemed that her crimes would go unpunished, at least before the justices of this world.

However, the authorities would later have their own suspicions about what was happening on at Buxton Hall. One of Hannah's former lovers had died under questionable circumstances. The man's sister refused to accept that his death was an accident; it was her insistence that prompted the police to reopen the inquiry years later. Just when the police felt they'd gathered enough evidence to begin a formal investigation, Hannah was unexpectedly found dead at her home. Her death was ruled officially as coming from natural causes. The allegations about the fate of the children were thereafter suppressed, the truth forever unknown. The facts of that ninety-year-old police investigation were not to become fully known until the island achieved independence. Such was the fear of 'repercussions', and the power of her family.

David found the tale a fascinating retrospective on the island's history. "Repercussions huh? You mean they were actually afraid of the slaves?"

"Well, maybe not afraid. They needed us to work the fields all over the island."

"A purely economic consideration, eh? Can't say I'm too surprised. Bill Redditch told me another story, about the Hancock woman's husband poisoning Hannah."

"That would be Sean Mack…His real name was Siann McFormorian. He was a bully-boss, you know, an overseer. He kept the plantation running and the workers in-line."

"So it was Sean Mack who did her in," mused David.

"That's one version. Old Matthew believed she poisoned herself to avoid a public scandal."

"That's all well and good, but nothing you've said answers the big question. Why would Hannah kill the children, or one of her lovers for that matter?"

Constance warned him that the tale got even more bizarre. Hannah was rumored to be deeply involved in the rites of satanic worship. The children and perhaps even her lover, so the story went, were her instrument to achieve the ultimate fallacy of pride: she was in search of eternal youth. According to Maureen Hancock, Hannah cruelly tortured the children, keeping them alive in agony for days for her profane purposes; she would later claim that their pitiful cries and pleas for help could be heard at night in the old house for years afterward. An Anglican priest was eventually called in to perform ancient rites of exorcism, setting the children's souls finally to rest. The surviving heirs of the Buxton estate eventually sold the house, casting off what had become a tarnished legacy; that was how Francis Hurrell came to acquire the property.

"…To this day, many people still believe that the old house is haunted by her ungodly presence. Have you heard anything at night?" she asked.

"No, but I'm a heavy sleeper," David replied half in jest.

Constance ignored the flippancy of his remark and went on with the rest of the tale.

Hannah had grown up with and gained the trust of her father's former slaves, mixing with them and attending their festivals as one of their own. But her attitudes towards them changed radically after she returned from school in Europe; she no longer cared for their feelings or their 'backward island ways'. The pleasant, red-haired child they had reluctantly sent away, that once they had raised with the milk of their own bodies, looked upon them with scorn upon her return. Oh, she made as much a show of concern for their welfare as was necessary, but they all knew the truth. Now they were workers, little more than a necessary part of the plantation her family owned.

"If the stories you told me about her were true, she had to be insane," David concluded. "How else could she have killed so many children?…She wasn't getting any younger. Couldn't she see that she was wasting her time?"

"What do you mean?"

"I mean couldn't she see that she was still getting older?"

"I'm not so sure. David, that picture in the living room of the house, I'm sure it was painted not much more than a year before she died."

"So?" quizzed David, unsure of what she was trying to say.

"I once worked at the library in town and I saw a copy of her birth certificate. She must have been at least sixty-five years old when it was painted."

"Oh come on, that's impossible! The woman in that portrait was no more than uh, thirty. Thirty-five at most." Then his expression changed, the confusion left his brow. "I think I have the answer." A smile came to his face. "So maybe she was sixty-something when it was painted, but hey, she paid for the thing. The artist painted the picture to flatter her."

He looked over to Constance with eyebrows raised; she didn't say anything.

"Yeah," he grinned, feeling rather pleased with himself. "It makes sense. If she couldn't turn back the years in reality, then she could always look at the picture, and see herself the way she wanted to be."

"Okay, I'd agree with you except for one thing. Even in her own day, she was well-renowned for her youthful looks."

"And how do you know that?"

"David, I said I worked at the library in Monmouth. It may not be very big, but there is a section devoted to our local history, complete with a collection of old photographs. I saw at least four photographs of Hannah. They were all dated."

"Connie, you can't be serious."

"Okay, so don't take my word for it. Go see for yourself."

David crawled into bed that night and fell almost immediately into a deep sleep. He was awakened prematurely in the dark early hours of the morning by voices out in the hallway. One was a woman; he thought it was the housekeeper on the phone or she maybe was talking to someone. In the stupor of his half-awake state, he simply wanted the noise to stop so he could go back to sleep. The voices were muffled; he couldn't make out what was being said. The next moment, the voices were replaced by footsteps, slow plodding steps that broke into a run, booming footsteps running loudly down the hall.

He called out to Jeanna, but there was no reply. His eyes were still almost closed as he got up and walked over wearily to the door. He composed himself, opened the door slowly and looked out. The hallway was quiet and dark.

Again, he called out for Jeanna, and again there was silence. He was almost fully awake now; he rubbed his eyes clear. There was no one there. His feet began to move with a will of their own, sending him down the hallway; he wondered who might be in the house so late. It wouldn't be burglars; they wouldn't make all that noise announcing their entry. As he got to the top of the staircase, he became aware of a lingering fragrance in the air. It was Country Lavender, just as sweet as the scent he'd noticed on his arrival at Buxton. The night outside was warm but not unpleasant; he assumed a window must be open, that the scent must be wafting in from the garden. He continued downstairs and approached Jeanna's room. He looked under the door for a light but there was none. He knocked and called to her first in a loud whisper, then full-voiced. The light went on. She called out a harried reply, eventually coming sheepishly to the door in nightcap and dressing gown clutched tightly at the neck.

"Mr. Llewellyn, Can I help you?" she peeked out.

"Hi Jeanna. Sorry to get you up, but, were you just upstairs?"

"No sir. I just wake up when you knock on my door. Why do you ask?"

"I thought I heard voices upstairs."

"I wasn't upstairs," she replied. "I been in my bed since eleven tonight"

"I was sure I heard voices, and footsteps in the hallway."

"Oh my gosh! Did someone break into the house?"

David hesitated as he looked down the hall. "No. I'm pretty sure there's no one else here."

"Well sir, I can assure you I wasn't upstairs." She paused patiently to collect her thoughts. "Mr. Llewellyn, this is an old house. The water pipes rattle when the toilet downstairs here runs. I have to get a plumber to come out."

"Water pipes...I guess that must be it." He apologized for disturbing her. "I'm a little hungry. I'll just get something from the kitchen."

"Do you need me to fix you something?"

"No, no. I'll help myself. You go back to sleep. Sorry again."

She closed the door, happy to oblige. David suddenly felt very tired, resolving instead to go back to bed himself. He climbed the stairs thinking of what Constance had said earlier about 'things going bump in the night', and decided that the suggestion had actuated itself in his subconscious. Jeanna was right. Buxton Hall was an old house; a water pipe's animated gurgling can be many things when you're half-asleep.

Two days passed before David felt up to going over to the library. Following Constance's lead, he sat down in the section on local history and with the librarian's help, located the photographs. Though none of the aged black-and-white images he saw was very large, the woman pictured and named as Mrs. Hannah Buxton-Taylor did not appear any older than the proud figure portrayed in the

Buxton Hall painting. Although this confirmed what Constance had told him, it established little else. Hannah was probably just one of those people who didn't show her years.

After a considerable amount of digging, he found copies of the handwritten parish birth and death records for the Buxton family. Sure enough, Hannah Alexandrina Mary Buxton was listed as the second of four children and the eldest of three daughters born to Joseph William Buxton and the former Francesca Saunders; Hannah's birth year was given as 1820. Reading on, he discovered that her elder brother and one of her sisters had died before either child saw a sixth birthday. Hannah's own death was recorded in the local newspaper in a short paragraph that ran a scant five lines. The notice was dated in October of 1887.

# CHAPTER 4

It would be Wednesday afternoon before David saw Constance again. He followed up on the invitation to visit Brendan's studio, and met her at the travel office in Monmouth where she worked. From there, Brendan's studio was a short drive down to the waterfront.

"I'm really sorry you didn't get to meet Mahernum," said Constance. "I think you and she are a lot alike."

"How do you figure that?"

"Well, she sees something good in almost everyone. After what happened the other night, I think you must be a very forgiving sort."

"Thanks…I guess."

"No, no. I do mean it as a compliment. I find it really admirable in a nice, maybe naïve sort of way."

"So now Mahernum and I are *naïve?*"

Constance laughed at David's irritation, explaining instead why she thought David should meet Mahernum. "She has a unique gift and uses it to help people. She can sort out what's going on, and help you put everything in context."

"Connie, I appreciate what you've saying. Sure, I would love to meet her from the 'meeting someone interesting' viewpoint. But," he smiled, "I can assure you, I'm pretty content with my life. I don't need someone to help me find myself. I know who I am, and where my life is going."

"That may be so," replied Constance. "But we can all use a little help to find our dreams."

She parked the car on an access road of what looked like an abandoned dockside warehouse, walking over to an unpainted metal clad door. While David stood assessing the exterior condition of the structure, Constance rang a doorbell and peered in through a grime-covered window. A minute or two later, Brendan met them at the door covered from head to foot in the powdered white detritus of chiseled marble. After apologizing for his appearance, he led his visitors through the dark, largely unused heart of the building, around to a separate area in the back. As they walked, the visitors began to be aware of the gentle strains of classical music floating faintly on the air.

"Rimsky-Korsakov?" asked David.

Brendan affirmed: the 'Prince and the Princess' from 'Scheherazade'. "It's a nice, relaxing piece."

"Oh, that kind of thing is okay but if you ask me," added Constance jiggling her hips, "it's kind of hard to dance to."

When they arrived at the workshop, the contrast with the rest of the warehouse was as clear as the difference between night and day. The walls and ceiling were painted a bright, flat white, and large skylights had been cut into the roof. Ultra modern living quarters were set off to one side, raised up on an elevated hardwood floor. Off to one side was a small fitness center comprised of free weights and a machine that looked designed more to torture rather than tone a human body.

All around the rest of the workshop were canvas tarpaulins draped over enigmatic, undulating shapes: works in progress assumed David. Positioned near the rear receiving entrance was Brendan's current project, surrounded by telltale piles of stone chips and dust; an array of mallets and chisels lay on a sturdy workbench next to the statue. The receiving door was raised open, allowing in a pleasant breeze from the sea. As he walked by, he grabbed and set into nearly noiseless motion a chain-block and pulley that hung from the beams above. David wandered over to check out and admire the view.

"It's a magnificent sight," acknowledged Brendan. "I can see most of the harbor bay from here."

David turned to take a closer look at the statue behind him; to his eyes, it was a tall, amorphous mass of stone. "Daphne and Apollo?" he asked.

"No," replied Brendan. "That's them, over there." He pointed over to the stockpile of covered works.

"It's going to be wonderful when it's finished," remarked Constance. She had just returned from the kitchen with a cold bottle of American beer for David and a glass of bubbling mineral water for herself.

"Don't I rate somethin' to drink?" smiled Brendan.

"You get cleaned up first," she said, "and I'll have a nice, cold brew waiting for you when you get back."

"Just as long as it's not any of that fizzy seltzer water you like to drink. I'll be right back. Why don't you tell Davie here about our latest project?"

David spoke after Brendan had left the room. "Here we are, alone once again. He keeps leaving you with me."

"Oh, do I scare you?" She winked an eye; he smiled a modest smile.

"What's this project you guys were talking about?" he asked.

"You're looking at it."

"You mean this?" He pointed at a rough-hewn block of marble in front of him.

"This is going to represent the friendly, blithe spirit of we simple island folk. He's going to embody the concept in the figure of a woman. I'm modeling for it."

"Simple island folk, huh?"

She hurried over to the table and brought back some sketches Brendan had made of her in semi-traditional island dress: a turbaned headscarf, a puffy short-sleeved blouse, and a long, multi-petticoated dress.

David smiled as he looked at the drawings. "I see. Looks like a nice idea, but that is not how I see you."

"Oh, how *do* you see me?" she smiled.

Before he could reply, Brendan returned to the studio looking a little more presentable. The tour of the workshop began now in earnest. The sculptures were uncovered one by one, as sketches conceptualizing each piece were displayed. All were in various states of completion. Brendan came off sounding like the proud father as he discussed his creations, but David didn't fail to notice that Constance seemed even prouder of their creator. She was practically falling over herself in singing the praises of his work. But she wasn't the only woman who had fallen under Brendan's relaxing, charismatic spell. David recalled the party at Hatherleigh, and how any number of the women they had met seemed entranced with the man. And why not, he sighed; he couldn't help but envy Brendan with his masculine good looks and cool, almost disinterested charm.

Finally, they arrived at one work David recognized without the need for an introduction.

"I know this one. This is your 'Rape of Daphne', right?"

"That you are. But I think that title engenders thoughts that are a little too violent. I intend to call my version: *A Prayer Answered*." He paused with his hands together hanging expressively in the air, awaiting a reaction. "Okay, maybe not that. But at least somethin' relevant to the storyline."

"You poor boy," Constance rubbed his back encouragingly and turned to David. "This is the piece I was collecting the driftwood for."

David tilted his head as his eyes followed the curving arch of the woman's body, commenting on how it melted effortlessly into the twisting contour of the olive tree trunk. "…It flows rhythmically, almost like music."

"Glad you like it. But for future reference that's a laurel tree," corrected Brendan.

"What? Oh yeah, a laurel tree. I must be getting old. Imagine forgetting my ancient Greek trees like that."

"I just like to pay attention to details. Over here is something I'm doing for Rhonda that I'd like you to see."

The trio strolled the few feet over to what appeared to be a covered bust. Brendan took hold of the top of the cloth, turned to David and then paused. "I'm going to cast a bronze from the clay. It's something I think you'll both find very interesting."

Without another word, he unveiled the sculpture and waited for a response from his guests.

"I've seen that face somewhere before," puzzled David.

The bust was of a woman's head down to the shoulders. Her hair was up in a very old-fashioned Graeco-Roman style. The features of the face were very natural, very graceful, and the expression was gaiety itself expressed fully in a delicate, thin-lipped smile.

"Wow Brendan…It's so real it's almost alive," replied Constance, barely able to control her glee. She grabbed Brendan's arm excitedly: "Will you tell him or should I?"

Both sets of eyes fixed on the perplexed figure, as he tried to recall the faces of the people he'd met during his time on the island.

"No…It couldn't be her?"

"And why not?" answered Brendan with the air of a challenge in his voice.

"What would Rhonda want with a statue of Hannah Taylor?"

"I think the question might be why *shouldn't* she want a statue of her."

David stood open-mouthed, waiting to be enlightened.

"Hannah was her Great-Grand Aunt."

"Okay, it's about time you guys leveled with me. What's going on here?" David's expression was now very serious; he felt as if they'd been planning this all along.

"Really David," added Constance reassuringly, "lighten up! I'm as surprised as you are to see this."

"She's tellin' the truth, man. Now, I've somethin' else to show you."

He led David over to a file cabinet next to the wall, producing a scrapbook filled with photocopies of articles and photographs; the collection was devoted to the life and family of Hannah Buxton-Taylor. Some of the photographs were copies of those David had seen at the library, most however were completely new to him.

Brendan pulled from the drawer a small photograph in an antique picture frame and handed it to David. "Be careful with it. It's very old. This is the photograph I used most to produce the likeness of her. Hannah was a beautiful woman, and not just for her day either. If she were alive today, she'd have the men linin' up at her door, just like our Connie here…"

"Where'd you get the pictures from?" asked David.

"I haven't seen them before either," added Constance. "Why didn't you tell me that you were working on a statue of Hannah?"

"It didn't seem important until our Davie arrived at Buxton," he apologized. "Rhonda loaned most of the photographs to me from her family collection. There're some interestin' pictures in here." He handed them an old album with polished wood covers.

"It's far too nice a day to sit in here and look at musty old photographs," huffed Constance. "Let's take them outside."

Following her suggestion, they moved out to the loading dock. They made themselves comfortable on straw beach mats thrown down on the hot concrete surface. Brendan said they were great for laying around in the sun, exchanging a smile with Constance.

"What about the rest of this story," inquired David, trying his best to ignore the latest flirtation between the two. "Does Rhonda know anything else about Hannah?"

"You mean those mindless stories about 'satanic' rites? Did Connie tell you everythin'?"

"In all the gory detail." He looked her way as he made reply. She sat in innocent silence a little apart from them; her chin perched upon her knees, her arms clasped about her legs.

"Workin' on the bust sort of brings her to life for me," continued Brendan. "I'd like to find out more about the woman behind the myths."

"You're starting to sound like a journalist," replied David.

"I'm serious here. There's a world of truth still to be told about Hannah. But we're goin' to need your help."

"Who's this 'we'?" asked Constance.

"Hannah and I…You know, ever since I heard the story, I've had my doubts. I've always thought she'd taken a bum rap to put it mildly. Sure she wasn't perfect, but who is? I'll need both of you to help prove it."

A smirk appeared on David's face. "You…and Hannah need help? Just what is it you guys want me to do?"

"I need you to help prove some ideas I have on this. I found an article in the library's archives of the Kirkmuir Times Gazette, written in June of 1853. It's only ten lines or so long. But here, I want you to take a look at this."

David read from a discolored copy of a microfilm document with Constance peering over his shoulder. The article was written to commemorate the first meeting of the 'Society of the Stone Circle', a group dedicated to the preservation of ancient Druidic traditions. Inaugural ceremonies would be held at sunrise on Fromesbury Hill. Two men, Lindsay Taylor and a Major Harold Ellis-Cairns, hosted the gathering.

"All that will get you a 'so what' from me," sneered David. "Where're you going with this?"

"Hannah was briefly married to Taylor, the first chairman of the Society. Old Lindsay died at sea in a shipwreck off the Florida Keys. And as for the Major, he was the man Hannah later supposedly murdered. It was his sister who got the police to reopen the case."

"Well okay," David sat up, his eyes keen with interest. "So she knew these guys from their 'tea socials' with this Society. Maybe they even knew each other well, and when her husband died, she got involved with one or the other of his old buddies. It happens."

"Yes," echoed Brendan, "life goes on. But there's more. In the memoirs Connie's famous ancestor here left behind in Charlestown, was mention of certain rumors."

Brendan thus explained that Matthew Lorrha was quite a meticulous investigator. In his notes, he had written down the dates and times associated with everything he was able to uncover, regardless of from whom or how unusual the disclosure. Maureen Hancock, the estate groundskeeper's wife, turned out to be his greatest source of information. Millie, as he referred to her, told him of bizarre rituals she claimed to have witnessed, involving some of the area's most prominent citizens. But no names were given.

"You can read the archives yourself if you doubt me. But from what I read, I had a feelin' that Millie did name names, but Matthew declined to commit them to paper."

"I'd say, given the times, it was probably the wise thing to do," added David.

"Okay," interrupted Constance impatiently. "So what's the upshot of all this, what are you getting at?"

Brendan sat back, his expression now more serious. "I believe that the Society or at least some of its members, were somehow involved in the children's disappearances."

"And not just Hannah?" asked David. "Based on what?"

"The documents I've read. The original accounts are in Charlestown."

"Okay," he exhaled loudly, "so what you're telling me is that you have a bunch of theories based on your interpretations of what you've read?"

"…Gotta start somewhere."

"What makes you think Millie was telling the truth about all this? She as much as said that she had a personal score to settle with Hannah."

"Yes, but Matthew considered that question too. He said he trusted in her sincerity."

"So Brendan, what you're telling me is that we have here a one hundred year old unsolved crime, involving a possible cover-up by members of the island's ruling elite, and with not much more than hearsay for evidence." He raised his eyebrows and smiled: "I think I like it!"

Brendan's face lit up at David's enthusiastic declaration.

"This has the makings of a good story," David continued. "It's almost like being back in junior High School, writing about what I did on my summer vacation."

They all laughed.

"Okay, great! Now David, there's one other thing I have to tell you, and this is the clincher." He paused. "I'm pretty sure that in one form or another, the 'Society of the Stone Circle' is alive and well, right here in Monmouth."

The revelation instantly unleashed in David a rush of ideas for an article of his own: "The Lost Children of Paradise," he mumbled. He had been considering the subject of what his next piece would be on when he returned home, but now that question seemed solved.

"What was that?"

"Oh nothing. I was just verbalizing a thought. You know, I think this has all the elements of a great little series."

"You certainly seem inspired," observed Constance.

"I am," David continued. "Just think of it: a class struggle, an unresolved wrong to right, and a slight touch of the macabre. Add to that, the legend of the ageless redheaded beauty herself. This could be good."

His eyes glassed over in expectation. Constance and Brendan could literally see the scenarios and implications whirring like cogs in his mind as he began to sort out the various angles he could pursue. Abruptly, he raised his head and stared coldly at them.

"Just what's in this for you Brendan? I mean, why hand this story over to me like this now? You've done all the digging, all the research."

A fervent but simplistic answer came almost immediately. "But you know how to tell a story, I don't. I want to see the truth come out. I want the world to know of the unbelievable hypocrisy that still goes on here. You're the writer, David. You got the connections. You can do the job one helluva lot better than I ever could."

"But I thought these people were your friends?"

"Oh no. If the truth be known, I can barely stomach their pompous asses! Most of these assholes act like they think they've still got a God-given right to rule the world…This is the *Twentieth* Century for Christ's sake. They're due a come-uppance."

"But what about the Toveys? I had the impression that you kinda liked them."

"And I do. Look, you've been here only a short time. There's a lot that goes on here you don't know about. Connie, why don't you tell him about that time we were near Charlestowne, when we were driving with your father…Go ahead."

"Oh Brendan, it really wasn't that bad. We *were* blocking the road."

"And so what?" he fired back, still very much disturbed by the memory of the incident. "We were visiting with Connie's father, and since I hadn't been there before, he was driving us around, showin' me some of the sights. Connie's father was a Member of the Assembly in the Parliament here, and he's pretty well known. We're drivin' along on this small road when this poor woman carrying a baby, with not even shoes on her feet, comes runnin' up to the car and flags us down. She'd recognized Norman and wanted to ask him to help her out with somethin', wiping her eyes with her one free hand. He stopped, rolled down the window, and was taking down notes."

He looked back to Constance for support, his blue eyes fired wide with emotion; she acknowledged the details with a quiet nod.

"Anyway, while we're sitting there, a car comes up behind us and starts blowin' its horn. There's this fat, red-cheeked bastard of an Englishman behind the wheel. He'd probably never done an honest day's work before in his life.

Norman then pulls completely off the road to let this fella get by. He turns around and tries to apologize: 'Hey man,' he says, 'I'm sorry if we were blocking the road', and then the bastard shouts back: 'Now there's a bright boy'.

He called Norman a 'boy'.

I mean, can you believe it? Here we had Norman Wellington Lorrha, a respected businessman and legislator with his 'Member of Parliament' plates on the car, a gray-haired gentleman deservin' of respect, and we have jackasses like that fat bastard acting like they still own half the goddamned world. He couldn't have been waiting more than thirty seconds, if that. I couldn't believe it. I was ashamed to be white."

David didn't know quite what to say. He had his suspicions as to Brendan's motivations before, but now he thought he was beginning to understand the man. The righteous indignation that Brendan had displayed at his memory of the incident had served to sway him.

# CHAPTER 5

"David!"

The voice belonged to Constance. She had been driving east on the Coast Road when she saw the familiar, pale-legged figure walking ahead of her. He stopped, turned around and waved as the car wound down to a noisy halt beside him.

"Where are you off to on this fine morning?"

"Actually, it's more a case of where I'm coming from. I got a call this morning from our Port William office to come over and pick up some things."

"A trip to the big city," he smiled.

"Yeah, well close enough to a city for these parts. So why are you on foot? Isn't Mr. Hurrell's shiny black Benz working?"

"Ah…The smoker?" he joked, referring to its diesel engine. "It's working fine. It's just that I almost had an accident in it the other day. I wouldn't want to damage it."

"What happened? Were you driving on the wrong side of the road?"

He looked back into her eyes, hesitated, and then admitted that the truth of the matter was much as she had guessed.

"That happens to Americans a lot down here. They think they're comfortable driving on the left side of the road, but going around a corner, or pulling out onto a road, they inevitably veer over to the right. You've got to remember: left, left, left. That's it in a nutshell."

"Yeah, yeah, yeah. Well, I have my own, more environmentally sound solution: it's called walking. Anyway, I wanted to come down to the beach and pick up some shells and coral as souvenirs. You er, care to join me?"

"Well, things *are* a little slow right now at the shop. I think I can hang out with you for a little while."

The decision thus made, she pulled completely off the road and locked up her car. They strolled barefoot across the sun-warmed warm sands, down to a nearby inlet sheltered by palm trees.

"At last!" he exclaimed.

"What's that about?" asked Constance, looking at the smile on his face.

"It is so good to have you all to myself, without Brendan around. Now don't get me wrong, I think he is one hell of a guy and artist, but sometimes, I mean he has a way of looking directly into your eyes…It can be very uncomfortable."

"I like it when a man looks into my eyes. It means that he's paying the proper attention."

"Well that's different."

"You'll get used to Brendan," began Constance. "He has a tendency to get his 'Irish' up at times."

Just to let him know where Brendan was coming from, she began to divulge what she knew of the man's family history. He was a second generation Irish Catholic, who grew up with an almost innate distrust of all things British.

"So you see," she continued, "it all makes perfect sense. He has an almost obsessive tendency to get involved in any cause which pits the little guy against the establishment."

"Sounds like you've got him pretty well psychoanalyzed. But then, why move to this place?"

"Because of his relationship with Francis Hurrell," she answered. "Frank is one of Brendan's strongest patrons. He loves his work."

"And I guess Brendan's still got to make a living. Paradise is as good a place as any, if you have to work."

Constance laughed at David, scoffing at the thought of Grand Kirkmuir as any man's paradise. But the smile on her face vanished almost immediately as her eyes fixed on the sky behind him. "Oh damn," she exclaimed in a low voice, "we'd better go!"

"What's wrong?"

She pointed back to the mountains; all of a sudden, a fierce bank of storm clouds had appeared over the ridge, and was gaining on them fast.

The normally clear blue skies were overcome in an instant by the dark menacing charcoal grays of a fast moving squall; the car was too far away. They began to run through the bushes towards a beach shelter a few hundred yards away; but it was too late. Heavy, wind-blown rains tumbled from the skies, thundering down upon their heads, soaking them through from head to foot before they could reach the shelter.

"I have never seen a storm move so fast in my life," panted David as he caught his breath. "Look at this," he said flexing his shoes with a squeak, "even my boats are filled with water!"

Constance had faired no better. Her hair was a wet bedraggled mess, and her yellow t-shirt clung to her body revealing the details of a lacey brassiere and the female anatomy beneath.

"Oh…You get used to storms like that around here. This is our rainy season. This island is so small, a storm can roll up over the mountains in minutes!"

David did what he could not to stare at her. He sat down to empty his shoes of water and sand, then took off his shirt and threw it across the back of a platform bench to dry. All the while, he focused on the top of her head.

"A great idea," acknowledged Constance. She began to slowly peel off her wet t-shirt, but snagged it on an earring. "Ouch! David, help me. I'm stuck!"

Being the perfect gentleman that he was, he raced to help her extricate herself from the tangle of wet cloth. She was frozen in place, arms in the air, the T-shirt pulled up over her head. He was momentarily amused.

"Now you just relax, I'll have you out of this in a second."

He could feel his own heartbeat picking up. He stood staring at the flowery yellow lace blossoming with the fullness of her form, as he slowly helped her to free herself.

"…All done."

"Oh, thank you." She began to carefully smooth the water out of her hair. "I hate it when things get stuck over my head. I should have taken these dumb things off first."

She pulled the earrings off in disgust and tossed them carelessly onto the wooden table. As she looked back at him, she saw the 'interested' expression of his eyes and laughed.

"David, you're gawking at me. Haven't you ever seen women's lingerie before?"

"…Of course I have."

"Pretend I'm wearing a bikini top or something, if it will make you feel at ease." She walked over and sat atop the table, resting her feet upon the bench.

David remained where he was, unable to move; his eyes still fixed in a boyish gaze. He began to back away.

"Where are you going?" She smiled and patted the table invitingly beside her. "Come and sit down. I promise I won't bite."

Her deep brown eyes sparkled with mischievous intent as she leaned back on her arms. He began to move towards her, stopping at the bench just in front of her feet. He could feel his heart pounding nervously in his chest. Reaching out with a trembling hand, he gently touched the side of her face.

She reached up and steadied his hand with hers, allowing her head slip back so that he would have to come in even closer.

He complied.

She stared enticingly into his eyes and spoke his name softly: "David…We're all alone."

He reached down and touched her knee, then slowly, as if waiting for her to stop him, he began to run his hand lightly up her thigh. Her eyes closed; she reached down and slid her fingers down from his navel, grabbing and unfastening the top button of his pants. He moved in towards her, bringing their lips together in that first, longed for kiss, tasting and savoring the passion he found there. Constance put her arms around his neck and brought him in to her as she lay back on the table. He climbed atop her and began to tenderly kiss her nose, her cheeks, then lightly below her ear. He reveled there in the rain-sweetened scent of her perfume, breathing in deeply as he lovingly caressed the supple fullness of her breasts with eager but gentle hands. With his lips he next began to softly explore her body, kissing her neck, the smoothness of her chest between her breasts moving lower, ever slowly, lower. She writhed in blissful ecstasy as he progressed down to experience the warm, moist pleasures of her womanhood.

This was what he had dreamed of in the unspoken thoughts of uncounted hours since he had met her. He raised himself up and entered her, locking his arms as he looked down upon the firmness of her mellow, brown body. His eyes were filled with her beauty; she was absolute perfection. She more than satisfied his dreams in releasing the willful desires of his fantasies.

Constance partially opened her eyes to watch her lover, delighting in the changing expressions of David's face, the depth and erotic fervor of his desire for her. She actively encouraged the avid lust of his lovemaking, for she relished being wanted and for now, enjoyed being taken. Together, moving to the rhythm of the rain beating loudly down upon the tin roof above them, they reached the peak of their shared passion as the clouds rumbled low with the distant sounds of thunder.

They lay in the closed embrace of each other's arms for untold moments until Constance pushed herself free and sat up. She had to return to her job; David had to reluctantly let her go.

"Well," she continued, "at least I know that you're not gay. Not that I ever had any doubts."

"Oh, is that was this was all about?" he joked.

"Of course not silly," she kissed him in frank reassurance.

"You know, all this time, I thought you and Brendan were, well, more than just friends."

"Oh, but we *are* more than 'friends'. We're very close."

He smiled back, satisfied for now by what she'd said.

"Okay," she announced. "Looks like the storm's just about gone now. We'd better hang these things up in the bushes," she said picking up their clothes. "They should dry quickly."

Within minutes, the horizons around them were hazy with hot, steamy evaporation as the tropical sun emerged to shine down even mightier than before. They sat and talked about the sky and ocean for a few more minutes before Constance affirmed it was time to move on. As she picked up her earrings, a large pearl-like adornment fell off one of them and rolled to a stop in a crack of the table.

"Oh hell," exclaimed Constance, trying to piece the earring back together. "I shouldn't have thrown them onto the table. I really liked these things."

"Don't worry," he took the earring from her. "Probably nothing a little glue can't handle. I'll take care of it for you."

She threw her arms around his neck and kissed him fully. Just as he was beginning to enjoy the embrace, she pushed away again, offering to drive him over to Buxton Hall saying 'it was time to return to the real world'. David declined her offer, deciding to venture back to the house via the seacoast. With that, they sadly and reluctantly parted company the way lovers so often do.

Buxton Hall was nestled on a high cliff, sheltered from the fury of seas by lines of trees planted as a windbreak. He began to climb the rocky crags up from the sea-sprayed coast when he found what appeared to be an old pathway that had not been used in a while. The course of the road then split, one route heading up to a grove of ornamental trees and hedges he had seen behind the house. Having nothing else pressing on his mind, he decided to follow the road to see where it might lead to. He was still about a quarter of a mile away from the house when he came upon a thickly wooded section of the grounds that had been allowed to return to nature's care. He soon discovered why.

Grown over by vines and thick scrub vegetation, almost hidden permanently from view was a small, granite-faced building whose impressive style reminded David of an ancient Greek temple. As he drew closer, he began to realize that this was where the Buxton clan began their endless journey through eternity; he had found the family's burial crypt. Immediately, he began to wonder if this was the final resting-place of Hannah Taylor herself; there was only one way to find out.

Pushing his way through the brush, he expectantly climbed a short bank of granite stairs up to the crypt's massive weathered-iron door. A panel above the door affirmed his discovery; in deeply chiseled letters, the name 'BVXTON' was spelled out in Latin fashion (with a 'V' substituting for the modern 'U' in the name). He reached out to test the door's large levered handle, and was surprised to find it unlocked. With a prodigious heave, the door creaked open on its massive, antique hinges.

He stumbled into the darkness of the crypt and momentarily held his breath: the air inside was stale. The size and shape of the chamber immediately struck him, the space within seeming so much larger inside than its outside dimensions would have had him believe. The outside of the building appeared rectangular in shape, but its inside was rounded and rose into a dome; it was an impressive architectural feat. His every movement was amplified in sound, which only added to the feeling he felt that he was an unwanted intruder, trespassing on the long undisturbed tranquility of the place. He reconciled reason to emotion quickly, since after all, he meant no harm. But it was still too dark to see anything clearly; he went back to the door and pushed it as far open as he could.

As he turned back around he was startled to see faces, staring back at him through the dark shadows; it was like a ghostly journey backward in time. All around the walls of the crypt were Romanesque stone busts of the male members of the family, their names etched beneath them, set in hollowed niches above the layered tombs. With his eyes straining to see through the poor light, he came upon the likeness of the Buxton dynasty's founder: Samuel Claymore. To David's eyes, the square jaw and solemn visage he saw befit the brow of a former merchant sea captain. This surely was a man whose will was strong enough to ensure that he got whatever he wanted.

Having put in his time at the library, David's task was made easier as he searched the walls for Hannah's name. There was Joseph William and wife Francesca, Hannah's parents, placed one above the other. He continued the search. Finally, his efforts were rewarded; as laid out in a burial space not far from her parents was the tomb of one Hannah Alexandrina Mary. Reaching up, he hesitantly touched the incised letters of her name; this was her final resting-place.

"Hello Hannah," he spoke softly, not wishing to disturb the silence of her long sleep. "I'm a visitor in your home, come to pay my respects. I've heard a lot of things said about you, about the things people say that you did. I want you to know, that I will be fair in what I write. I want only to present the truth."

Thus, having said his piece, he decided to end his intrusion and leave this dark place of solitude to the Dead. He closed the crypt door as gently as he could, glad again to once more to be out in the warm sunlight.

He was no sooner out of the thicket that surrounded the burial crypt than he came upon a second discovery. Sitting in the grove of trees was a huge bronze sundial, turned almost completely green by action of the elements. He wondered at first why he hadn't seen it before from the house, but a second look at the weathered exterior explained how it would have been difficult to see, blending so well with the natural greenery of the trees. The sundial was made even more curious as all of its aspects spoke of the moon. A large, stylized representation of the crescent moon served as the gnomon, and rose at least four feet in the air. The plate section sat on a low pedestal, the sides of which were covered in strange cursive, leaf-like designs. The hour marks on the plate were fashioned after the phases of the lunar orb, marking the gradual progression from new to full moon.

David continued on up to the house, thinking that he should invite Constance out to the grove for a champagne picnic one afternoon; the sundial would serve for a pleasant backdrop.

# CHAPTER 6

Almost two days passed since the rainstorm. Constance had barely returned home to her store-top apartment when the telephone rang. On the phone was an animated David; he said that he'd been trying to reach her all day. She explained that she had been visiting with Brendan, and that he'd discovered some new information on the Stone Circle Society. David shrugged off the news, suggesting instead that they meet for dinner to discuss in person Brendan's revelations. The time and place were easily arranged.

Breaking with the usual dating traditions, Constance drove her car over to pick up David at Buxton Hall. He greeted her with flowers and a kiss, but she quickly persuaded him to switch to the old black Benz if for no other reason than to get it some exercise. But in truth he knew that Constance, like everyone else on the Island, was very much aware of 'appearances'. They were soon on their way to dine at the Somerset House hotel restaurant, in the very best part of town. It sat majestically on the great hill overlooking the entrance to the Monmouth harbor. In another time or place, a fortress with black iron cannon might have graced the heights, as the town saw its real beginnings as a provisioning stop for merchant and naval ships alike to take on fresh fruit and sweet water.

Every place and thing in Monmouth had a story it seemed, as Constance filled David in on the history of the hotel. Somerset House was built in the later 1920's by a well liked but frail young man fondly remembered as 'Fritz'. He hailed from an old Swiss hotel family, and had reportedly come out to the islands for reasons of health. As it was, the owner happened to be a fan of the English writer W. Somerset Maugham and named his new hotel after him, deciding it to be totally appropriate upon getting to know a few of his neighbors. Unfortunately, his migration to the Caribbean did him little good, as he died less than five years after construction on the hotel was completed. His family had little interest in continuing the ownership of such a faraway property, and allowed the Somerset to be sold at auction.

Though the hotel was plainly visible from the town below, the way up to the Somerset was along a narrow winding road. The sun was starting to set, and street lighting in Monmouth was inadequate at best. Constance warned David that two large lanterns atop the wall either side of a tree-lined driveway marked the entrance to the hotel. Nonetheless, David slammed on the brakes to avoid driving by the gateway.

Up close and personal, everything about the Somerset spoke to the era of opulence and showmanship in which it was built. The current owners apparently were attuned to the dignity and tradition that the Somerset represented, and spared no expense in maintaining the look and feel of the place. David now understood Constance's reasons for wanting to arrive at such a place in style, and even he felt a little of the patrician's pride in being there.

"There's a picture of Fritz over there," Constance pointed to a nearby wall as the couple waited to be seated.

David happily followed her direction. Across the candlelit foyer was an old ebony-framed photograph of one Karl-Heinz Wilhelmenius, wearing a gaunt-faced smile behind dark, thin-rimmed sunglasses. It was a face that seemed vaguely familiar in its angular lines, but he couldn't think from where. A small bronze plate below the picture was captioned plainly 'Fritz'.

They were escorted past a woman resplendent in a black evening gown playing an open grand piano, to a table near an open verandah that looked out across a calm evening sky, down onto the gently swaying lights of the harbor below. The dining room was sparsely filled with well-to-do patrons, quiet in their enjoyment of the good food and soft music. David selected the wine and began almost immediately to relax into the high-browed pleasantry of the surroundings.

"Right now," he paused to look around, "the real world is pretty far removed from anything in this room."

"Okay, but you've got to admit the atmosphere in here is very nice. And a lot nicer than Bel Rios!"

"Oh yes…Bel Rios. Do you remember that assignment I told you about surviving day-to-day in a black ghetto in the city? What I didn't tell you was how afraid I was when I began the assignment. Poor people used to scare me. Poor people of any kind. I grew up in an all white, middle-class neighborhood in the Midwest, and to be honest, I didn't get exposed to very much.

That all changed when I was on a high school trip when the bus broke down. We were passing through this little backwater of a town on an Indian reservation. The place was a disaster: no real stores or businesses. Most of the buildings in the main part of town were boarded up. I will always remember the way the people there looked at us. Their eyes, I remember, had this strange, empty expression. It was hopelessness. I mean, real hopelessness.

As I look back, I think that was the really frightening thing. Those people were resigned to living out their entire existence with no hope of anything better. You know, when we first saw those guys in the Highlands, I saw that same look again in the eyes of those young men.

We could fix our bus and head home. But they would be stuck there, maybe forever."

"I see what you mean. I couldn't imagine being born and raised on a reservation. The whole thing smacks of a prison camp to me," she muttered. "But even if they left the reservation, would life have been any better for them somewhere else?"

"No, not back then. I like to think that things are changing. But my last assignment showed me how really difficult it can be to change people's attitudes, to get out of poverty. Unless you have help, or just the plain gumption to fight your way out of that kind of existence, I understand why some people take the easy way out."

"It's interesting that you said that. I think Brendan's a fine example of life showing you a way out."

David would find what Constance next told him to be a true revelation. Brendan admitted to her that he wasn't always the 'socially enlightened' soul she now knew. In the neighborhood he grew up in, you trusted no one other than the people you knew on your street or went to Sunday Mass with. Brendan said outright that his father was one of the most bigoted people he had ever known, passing on to her the only words of advice the man had ever given him: "Take nothin' from no one." And those sage words he followed regularly. He recalled being suspended at least three times for fighting before he even got to High School and the only thing his father ever said was that he hoped the other guy looked worse. Brendan said that he couldn't even recall why most of the fights got started.

The turnaround in his life came after he got to High School. He unhappily was required to go on a school trip to an Art Museum, and saw for the first time in his life reproductions of Michelangelo's finest works; he was very much impressed. He always liked to draw pictures of people and animals as a youngster, and found himself sketching images of what he remembered of the statues in other classes. One of his impromptu sketches was confiscated while in a history class, but instead of getting him into trouble, the incident ended up changing his life. The History teacher kept the sketch and later showed it to a friend in the school's Art department, who later contacted Brendan and arranged for a meeting. The History teacher was a Black woman, the Art department instructor was Jewish. Together, they made sure he understood that he had the talent to make something of his life, if he had the desire and the guts to try.

His father ridiculed the idea from the very beginning: College? No, not Brendan; he told him point blank that he was wasting his time, that he would never succeed. He said that they were having their fun with him, and should be ashamed of themselves for filling his head with dreams like that. Brendan said that he would have given up the idea right then had it not been for his mother, who stood up to her husband. If one of her sons had a chance to make something of himself, then he was going to take that chance. His mother went to her grave, still encouraging him to try and be the success she knew he could be.

"Brendan tells me that 'dear old Dad'," she continued, "to this very day, tells him that he's wasting his life and doesn't care to understand anything of who he now is, or how he lives his life."

It was at that moment that the waiter returned to present the wine. While David was talking with him, he noticed that his dinner date's attention was focused on something other than the menu in front of her. She was staring off towards the middle of the room, at something or someone. He turned his head to look as soon as the waiter walked away.

"What's wrong?" he asked.

"…I just saw someone I know: Warren Stephenson. He's the only physician we have in town. Maybe I'll introduce you later."

David perked up: "We should go over now. Where is he?"

She pointed him out, and waved a subtle greeting to a couple seated across the floor. A dark man wearing glasses bowed his head in acknowledgment, holding his gold-rimmed spectacles in place as he did. He had a receding hairline, to which was matched a close-trimmed beard to frame his long face. He was perhaps thirty feet away with a beautiful young woman of perhaps partly Asian extraction as his companion.

"Maybe we should go over and say hello," David repeated.

"No, not now. They've already started their meal. It wouldn't be polite."

"Oh come on, let's go over and be sociable."

With that, he began to reach for Connie's hand to make her to go along with him, but she was quicker. She nimbly avoided his grasp and firmly pressed his hand down onto the table with an 'I said no, David' affirming her decision.

He conceded, and after a moment, tried to continue talking about Brendan. But the mood of the evening was changed thereafter; the rapport he had taken such great pains to build with Constance was disturbed. All through the meal he felt as if a pair of unfriendly eyes was staring hard in his direction, scrutinizing his every move. On the one occasion that he dared sneak a look over, he saw the good Doctor's head snap back, proving to his satisfaction that he wasn't imagining things.

They had almost finished their own entree when the Doctor and his friend across the way got up to leave. David promptly alerted Constance to the couple's imminent departure, and swallowed hastily preparing for the introduction he was sure would come. But as the couple passed by the table, a glance and a nod were all that was exchanged between Constance and her friend.

"So, that's it?" asked David." I thought you wanted me to meet the guy?"

"Really? Was it Warren you were so keen on meeting."

"How's that?"

"Oh come on David, I saw the way you were salivating over that girl he was with. I don't understand how you could do that to me," she feigned injury, "how could you look at another woman when you're out with me! That really isn't very nice."

"Connie, I apologize if in any way I gave you that impression. That's not how it was. How could I possibly even think of looking at another woman when I'm with you? You are by far the most beautiful woman on this island!"

"Now that's better. Thank you."

"You're welcome. Oh, by the way, just out of curiosity, you wouldn't happen to know who she was?...Ouch!"

His last question was answered decisively by a pointy-shoed kick to his shin. Constance's sense of humor, it seemed, was not limitless.

It wasn't until they were on the way home that David remembered her visit with Brendan earlier that day. Constance eagerly disclosed the details of the discussion with an announcement: this was the second month of Beltain. Since the significance of the date was meaningless to David, she continued, revealing rumored plans for a ceremony by the modern-day Society. But it had to take place before the ancient Feast of Lugnasad.

"Beltain?" He looked back at her confused. "*Loog* what? Connie, what are you rambling about?"

She freely acknowledged not being an expert on the topic. All she knew was that Beltain and Lugnasad were ancient Celtic religious feast-times, and that the timing was crucial. She pulled from her purse notes Brendan had written and read it aloud: "There were four main feasts in the old Celtic year. Beltain was held on the first night of May; the next feast was Lugnasad, three months later on the first night of August."

"Celtic festivals?"

"No, *feasts*."

"Connie, you're starting to scare me. You sound like you're beginning to take this stuff seriously…"

"All I know is that Brendan's heard these people are going to perform some kind of ritual, and it has to be done around the time first full moon shows up in August."

"Okay, so that's weeks away. Since Brendan seems so well connected, maybe he can he fill in the most critical piece of information."

"What's that?"

"Who these people are. And while we're at it, what exactly is this ritual these crazies involved with?"

"You'll have to talk to Brendan about that," replied Constance. "He said he'll drop by to see you."

"Great! You had me really worried I'd have to research ancient Celtic dinner menus," he laughed.

They soon arrived back at the grounds of Buxton Hall. David drove slowly around to the back of the house and parked behind Constance's Volkswagen. They lingered nervously in the car like two inexperienced teenagers at the end of a first date, one person patiently expectant of an invitation the other was wholly unable to make. Finally, when it looked like Constance was about to go home, David overcame his fears enough to give voice to the desire within him. He invited her inside; she accepted.

They entered the kitchen and settled in as David looked to brew a pot of decaffeinated coffee. As he noisily searched the cabinets for coffee mugs, Constance revealed almost casually that she was thinking about returning to school in the States.

"Going to Law school, in California?" asked David.

"Right on both counts. Why, can't you see me as a lawyer?"

"Of course I can. It's just Los Angeles, that's a long way from home." He returned to sit with her at the dining table. "I guess this is something you've been thinking about for a while."

"Yes."

"Well, in a very selfish way," he said, staring into her deep brown soulful eyes, "I'm glad you are."

"And why is that?" she asked leaning forward.

"Because you'll be that much nearer to me…"

The next afternoon found David outside on a lounger, comfortably stretched out amidst the bright tropical flowers on the long back veranda of Buxton Hall. A small table beside him was covered with papers. Jeanna appeared from the living room to inform him that he had a visitor.

"Mr. Llewellyn I presume," sounded out a familiar voice.

It was Brendan. He walked around and playfully slapped Jeanna on her rear as he did; under his arm was a stack of books.

"What're you doing out here with the hummingbirds and lizards?" he asked.

David looked up a little confused: "I wasn't expecting you for another hour. I'm just going over some things I'd brought along from the mainland."

"That's what I thought. Man, what is wrong with you? You look too much like you're workin'. Remember, you're here on vacation!"

With a huge sweeping motion of his arm he proceeded to clear the table, ignoring David's feeble protests, plopping down his own bundle of books and papers.

"Now, I've got something here I know you'll find one helluva lot more interestin'."

He casually picked through the unorganized pile, handing David a book on Celtic mythology.

"What's this?" David asked, reading the title aloud: "*'Ancient Chronicles: The Legends of the Gaels, Scots and Britons'.*"

"Yup, that's what it says. You might want to read this stuff over the next couple o' days. It'll give you some background on what we've been talkin' about. But before all that, did you and Connie enjoy dinner last night?"

"Definitely. We went up to the Somerset House for dinner. It's a pretty ritzy place."

"That it is, Davie, a very nice place…But I still think you've been workin' too hard. It's time to get some air." He leaned over, grabbed David's arm and pulled him up out of his chair. "We're gonna take us a little trip. I want to show you somethin' and introduce you to someone."

"Oh. What and who?"

"Mahernum Foster: she's the 'who'."

David squinted and repeated the unusual first name with an expression of disbelief. "Is that the 'Mother Foster' Connie was taking me to see?"

"The very same. 'Mother Foster' is how folks here usually refer to her. 'Mahernum' is probably some old English or Biblical name or somethin'."

"What is with you guys? What's so important about meeting this woman?"

"For starters, she's a friend. Mahernum's renowned for having the gift of spiritual insight. She uses her gift to help people. But I think that meeting her will really help you understand what makes this little island tick."

"You mean there's something else I don't know about?"

"Well Davie," he laughed, "in case you haven't noticed, there's trouble brewing in Paradise."

Brendan proceeded to fill David in on the three-way power struggle going on for the control of a large old estate called Blagdens Shoals, located in the neighboring county of Falmouth; the entire property was up for sale. It was a battle between the old and the new established orders on the island, with a loose coalition of the island's have-nots led by Mahernum Foster, representing a formidable obstacle in the way of the two larger factions.

The members of the 'Old Guard', as they referred to themselves, were chiefly drawn from the remaining diehards of the pre-independence white power structure. They were people like Rhonda Tovey, who were bent on turning back the hands of time to virtually keep the island's social and political hierarchy much as it had been fifty years earlier. Their major opposition came from a growing alliance of mostly black young professional types who'd joined forces with like-minded bankers in a plan to develop the prized property into a profitable condominium resort. They were officially known as the 'New Deal' coalition.

"Both groups are opposed by Mahernum and her people. They want the estate house turned into a community center and a school, and they want to build a medical clinic."

"Then why all the fuss? Seems to me that there's plenty of land around here to go around."

"Ah no, that ain't quite so. I know it looks that way, but most of the land on this island is still owned from 'sea to shining sea' by the old plantation families. Sure," Brendan continued, "once and a while, a situation like the Blagdens happens, and the old crooner that owned the place kicks the bucket without an heir or a will."

"Is that what happened?"

"That's exactly what happened. I heard about a similar situation a few years back in Stonebridge near the capital. The county government took over the estate, carved it up and built a golf resort."

"So what's wrong with that?"

"Nothin' at all, except that the profits from the work stayed mostly in white hands. Officials planned for most of the work to be handled by small black-owned companies, but the companies awarded the work were mostly fronts. Things got pretty nasty when the truth come out. The government had to step in and promise that an official investigation would be made."

"Did anything come of it?"

"What do you think? Money bought out and watered down any real action. The blacks had their eyes opened again to the power that comes with wealth. Most feel they've been excluded from the real power here even with independence from Britain. They learned the lesson: money opens doors. The GAMMBY's want their slice of the pie."

"The what?"

"Not what, David: Who. GAMMBY's is an acronym,...right, for the Greater Antilles Maritime Merchant's Bank. That's the largest non-government financial institution here. GAMMBY's is sometimes," he paused, "okay, usually a derisive term used by the whites to refer to the coalition of black professionals and the bankers. And I can see from that smile you think the name is kinda stupid. But the GAMMBY's have turned the joke into a mark of pride. To them it's a reference to their origins in Africa."

"Africa? Oh, I get it. Gambia: the country in West Africa."

"I guess. Pride in their roots. Anyway, a lot of this is obviously racial. But a lot of it is personal too, especially where Rhonda is concerned," added Brendan.

"Rhonda? The Tovey's seemed to me like they got along pretty well with everyone at the party."

"For *appearances*, Davie. Come on, you know things aren't always what they seem. Did I tell you that Norman Lorrha is one of the leaders of the GAMMBY's? And Connie's ex-boyfriend, the doctor, is a big time investor in the group."

"This is good stuff Brendan. But you guys have got to stop feeding me information in these little bits and pieces."

"I'll tell you whatever you want to know along the way. I told Mahernum we'd be there before evening."

Minutes later they were in the yellow jeep, driving along a high-hedged road in the direction of the town. Brendan began to reminisce, telling David of how the scenery in this part of the island was reminiscent of the checkerboard farm-country he had seen on a visit to Ireland. "...Hey, have you heard anythin' I said?"

"Sorry. Just had some things on my mind."

"Problems?"

"No. It's just that she's a hard woman to understand."

"You mean our Connie?" He quickly glanced over; David was staring straight ahead. "But aren't they all?" he laughed.

"Yeah, guess so."

"Welcome to the world, Davie...."

They continued to drive until they were about a mile or so from Monmouth's downtown. Brendan then abruptly pulled over to the side of the road and made an announcement: "Here we are—Fromesbury Hill."

"Why are we stopping here?" asked David. "Aren't we going to be late?"

"This won't take long. I said I was gonna show you somethin'. This is the 'what' of the 'what and who'." He glanced up towards the hill as he set the parking brake. "It's up there."

They got out of the car and began an unexpectedly difficult climb up the slope. David watched as Brendan took to the ascent with the ease and grace of a natural athlete, and grew envious. There he was, everything David himself was not: handsome, in great physical shape, a man who was both wanted by and at ease with women. He lamented the misfortune of his own physical inadequacies with each and every tortured step.

An expansive, rocky plateau crowned the summit of the hill. As David stood bent over trying to catch his breath, Brendan continued on, calling back occasionally, encouraging his companion to follow. David grumbled to himself how it was much too hot a day for anything so strenuous. As he fell further behind, he began to wonder if Brendan was deliberately trying to show him up. Eventually, they came to a stop near the opposite edge of the plain, in the middle of a small, well-kept grassy field.

"At last!" Brendan was standing with his arms crossed; he unfolded them to look briefly at his watch. "My friend, you stay out here with us a couple more months and I promise I'll have your butt whipped into shape in no time at all."

He winked his eye to signify he was joking, but David was far too winded to see any humor in the remark. Brendan waited for David to recover his breath, and then told him to step off about seven paces and walk around in a circle.

"Why?" puffed David. "What am I looking for?" Almost as soon as the words left his mouth, his eyebrows raised up in a graphic moment of understanding: "It was here, wasn't it?"

"He's finally caught on. Yes Davie, the infamous 'Stone Circle' was right here. The holes which the stones were originally set in are still here, filled in with rocks and powdered white chalk, as you can see."

"But why do that, unless there's a plan to re-erect the circle."

Brendan shrugged his shoulders; he couldn't say or didn't know. David looked out across the plain, down onto the surrounding hills turned brown by the sun and the rolling sea beyond. Fromesbury Hill certainly held a commanding view of the area.

"Who owns this place?" asked David.

"I'm pretty sure it's the town of Monmouth," replied Brendan. "I've seen uniformed workers up here clearing the weeds."

"What do you think happened to the stones?"

"Couldn't say for sure, but I have heard rumors."

Brendan had heard that the Society membership took the circle down, moving the stones and even incorporating some into the structures of their houses. It had all happened quickly and quietly after Hannah's inauspicious death. He guessed that they just didn't want to draw any further attention to themselves. David readily agreed on that point; he got down on his hands and knees and began crawling over the rough ground. The holes in which the stones had once stood were uncovered each in turn; thirteen altogether were counted set in a small circle with perhaps a thirty-foot diameter.

"From what I remember about the layout of these things," continued David, "shouldn't there be a secondary alignment of stones inside the bigger ring?"

"Not necessarily. You're thinkin' about Stonehenge now."

"Yes, as a matter of fact. I saw Stonehenge when I was vacationing in England a couple of years back. My mother was born in Wales and came to the U.S. as a teenager. I went over to see her hometown and meet my relatives," he smiled. "Now that was an experience. Her maiden name was Gwyddion. Your friend

Francis told me that the Gwyddion's are descended from an ancient line of Celtic kings."

"Okay," laughed Brendan, "so now he's my friend?"

"Alright, *our* friend."

"So it's your ancestors that built Stonehenge?"

"Maybe, maybe not. I saw something on TV that said the Celts arrived in the British Isles a few centuries after Stonehenge and the other big circles were built."

"You saw all this on television?" mused Brendan.

"I visited some Neolithic ruins and I think most of the larger rings had inner circles," continued David, "I remember seeing a few rings about the same diameter of this one. But from the size of these indentations, these stones must've been a good size."

"I hear they stood at least ten feet tall. Maybe weighed a ton or two," speculated Brendan, "maybe more."

"A couple of tons?" David uttered in disbelief. "Hell, most of the apartment buildings in New York City will shit bricks if you try to move a waterbed in."

"You seen the size of some of the houses 'round here, Davie. It wouldn't be too hard to hide somethin' like that."

"I guess you're right. A house that has a church parish named after it could probably hide an elephant."

"Okay then. You seen enough here?…So let's go meet the lady."

They began the trek down the hill with Brendan leading the way. But David was determined not to be embarrassed this time, and abruptly broke into a run.

"Hey! Slow down," shouted Brendan as he took off after him. "Man, if you break your damned neck, I swear I'll leave you for the buzzards!"

The warning proved almost immediately prophetic. David pushed a little too hard; he tripped and began to tumble, then slide awkwardly down the face of the hill. He ended up on his back, sprawled out at the bottom of the hill. Brendan clambered quickly down the hill after him and stopped a few yards away.

David wasn't moving. He was just laying there, the frown on his face showing as much humiliation as pain in the distorted contour of its lines.

"You okay, man? You kicked up a big enough cloud of dust," Brendan joked. No reply came. He walked slowly up to and leaned over the prostrate figure.

David opened his eyes and moaned, saying something unintelligible. Brendan attempted to prevent him from getting up too quickly but again, the advice was ignored. Gradually, David regained his senses and asked a not too unexpected question: "What happened?"

"You idiot!" shouted Brendan. "Do you have a death wish or somethin'? I told you not to run down the hill. Man, you could've been seriously hurt."

"Uhh...Have a little sympathy."

"You okay?"

"My back is killing me..."

"You must've hit your head pretty good too," Brendan announced examining a swelling knot on the back of David's head. "It'll take a while for that to go down." He began to help him over to the car. "How are you feeling? Your eyes don't look too good."

"I'm fine," David answered defiantly. But all of a sudden, he felt his knees buckling.

"David!"

Brendan had to practically carry him the rest of the way with David apologizing incessantly for his stupidity. He all but passed out as Brendan strapped him into his seat.

"David: look at me. What's my name?"

"Your...name?"

"Okay, that's it. I'm taking you to see the doctor," he said as he started up the car.

"Brendan, I'm okay. I was playing with you."

"Sure, sure!"

"Where are we going?"

"To Doc Stevenson's."

"I know that...What did you say his name was?"

"...Warren Stevenson."

"Stevenson?"

"Yep, you know 'im?"

"The name sounds familiar. Where are we going?"

"I just told you. Don't talk, just sit back and relax."

David complied. He closed his eyes and lay back in his seat for a minute or so before he spoke again. He began to babble, trying to apologize again for acting so foolishly.

"What are you trying to say?" asked Brendan.

"I want to say...I think I'm gonna be sick."

"Oh Jeez…Look, we'll be at the Doc's in a few minutes. If you think you're gonna barf, just do me a favor and try to lean out over the road, huh…No, on second thoughts, just tell me so I can pull over. Okay?"

They'd entered the town limits, and were driving by one of the three old local churches when David saw something of an unusual sight for a weekday afternoon. Several young black girls all dressed in white, were standing out on the church's stone steps, waiting beneath the green-leafed shade of a large tree. They all wore sheer white veils upon their heads, lacey white dresses, white handbags, stockings and shoes, some with white ribbons in their hair. All were carrying what looked like small books in their hands, bibles he assumed. The children seemed to be coaching each other, practicing for some church ritual perhaps, for two of the girls were facing each other, holding their hands up clasped together in the attitude of prayer. His head turned and he stared back at the church as the car carried him further and further away. The whole scene appeared to progress in slow motion. The girls themselves seemed somehow 'other worldly' dressed as they were, their lithe, vibrant features rendered into dull, lifeless grays by the shadows cast by the old tree. He thought that somehow, the images that he saw were not too unlike a series of old-time still photographs.

"Davie, how you holdin' up over there?"

Brendan's keen New England brogue was like a sharp elbow to his side, jarring his thoughts into focus once again.

"David, how are you feeling?" he asked in a commanding voice.

"What? Fine…I'm fine. I just need to rest."

"Stay with me, fella. We're almost there."

They turned a corner and parked quickly in front of a flat-topped white building which looked to have been a residence at one time. Some workmen were gathered out front finishing up on a small job. Where the house's rocky lawn had once stretched down to the road, was now a freshly sealed asphalt parking lot. Brendan hustled David through the men and within seconds, they were seated in the doctor's waiting room. Fortunately, it was almost deserted. David lay back in his chair and rested his head sideways against the wall, as Brendan went to inform the nurse of what had happened to him.

"Hey man," a voice spoke out. "What you doin' here?"

David opened his eyes to see a familiar face smiling at him. "Bill, it's good to see you," he spoke deliberately, careful to enunciate his words. "It's been a while."

"Jus' a few days. Man, you don't look too good," he said looking at the general condition of David and his clothing. "What happen to you?"

"I think I did something a little stupid."

"You bet you did," added Brendan. He had returned from his talk with the nurse; he reached out to shake the old man's hand. "Mr. Redditch, it's a pleasure to see you again. I hope everythin's well with you, with your bein' here I mean."

"Oh, I'm fine. I jus' come over to talk with me nephew the doctor 'bout a small matter."

It was at that moment that a man emerged from the office with a middle-aged female patient; the nurse referred to him simply as 'Doctor'. He was a tall fellow with a lean build, who appeared to be in his early to mid-thirties. Though his manner of dress was *almost* relaxed, the seriousness of the expression behind the gold-rimmed glasses said that he was solely about business.

After delivering the woman into the care of his nurse, he spoke with her momentarily before he turned to walk over towards the two Americans. After a bout of courteous smiles and polite hellos, he introduced himself formally and escorted David into his office. The two men sat down in chairs directly across from each other. The doctor asked David to tell him what happened, and began the examination by shining a penlight into David's eyes.

Even with his faculties in a light fog, David still discerned Warren's less than friendly demeanor, but he dismissed his aloofness as being typical of the medical profession. It was then that David remembered that he did know the good doctor. He reminded Warren that they'd met a few days ago albeit briefly, and complimented him on his choice of dinner guest.

"Very good," quipped Warren. "Your near-term memory seems to be unimpaired."

"Then I don't have a concussion?"

"I didn't say that. Some of the symptoms you've described: the nausea, the delay you experienced in cognitive perception or the apparent 'slow-motion', would lead me to suggest caution at least. You say you never lost consciousness?"

"No, I don't think so."

"Good." He got up and began to examine David's neck. "I have to commend you on your own choice of companion."

"Oh Connie…"

"Yes, Constance."

A moment of uncomfortable quiet ensued.

"You must've spent some time in the States," observed David.

"Why do you say that?" he asked almost dismissively, examining the lump on the back of David's head.

"Your accent, it's not—"

"Oh having trouble finding the words? Let me help you, 'not very black'?"

"Ah…" David literally felt his face blush beet red; what could he say? He seemed to be making a habit of sticking his foot in his mouth.

Warren charitably decided to help him out of the rut he'd dug for himself. "Actually, you're correct. I did my pre-med studies in Maryland and completed my residency at a hospital in Washington, D.C."

David looked up at the wall behind the good doctor; sure enough, figuring prominently among a meant-to-be impressive display of degrees and certifications, was a diploma from the Georgetown School of Medicine. That was about all Warren said in a sociable way. The rest of the time he prodded and pulled, poked and stretched David's self-abused body, concluding the examination with an observation his patient could well have gone without hearing.

"The nurse will clean up those abrasions for you. You'll probably be stiffening up soon. A warm bath in mineral salts might help. And by the way, you could probably stand to lose a little weight."

He sent David away with instructions to go home and rest in bed, cautioning him to stay out of the sun for the next few days. As it was, he wasn't really didn't mind the advice; it would give him the opportunity to get caught up on things.

It was a long ride back to Buxton. Brendan was apologetic for his part about David not being able to meet with Mahernum, especially since it was a promise he had made to Connie; but there would be other chances to get them together.

At the mention of Constance, David remembered her having said something about living in the Washington D.C. area. He raised the point with Brendan who laughed: "Nothin' slips by you does it? Yeah, I believe they were pretty close at one time."

He explained how Warren and Constance went to the States and lived together while she was at college, and he completing his medical internship. He reportedly became dissatisfied with the situation, and asked her to lighten her study load so that she could be 'little Miss Housekeeper' too. Warren reportedly went as far as saying that she didn't really even need a degree if they were eventually going to get married.

"And you probably can guess how that went over with Connie."

"Yeah, she's not exactly the type I'd picture happy playing 'little Miss Homemaker'."

"No. Warren's got maybe a decade on her. He's been around, played the field…And still is, as I hear. I suppose it was a situation where he was in a settlin' down mood, and she was just getting started out in life."

"So if they broke up, how come they both ended up back here?"

"I don't know," he laughed. "That my friend, is somethin' else entirely. You'll have to get our Connie to fill you in on that."

# CHAPTER 7

Brendan dropped off his ailing comrade at the front door of Buxton Hall, delivering him quite literally into Jeanna's very capable hands. As she helped him by the living room on the way to his upstairs bedroom, David looked up and glanced over at Hannah's portrait; something about the face caught his attention. He left Jeanna standing in the hallway and hobbled into the living room, stopping a few feet away from the fireplace mantle. He stared up at the painting. Perhaps it was some unusual afternoon refraction of the mercurial Caribbean light, but the picture seemed to be strikingly different. Her red hair and pale white skin seemed to be glowing in a way that made the face seem eerily more real.

Suddenly, he drew back in disbelief...For a brief instant, he thought the expression on the face had changed. For one astonishing moment, he was sure that the face *had* come alive.

"Mr. Llewellyn, is something wrong?" Jeanna asked, touching his arm timidly. She had followed him into the living room.

"I must've been seeing things. Her face, I mean the painting—I could've sworn she...smiled at me."

"I beg you pardon sir?"

"...Nothing Jeanna. I'm not feeling well. Can you help me up to my room?"

As they climbed the stairs, though he kept his silence, he stared back at the gilt-framed canvas as long as it was in sight, watching intently for any changes of expression on the face. But by the time they reached his room, David had convinced himself that the blow to his head was the cause of his imaginings. He stepped out of his shoes and crawled onto the bed, collapsing face-down into a pillow.

The long shadows of eveningtime had stretched over the island when David awakened from a short, hard nap; he reached over fumbling for the switch as he turned on the bedside lamp. His eyes closed as he lay back, his body a throbbing mass of aches and pains. Eventually, he recalled with embarrassment the day's events as they flowed inexorably back into his thoughts.

On the nightstand beside him was the pile of books Brendan had brought over earlier in the day. He reached over half-heartedly and began to paw through the pages of the book with the nicest cover; before long, he was reading intently about Celtic civilization. Theirs was a harsh and brutal world judged by the standards of today, the passage of time marked in their calendar by bloody human sacrifices. He read with both fascination and disdain how the Druid priesthood might stoke up a bonfire to burn a chosen individual alive whilst suspended in a basket, hoping to gain some portent of the future or other insight from a ritualistic examination of the remains. And even more disturbingly, the author left no doubt of his suspicions of cannibalistic rites.

But David was still tired. It wasn't long before his mind left the transcribed pages of the Celtic past, slipping once again into the world of dreams. As he traveled deeper into the enigmatic otherworld of his subconscious mind, images of a different kind of reality began gradually to emerge…

He was in Monmouth town again, enjoying the tropical sunshine as he walked the narrow streets. He stopped across from the old stone church he'd driven by just hours before. Still happily playing children's games were the same young girls he'd seen earlier, all dressed in brilliant white lace dresses while they waited on the church's gray slate stairs.

All of a sudden powerful winds came up, pushing before them bellowing black clouds that darkened the skies above in an instant. Thunder raged in mighty tones that rumbled across the island's low landscape. David thought at first that they were in for another of those flash rainstorms that had a habit of appearing from nowhere. But he was wrong; there would be no rain.

Instead, violent winds rushed down from the mountains, pushing ahead blinding clouds of dust, leaves and a chaos of dust and debris into the once tranquil streets. He covered his face and struggled to stand his ground. He heard the high-pitched screams of children—it must be the girls! He tried to make his way across the road to get to them, but he could barely see where he was going.

There they were…He could see them huddled together at the foot of the stairs, clinging desperately to the post of a stair railing, afraid to move from where they were. He called out to them, trying to tell them to stay where they were until he got to them, but the noise of the storm was deafening. They couldn't hear him.

He started out their direction.

When he was almost within reach of them, a sudden, tremendous blast of air bowled him backwards, tossing him haplessly back onto the road like an unwanted rag doll. Banged up, and feeling helpless, he began to crawl on his hands and knees over to a street light, there to hang on for dear life. He had almost been within reach of the girls!

But something was happening across the way. The church's high arching doors were slowly opening up; a dark figure emerged. David shielded his eyes and strained to see through the hail of wind and flying debris. It appeared to be a tall woman, dressed in a flowing gray gown, her face and head covered with a coarse, dark veil. Though he couldn't make out her features through the veil, the very sight of the woman filled him with apprehension. She stepped forward, seeming to ignore the bedlam around her, motioning to the children to go inside.

But somehow David knew that only evil awaited the girls in there. He tried to shout out to them to warn them away from the woman, but his voice was drowned out by the baleful drone of the winds. Without lifting their heads to cast a second look upon the woman, the girls ran towards the promise of safe haven; all they cared about was finding shelter from the savagery of the storm. As they disappeared into the church, he knew deep in his heart that they would never be seen again.

In the next instant, it was as if a tremendous shadow had overcome the entire town; he could no longer make out the physical details of the church or any other building. The skies, which had once been a clear summer blue, were now as black as a moonless winter night. All was darkness, save for an unearthly, yellowish light pouring out of the church's opened doorway, silhouetting the strange woman in a cloak of ghostly radiance.

David looked around the dark streets; there was no one else in sight. The woman began to walk down the stairs, undaunted by the raging tempest still swirling about her. He called out to her at the top of his voice: 'Who are you?— What did you do with the children?' She did not stop to pause or make reply.

He saw that she was holding something in her hand; he strained to see what it was. But the object remained hidden in the wind-blown folds of her gown, until she began to pull her arm clear: it was a long, narrow bladed dagger.

She meant to kill him, he knew it. He tried to turn to run away but couldn't. The storm suddenly raised up thrice fold in its fury—the harder he tried to move forward, the more the winds pushed him back, back towards the advancing apparition. Fear and futility grabbed hold, reaching deep down into the bowels of his soul. He knew this was a dream, it had to be! But he couldn't wake himself.

She walked towards him with her arm now thrown clear of her body, the dagger glinting menacingly in the ghostly light…He had to wake up.

The closer the woman came to him, the taller and more threatening she became. She was coming to take his life; he knew it. She meant to take his life, and he didn't know why. She stopped barely an arm's breadth away and stood ominously still.

Then, without the slightest sound or warning, she grabbed him by the wrist! Try as he might, he could not break free of her; the strength of her grip was incredible…He was helpless before her, being little more than a child subject to her rage.

She jerked his arm straight, pulling it high in the air. She practically lifted him off his feet: he thought she meant to rip it from his body. He grimaced in pain as he turned his head to look back at his tormentor; a ringing numbness began to overcome his body from head to foot. Though he wasn't at all sure, the rapid pounding in his chest assured him that he was still alive.

He stared in terror up into the featureless contours of the cloth-covered face, certain that what he beheld was the frightful mask of Death itself. Although he could not see the woman's face through the veil, he could feel from her a burning, smoldering anger behind the veil, fueled by the full passion of hatred. Slowly, she raised the knife and—

David woke abruptly in a cold sweat, his body completely wrapped up in a chaos of bed sheets. He was confused, the darkened room around him seeming momentarily unfamiliar; he freed himself from the tangle of linens, tossing them aside. He was shaken by the sheer malevolence of the specter; this was not at all the romantic image he had heretofore held of Hannah! The solid feel of the floor beneath his feet assured him it had all been a dream; he took great solace in that.

The warm night air had left his throat dry. He thought about ringing for Jeanna, but it was late and she was probably asleep. He walked down to the kitchen, pouring for himself a cold glass of orange juice from a pitcher in the refrigerator. He deliberately left the lights off, careful to make as little noise as possible since the door to the servant's quarters was a few feet away. As he placed the glass down gently on the counter top, a thought struck him.

How could Brendan have known about the disposition of the stones from the circle? There was little enough written about the Circle in anything he'd read, let alone the disposition of its stones. Indeed, the man's knowledge of the Society and Hannah Taylor was impressive, certainly surpassing that of all others he had spoken to. But he began to rationalize: Brendan had been on the island for a while now; it was only natural that he had heard a tale or two. That would be something he would certainly ask him about the next time they met.

Sitting around the house, however, was not something David proved to be very good at. He soon tired of following doctor's orders and decided that this would be an excellent time to take Rhonda up on her invitation to tea at Hatherleigh. He had thus been presented with the perfect opportunity to scope out first hand what the lady's true feelings were towards the progression of island life and society. He telephoned early in the day to ensure that his visit would not inconvenience the Toveys, and arranged to come over later that afternoon.

Jeanna then took it upon herself to sit David down and explain to him that he had actually been invited to 'High Tea', which at Hatherleigh was always a very formal affair. That meant that the beverage would be served on fine china accompanied by small sandwiches and cakes, in accordance with British custom. She suggested that he avoid bringing up any topic that might tend to make his hosts uncomfortable. David could not help but smile for she clearly understood something of his purpose without being told; he gave Jeanna his promise he would be tactful.

He arrived at Hatherleigh wearing a white shirt and tie, and the only pair of long trousers he had brought over from New York. He was met at the door by one of the servants and escorted to the 'Morning Room', ever watchful for the cats that Brendan mentioned roamed free. As he walked through the door, Rhonda greeted him warmly and immediately offered regrets.

"William so wanted to join us," she explained, "but he was called away on an urgent business matter."

She stared at a bruise on his cheek but said nothing, bidding him to sit on a separate settee across from her. A cocktail table between them was covered with the expected silverware and plates filled with small cakes and some typically English cucumber, watercress and salmon pate triangular crustless sandwiches. Before his tea was even poured, David consumed several of the dainty mouthfuls without a thought.

Once presented with a delicate cup and saucer with the steaming brew, David sat back and began to study his hostess. She was a fairly tall woman, probably fifty-five to sixty in age he guessed, elegant and angular in her looks which were not bad for a woman of her years. Although he had not seen the Tovey's since the San Sebastian Day party, he assumed that she was some ten years younger than her husband. And there was, to be sure, in the proud cheekbones of her face, something of a resemblance to Hannah.

The conversation started off as would be expected, with Rhonda asking him how he liked the island and his accommodations, and then progressed to the more personal as she politely asked about his family and social-marital situation. He answered as candidly as he could without revealing too much or being rude. And thus, given the opening, he began to inquire *politely* about Rhonda's life and family, explaining he was interested in writing a piece on the island and its recent history. She seemed enthusiastic and eager to help, readily confirming much of what he had already learned, verifying her own kinship to the Buxton line and her husband's Naval background.

William Tovey was educated at Cambridge, and became something of a 'self-made' man, earning his money after retirement in development of vacation resorts. That business brought him to Grand Kirkmuir in the first place and had taken him away from Hatherleigh for the day.

"That's really remarkable for a man his age," commended David. "Most men in their sixties would be content to sit back and quietly smell the roses."

"That's very astute of you, Mr. Llewellyn."

"Pardon me?"

"Your observation about roses. We're both very fond of roses. If William were here, he would be more than happy to show you his prized Orchid collection."

"I understand that orchids are notoriously difficult to grow."

"Oh no, that's really not so. Not if you know what you're doing. It's a labor of love for William, and a splendid hobby."

"And how do you keep yourself busy?"

"I'm very active in several civic organizations we have locally."

"Such as? I'm wondering if you have the same clubs as back home like the Shriners..."

Rhonda smiled, almost as if she enjoyed the little game they were now engaged in: "No. I'm involved here with the Saint Bartholomew's Ladies Club: a similar, charitable organization. And then there's my Bridge club. Do you play?"

"Play?"

"Bridge," she affirmed.

"No, never quite got the hang of it."

"It's really not that difficult a game," her eyes twinkled, "not with the proper person to teach you. I would be more than happy to give you a lesson."

"*Er*, thanks. Maybe I'll take you up on that sometime." He took a sip of the still hot tea. "Are there any other organizations you belong to? I mean, the ladies club and Bridge probably don't keep you all that occupied."

"Well, Mr. Llewellyn, Hatherleigh is a working estate. We do more here than throw parties and attend church socials. We have a dairy here that produces many of the milk products sold locally. The cheese you're enjoying is our own variety of Stilton. It's very difficult to run a dairy successfully here, given the hot temperatures we can have and the low rainfall most of the year."

He acknowledged her observation, taking up a spoon and stirring before taking another sip of the hot tea.

"And I am politically active, you know. I'm one of the founding members of the Old Guard."

Finally they were getting somewhere. 'The Old Guard?' He pretended not to know of what she spoke.

"Yes. It's a relatively new organization. We borrowed the name from Napoleon Bonaparte's bodyguard of honored, veteran French troops."

"Oh, I see."

"Do you indeed," she smiled. She continued before David could say another word. "We're dedicated to the preservation of our revered institutions which thrived under British rule here. For example, the Cane & Molasses Exchange, and the Commonwealth Mercantile Association were two organizations that existed here *for well over two hundred years*. Both have disappeared in the last five years. And many other institutions that exemplified our island society are beginning to struggle in the face of change."

"So you're seeing a lot of negative changes occurring?"

"Without a doubt. But much of what's happening is influenced by outsiders."

"Could you elaborate?"

"Well, for one thing, there's the influx of American money and influences. Not all of the things made in America are beneficial, you know."

"You mean like ideals of freedom and democracy?"

"Oh come now Mr. Llewellyn, let's not get carried away with flag waving and 'Mum's apple pie'. The love of freedom and democracy are traditions your ancestors shared with my own. I suggest you look up the Monmouth Rebellion in the history books. People in the southwest of England rose up on more than occasion to defend their beliefs. That heritage lives today in hearts of the people I call friends in my Monmouth. And after all, your American ancestors began protesting what they decried as the loss of their rights as *Englishmen*."

"Okay, I won't debate that point with you. I don't know enough about it to argue what their motivations might have been. But shouldn't those same rights extend to all men and women?"

"I believe that our institutions are what they are, because they developed simultaneously with the evolution of British society. We earned the rights we have today through the blood and perseverance of our ancestors. We enjoy these rights," she smiled, "Mr. Llewellyn, because we earned them."

"Ah, excuse me Mrs. Tovey, but let me understand you. I wouldn't want to put words in your mouth. Now, are you saying that the Whites on Grand Kirkmuir have earned the right to rule, and the Blacks here have not? Are you saying that the institution of slavery did not exist here?"

David braced himself for anything; he wasn't sure how she would react to the directness of his questions. She raised her head and looked back with a proud, confident smile.

"Mr. Llewellyn, did I tell you that I was born and raised on this island?...Well, I was. I was born not twelve miles from this very spot. When I was of a suitable age to go to school, I attended the church school established and administered by St. Bartholomew's Church. Matriculation was open to everyone without cost, regardless of class, social standing or race. I think you'll agree that fifty years ago, blacks and whites attending school together was very unusual,...even for the land of freedom and opportunity from which you hail. Oh, by the way, one of my classmates happened to be the father of one of your acquaintances, Constance. It helped give Mr. Lorrha his start in life.

Now understand, my parents weren't, I believe the fashionable phrase is, 'bleeding heart' liberals. But they did believe it was important that as Kirkmuirians, we had a common heritage that should be learned and shared together.

What I am trying to say is this: I believe that at heart, most people here on this island appreciate the institutions and traditions that make us all proud. It is that heritage which makes us distinctly Kirkmuirians, it makes us what we are. But, there are others, who for whatever reasons, have turned their backs on those same traditions. I, and people like me, want to see to it that our children, and our children's children, will be able to enjoy the very same institutions that we have enjoyed in our own lives.

Now David, if I may call you by your first name, I may be old but I am not a dinosaur. I realize that the march of change is inevitable as the tides. But I will not stand idly by and allow anyone to destroy the good that is my island. This island is my home, my country. I understand your point of view. It is true that the Old Guard is an "all-white" organization at present, and we do recognize the…handicap, that our current make-up presents. We'd like to recruit like-minded members of our colored citizenry, but realize that will take time. But we are working to change and rectify the situation as soon as possible."

David listened very carefully to what he considered her very eloquent defense of self and beliefs. He saw, however, that he was not getting anywhere with Rhonda this day and so resigned to sit back to enjoy the hospitality of the afternoon. She was obviously a very shrewd lady, well prepared to answer any question he might put to her this day. Nonetheless, he found it most interesting that her stated reasons for forming the Old Guard did not include her own family's loss of home and heritage, and the attendant tragedy of her brother Michael Edward. His time however, was not wasted; she did say that she had first attended school some fifty years ago. He was gratified to have at least verified his initial guess at her age.

A few days later, Brendan telephoned David on a Saturday telling him to drop everything he was doing, which wasn't very much as it turned out. The call was to reschedule the missed meeting with Mother Foster. Brendan arrived with Constance in tow as an unexpected guest, much to David's delight. They traveled west for miles along the coast, down narrow, winding roads, dodging in and out of what passed for highway traffic on the island. Almost ninety minutes later, they arrived in a small settlement called Betheltown, just outside of the harbor town of Falkirk. Connie explained that it was not truly a town in the proper sense: no map marked the hamlet's existence, no elected government existed to serve the needs of the populace. The houses that surrounded them, from the ramshackle walls to the gray corrugated tin roofs satisfied in every aspect the definition of the word 'shanty'. David was temporarily stunned into silence; he had seen urban poverty before, but this was destitution of quite another kind. The raw rising stench of the place was unbelievable. Shallow hand-dug ditches, wrought from the rocky earth by pick and shovel, served as stagnant open canals that trickled away the waste products of daily life and living.

David timidly asked a first question: "What are those barrels for outside of the, *er*—"

Brendan finished the sentence: "There're called shacks. The barrels are for storing rainwater. Most of the drinking water here is captured rain runoff. I don't think anyone here has indoor plumbing. A stream down the way there serves most other needs, but it's nothing more than an untreated sewer. These are some of the poorest folk on Grand Kirkmuir."

"What keeps them here?" he asked.

"Hope," replied Constance.

Her simple answer was as much of a shock to David as the sun-ripened odors affronting his nose. "Hope of what? I don't see very much around here to be hopeful of."

"There's a chance they can get work by staying here," she replied.

"And the price of the rent is right too," came a practical consideration from Brendan. "But I guess that's somethin' you've never had to worry about, paying the rent I mean," he added with a grin.

"Hey, now that's not fair," objected David. "My mother and I had to struggle to make ends meet many a time."

"…Sure you did."

"Okay boys," interrupted Constance. "Stop it. The people out there are the ones you should be concerned with. They're the ones who've really had it rough. They could teach us all a thing or two."

They drove onto a rough, unpaved road, washed out in places by the recently fallen rains. Brendan's Jeep proved it's off-road worth, traversing the smooth as well as it did the rough. They passed women and children carrying foods and all manner of boxes and containers on their heads. David slowly began to understand. These were not the same semi-complacent townsfolk he had become accustomed to seeing in Monmouth. These were the poor people of the countryside: these were Mother Foster's people.

They continued up to the front of an old white trailer permanently, it seemed, raised up on concrete blocks. A long green and white striped awning hung from its front. A line of people stretched out from the awning; apparently, a distribution of donated goods was underway.

Standing in front of the trailer, giving directions to several helpers was a middle-aged woman identified by Constance as Mahernum. On her head was an old straw hat, which though unraveling at the back, still served its purpose well. She was wearing a white, loose-fitting summer frock and an old pair of shoes flattened at the back like sandals. In short, her attire seemed entirely appropriate to her surroundings.

Mahernum smiled as this new group of people got out of the car and approached. Brendan hurriedly whispered to David in jest that she was 'single' and slapped him on the back. Constance introduced David to her as an important American columnist and writer, which made him blush slightly.

Before David stood a dark, small-framed woman whose sparkling eyes and energetic demeanor seemed to belie the prodigious efforts of her struggle. From her composed presence and very proper Caribbean-accented speech, David immediately perceived that there was more to this leader of the island's forgotten masses than he had first believed.

"How long will you be staying with us on Kirkmuir?"

"I originally came down for a six week vacation. I've got about three weeks left."

"So you'll be leaving us soon?"

"Probably not." He looked over at Constance; they exchanged a quick smile. "I'm planning on staying a little longer now. You people have some pretty interesting things going on."

"I'm glad these young people are keeping you informed as well as entertained. Good, there's nothing worse than a boring holiday. Tell me," she continued, not allowing him time to make reply, "what do you think of Betheltown?"

"It's…a remarkable place," David replied.

"Come on now, you don't have to be polite."

"Okay. Honest opinion—I think this place is a disaster waiting to happen. There's no fresh water, filth is accumulating in ditches ready to create disease: basic human needs aren't even being addressed let alone being met. It's a crime."

"My word," Mahernum exclaimed. "You certainly don't pull any punches. But I completely agree with you! It is criminal that a government could sit back and allow its people to live this way. That's why my co-workers and I are staying here. Those of us that are able to help others, should. And I hope that's why you've come here today…"

Old Mother Foster wasn't at all what he expected; he had already begun to take a liking to her. Constance and Brendan excused themselves and wandered off chatting with a member of Mahernum's staff, leaving the two alone.

David learned that she had once been a tenured professor and lecturer in Economics at the prestigious University of the British West Indies. With the pain and emotion expressed with every word, Mahernum detailed the years she had struggled to achieve that goal, overcoming obstacle after obstacle that was set down into her path. This 'little bush woman', as she had once been decried, was not welcomed with opened arms into the bosom of either academia or society. Unfortunately, her own individual victory would have shallow rewards. She told of how having attained her goal, the social and profession isolation she felt made her realize that regrettably, her place was not in that world.

The small woman before him was no backwoods fool. He now understood why it was that the other parties in this island power struggle feared her.

But as David pressed to find out more about her personal life, he quickly found the tables turned. Instead, she began to interrogate him, to delve into areas of his personal life he would not normally discuss. He told her of his deteriorating relationship with his mother, of his last failed relationship, and why this trip to the island was for more than a rest from the rigors of his work. When he mentioned where he was staying, her small black eyes momentarily opened wide.

"Does everyone on this island have that reaction to Buxton Hall?" he asked.

"David, I apologize. I'm sure that you must know by now the story of the woman that lived there. After all these years, people feel that house still has evil in it. The stigma remains."

David could not hide his skepticism: after all, how could an inanimate thing built of bricks and mortar actually be evil? Mahernum, for her part, refused to accept his cynicism, saying: 'You are like the young bird that has not seen the hurricane'.

"Huh?"

"To put it into other words: there are more things in heaven and earth than the mind of man can ever know. Or, would you deny even the possibility that such a thing may be?"

"Of course not. It's just that—"

"Yes?"

She looked back at him convinced that she was right; it was all in keeping with being Mother Foster. The assured quiet of her expression said that she was always supremely confident in herself: she *knew* she was right: there could be no argument. David lowered his head and massaged his eyes; this was not going to be an easy interview.

"Are you okay?" she asked.

"Yeah...Sure, it's just that I had a rough night."

"Bad dreams?"

"No....Well, yes. You could say that."

"Give me your hands," she ordered.

"What?" He straightened up.

"Don't worry," she smiled, "I'm not 'making a pass' at you. Your hands: give them to me."

"Why? I mean—"

"I have the gift of the second sight."

"I kinda heard that."

"Now, don't tell me a big man like you afraid," she smiled.

"Afraid of what?"

"Then give me your hands."

Now the mystical side of the woman he'd heard so much about began to show itself, as Mahernum began to take on almost an entirely new personality. Taking both of his hands firmly into her own, she exhaled some words he had no hope of understanding, and then stared up, studying it seemed every line and detail of his face. David wasn't at all sure of what kind of show she was going to put on, but he was convinced that it was all contrived for his benefit. She began to take in a series of long, deep breaths; her head rolled slightly back and her eyes closed as she spoke.

"I see a dark cloud descending around you boy. I sense evil in this cloud. I warn you to be careful!"

Her grip began to tighten.

"This is a cloud born from fire, a fire burning slowly, stoked high by lies and deceit."

Her eyes opened wide, fixing directly upon his as she spoke: "Take care David, the bloody hand of the devil is reaching for you. His circle of evil has you in its sights…"

Mahernum released his hands and took a half step backward, her wild eyes coming to fix upon his, as she solemnly repeated her warning. David stood motionless, his hands hanging in the air where she had left them; he was somewhat surprised by what she had said. He wasn't sure what had he just experienced? Sure, he knew Constance and Brendan wanted to enlist him in Mahernum's cause, but why go to all the trouble of arranging such a performance? If they really knew him, just seeing the squalid conditions that the people of Betheltown had to live in would have been enough; he was an easy sell. But all that was assuming that the exhibition was nothing more than gamesmanship. The moment of uncertainty was dispelled in an instant as the small woman's once deadly serious expression suddenly softened, broadening into a smile.

"Well, Mr. Llewellyn, for a writer," she quipped, "you sure are tight with the spoken word."

# CHAPTER 8

The road home proved long and silent for David. He excused himself from the lighthearted conversation of Constance and Brendan, claiming merely that he was tired and had tried to do too much, too soon after his misadventure on Fromesbury Hill. The truth of the matter was that he was more troubled by what Mahernum had said than he was allowing anyone to know. He was convinced that there was more substance and purpose in the little woman's warning than the melodramatic performance he had first taken it for.

Buxton Hall soon came into view, rising majestically over the high, tidily trimmed bushes that hid the grounds from the road, its white-painted walls tinged pink reflecting the setting sun. David stared at the old house, recalling how Mahernum had claimed that the old house was 'evil'. To him, as grand and as filled with history as the place was, it still appeared nothing more than a well-ordered pile of mortar and bricks.

But as his footsteps sounded on the marble tiles of the foyer, he remembered the proud lady who once lived in this house, and the appalling things she was said to have done. He made his way across the living room to stand before Hannah's portrait. As Mahernum had studied his face, he in turn studied the face of the woman so skillfully portrayed on the canvas. In the yet admiring gaze of his eyes, she was as a beautiful woman as he had ever seen, her smile seeming so carefree, so ingenuous.

"Could you really have done the things people say you did?" he wondered aloud.

"She did all that and more, sir," came a whispered reply.

The voice came from behind; David turned around quickly. "Jeanna...You surprised me."

"Oh I'm sorry, I didn't mean to sneak up on you. Would you like something to drink?"

At first he was going to say 'yes', but then he caught himself before the words slipped out. "Jeanna, can you quit playing the 'faithful servant' bit for once. Please," he motioned for her to come over to have a seat, "tell me what you know about her. I mean, you grew up here on the island."

"I did more than just grow up on the island, Mr. Llewellyn. I grow up right here in this house...Hah," she laughed, "I could tell you some stories."

"I wish you would. I want to hear it all."

Repeated were the oft-told tales of Hannah's husbands and lovers, the stories of their untimely deaths, and the many rumors of her involvement in witchcraft and black magic. But beyond that, Jeanna knew something of the recent occupants and history of Buxton Hall itself. She told of stories the older servants had passed on to her of strange cries and voices in the house, voices heard behind the closed doors of empty rooms. She told him of people finding themselves inexplicably locked in rooms, of items of furniture mysteriously moved during the night.

The bizarre happenings were not limited to the confines of the house itself. At one time, a cleared grove had existed out beyond the imported olive trees on the east edge of the lawn. Hannah's mysterious groundskeeper, Sian Mack, forbade the servants and workers access to the grove. On certain nights, back in those days, the shrill laughter of ungodly revelry echoed loudly from the anonymity of the gardens. That same wicked laughter, it was long said, could still be heard there, carried aloft on the warm winds of the darkest midsummer nights. While she herself had not borne witness to the stranger occurrences, she had on occasion caught the faint but distinct scent of Country Lavender, lingering in the air of Hannah's former boudoir.

"Lavender?" queried David, remembering his most recent fragrant encounter.

"It was so sweet, it almost make me sick," she continued. "English Lavender, it was one of her favorite fragrances...She used to have the plants them growing all over the house." She paused. "I used to hate to go into that room."

"Is her room in the closed part of the house?"

"No sir. It was converted a long time ago. It's the Reading Room now."

"You mean the library upstairs?"

"Yes, the room you like to study you books in."

"Uh…That's comforting to know" he remarked satirically. "Is that the only room in this house with problems?"

"Well sir, if the truth be known, I'm not that happy about the wine cellar either. I think it the worse place in the whole house."

"Why, what happened?"

Going back across the years, Jeanna recalled an incident when she was eight or nine years old; a man named Harry Cullainan owned the house in those days. Jeanna was helping her father in his work around the house.

"Anyway, my father send me down to the wine cellar to get Mr. Harry a bottle of his brandy. I go on down to the cellar, and was walking towards the back when the lights them all of a sudden just go out. I couldn't see my hand in front of me face it was so dark. I was walking, feeling me way along the racks, when someone reach out and grab me hand! Oh God, I was so scared. I start to scream as loud as I could. Whoever it was almost pull me arm out of the socket!"

David shuddered as soon as the words left her mouth; the description of the incident was strikingly similar to the episode in his dream. "What…happened then?" he asked.

"I don't know how I did it, but I break free and I run upstairs as fast as I could!"

"Did you tell anyone about what happened?"

"Of course! I tell Mr. Harry and me father. They all go down into the cellar, Mr. Harry carrying him shotgun. But they find *no* one."

"So there was no one there?" he repeated.

"Nobody at all. Mr. Cullainan turn around and tell me that I make the whole story up…I hated that man. Me father tell me later to pay him no mind. He believed me. He told me that I shouldn't go down there alone again."

"Did anything like that ever happen again?"

"Mr. Llewellyn," she looked straight at him, "I was so scared that night, it was years before I would go down there again alone."

David had no problem understanding that.

"Well," she got up slowly, "it's time for me to leave now."

"Why?"

"It's Saturday night. You know I always spend the weekends home with me family. It's almost eight-thirty. Me husband George will be here to pick me up soon."

Jeanna's husband arrived right on time, leaving David alone to reflect on her vividly told tales. He tried calling Connie but she wasn't home; leaving a message seemed pointless. He sat slouched down in what had become his favorite tall-backed leather chair, staring up through the dark amber of the port wine in the glass he was holding at arm's length, symbolically moving it back and forth across the painting of Hannah Taylor on the wall. He was of two minds about the situation. On the one hand, many of these yarns were clearly nothing more than stories made up to explain and embellish the many mysteries surrounding Hannah; he laughed at himself for taking them seriously for more than a moment.

But here he was an educated man, almost ready to believe stories of things he knew just weren't possible. By the same token, there was his dream and here this very day, two different women had related to him some detail of that same dream, a dream he had mentioned to no one. Earlier that evening, he had seen the white walls of Buxton Hall tinged with the clinging crimson red of the sunset. Perhaps, it was a mark from the bloodstained history of the place just as Mahernum had suggested. He wondered now if she could indeed be right; that a house could be evil.

David remained in the study a few hours longer, until the bottle he was sampling was almost empty. He finally pushed himself up from his seat with every intention of heading on up to bed but when he reached the foot of the stairs, he stopped. Down the hall, a sliver of light shining from beneath the kitchen door caught his eye; Jeanna must've left the light on in her haste to go home. His head began to swim. Although he knew that he had partaken of a little too much drink, he was sure that he was still in full control of his faculties and left the stairs heading down the hall. Jeanna's childhood memory of the incident in the wine cellar came to mind as soon he entered the kitchen. He paused as he reached the cellar's entrance, putting his hand out onto the door's white-painted frame to steady himself. He stood there for a moment before deciding to go down, without thinking about what, if anything, he expected to find.

Curiosity had set his wheels in motion. The door was unlatched and very carefully pushed open; he was surprised that the hinge didn't creak. He put the light switch on. Everything below appeared clean and dry, so he held onto the handrail and ventured down into the cellar one step at a time.

David congratulated himself on reaching the bottom of the stairs without incident, and remained there a moment as he took a good look around. An old mahogany credenza with two antique oil lamps was set against the wall nearby; he assumed that it was there in case the people in the house had to seek refuge in the basement from a hurricane. The cellar walls were painted a dull, flat white that almost melted into the checkerboard floor of ancient black and white tiles beneath his feet. From the look of things, the paint on the brick walls had built up layer upon layer over the many years. Wine racks of unusually rough-hewn wood stretched in several long, well-stocked rows running parallel to the cellar stairs. David made a quick estimate of the number of bottles and wondered if his host wasn't pressing and bottling the stuff himself. He walked down the center aisle enthusiastically perusing the dust-covered labels, debating which vintage he might try with dinner the next night. Then, as he made the turn into the next aisle, he practically tripped over his own feet and tumbled into the wall. As he righted himself, he noticed something peculiar about the surface of the wall.

For a span of about four or five feet, the surface was unusually smooth; unlike elsewhere, the wall here had no brick and mortar pattern at all. At first, he thought that he'd come upon a structural feature, but as far as he could make out, it stopped a few feet short of the ceiling. Though painted over, there was a small but discernible indentation in the wall all the way up on both sides; he took a credit card from his pocket and pushed it through...It had to be a door.

Just maybe, he thought excitedly, he'd found an entrance to a concealed vault; he wondered what might be hidden there. Everyone had heard stories of the exploits of the renowned Caribbean buccaneers that once had roamed the local waters. According to a rumor he'd either heard or read somewhere, the Buxton fortune itself was founded on the ill-gotten proceeds from smuggled or pirated goods. In his imagination, he began to conjure up images of what kind of magnificent treasure might be inside. His hands pawed at the door's edge as he probed for a hidden handle or lever without success; then another thought occurred to him. Perhaps the door was set on a pivot; he put his shoulder to one side of the door and leaned into it with all his weight. Nothing happened. So he tried the other side and slowly, it began to give. He managed to push the door open a few inches, then a foot or so, but that was all. Exhausted from the strain of the unaccustomed physical exertion, he stepped back to wipe the sweat from his eyes, then peered in.

It was dark inside, he couldn't make out very much. Remembering the oil lamps, he hurried back to the credenza by the stairs.

"Dammit!" he exclaimed. Both lamps were empty. He threw open the credenza's doors and was overjoyed to find a battery lantern. He switched it on and fortunately, it was in good working order. He ran back over to the doorway and squeezed through the opening.

The air inside the vault was heavy with the damp smell of rotting vegetation but not really stale. He assumed that air must be seeping in from the outside, perhaps even through some other passageway. He shone the lantern around to discover a large, mostly empty space, with a few long, fibrous roots of plants hanging down from cracks in the ceiling. Across the way were three alcoves, one larger than the other two, all deeply recessed into the far wall.

Then he made an even stranger discovery. Off in one corner stood a baroque, floor length candelabrum, apparently fashioned in style after a deciduous tree of a sort. He walked over to examine it more closely. The wax in the candle wells was dry and brittle from age. He brought the light closer. From the greenish oxidation on the surface of the thing, he reluctantly concluded that it must be made of bronze.

"No treasure here. Guess they could've used it for a Christmas tree," he thought in amusement. "Packed it away in here and forgot all about it."

He directed the lantern's beam over into the opposite corner of the room, and as he did, something small glinted on the vault floor. He hurried over and found the scratched surface of a large metal ring. His first thought was that it was a retaining ring of some kind, intended at one time to hold something down on the floor. But then, why was there only one ring? Perhaps, it was some kind of old-fashioned door handle he next thought. If that was the case, then it was his duty to open it. There was probably another cellar or passageway beneath the floor. He reached down and pulled with one hand. Nothing happened, he couldn't move it. The hinge holding the ring was rusted, which was not surprising since it presumably had not been used in a good long while. He put down the lantern, gritted his teeth and leaned back…Again, nothing happened; the ring would not budge. He gave up the effort as his head began to ache, concluding that it would probably take some kind of lever to free it.

Just as he turned to leave the vault, a loud, grinding moan wrenched his attention towards the back of the vault; the panel at the rear of center alcove was opening up. He stood back and watched as it opened up onto a huge, uninviting blackness that lay beyond.

"…Probably the gateway to Hell," he thought aloud. "Nothing ventured, nothing gained."

With only the sound of his own voice to urge him on, he ventured through a short tunnel down a flat bank of stairs hewn from the bedrock; the stairs led into a huge underground grotto. Glistening stalactites and stalagmites protruded from above and below like teeth from the gaping jaws of an angry snarling beast ready to consume any unsuspecting prey. All around him in the unseen darkness were the sharp, distinctive echoes of water dripping into gathering pools. It was apparent that it was the rainy season down here too, as occasionally a droplet would fall unexpectedly from above and land upon his head, then slither coldly down the back of his neck. The cave was descending, probably down to the sea he assumed. Directly ahead, his lantern revealed what appeared to be a clear, traversable path but nevertheless, he would have to tread carefully because it was very smooth and wet.

Suddenly the light from the lantern dimmed noticeably; the battery was dying. The question now was whether he should go back. There was no way of telling for sure how far the cave went, but he was sure that it couldn't be much farther since that side of the house faced the sea. He made up his mind to go on, with hope upon prayer that the lantern would not fail him.

But that was not his only problem; the cave was growing noticeably warmer. In the back of his mind he began to fear that there was no outlet to the sea, that the breathable air was getting dangerously thin, that something would happen to him, and this foolish decision would mean that he would never get out of there. But he convinced himself that he had to control what were plainly irrational fears; that he must go on. He reminded himself that a key to a long lost treasure could be just ahead. Around every corner, he half-expected to see some smuggler's bones turned brown and brittle with age unburied on the cave floor, or at the very least, colored shards of glass from a lost, broken bottle of untaxed, contraband rum. But no such relics were found.

His eyes began to stare up at the undulating stone ceiling, but search as he did, he saw no evidence of those winged denizens of similar isolated places: bats. This fact served only to add to his very consciously suppressed fear of the place. The farther he went the more the unnatural stillness of the caves bothered him: why were there no living creatures down here? He didn't like it. The damp clay smell in the air disagreed with his wine-rotted stomach, evoking further, lingering fears of death.

These thoughts did not remain long in his conscious mind, as he was abruptly faced with a decision. The cave had opened up into a huge, dome shaped "room" like a grand dining hall, shimmering in the glow of his lantern like the light of a thousand candles. From here the room appeared to lead on to a series of connecting caverns beyond.

But the best way forward was no longer clear. At any other time, in a clearer state of mind, he would have chosen prudence and returned the way he had come. But whether it was the alcohol, a lack of oxygen or the sudden onset of fatigue, a muddled decision was made to press on. He had recently climbed the rocky hill from the coast to the house; he reasoned that the outlet to the sea could not be far off. It had to be the path straight ahead.

This quickly proved to be the wrong choice. Though the cavern seemed at first to continue the path's easy descent, the gentleness of the incline vanished into a maze of bewildering rocky intrusions. The cave was closing in on him. By the time David realized his error, the way back had become a treacherous, slippery climb.

He was almost back to the 'dining hall' when he stumbled reaching for a hold on a rock. He dropped the lantern as he fought to regain his balance and then, all of a sudden—he fell! He slid uncontrollably backward, clawing and grabbing at everything and anything...until his head and back abruptly ended a hard fall.

For a few brief moments, all went black. His eyes reopened to watch the lantern flickering a few feet way, until its light finally went out. He was helpless, unable to move, his mind teetering on the edge of consciousness as the swirling darkness of the cavern began to close in around him...

From off in the distance, he thought he could hear the sounds of footsteps approaching, but he could not summon the strength to call out. Someone must have found the vault door open and was coming to mercifully rescue him. The footsteps drew nearer; he could hear the sounds of voices talking softly. At first, the voices seemed to belong to two women but as he strained to listen, he was certain that the second voice was that of a child, a young island girl.

But there was something strange about the child's voice; she sounded disturbed by something, almost frightened. She was almost certainly crying. David didn't recognize the woman's voice at all, and although he couldn't hear the words she spoke, the very sound of her voice seemed foreign.

Gradually, the whole chamber began to fill with a soft white light: David was sure that the woman and child were his salvation. He struggled to raise his head expecting to see the faces of his rescuers, but he was completely unprepared for what he saw.

Standing before him was a tall, thin woman in a long dark dress; a white scarf or veil covered most of her head and hid her face from sight. Trailing at a straight arm's length behind her was a small black girl, clothed in the most wretched of rags; both were standing in a weird half-light that glowed iridescently around them. He ascribed the glow to his eyes being unfocused, maladjusted to the new light. But even so, he saw that the woman held such a determined grip on the girl's wrist that the skin on her own pale wrist was pulled tight to the bone; the child's miserable expression told of the pain she was in. Then it struck him that neither of them was carrying a lantern. His failing senses were slow to put it all together—somehow, he knew this woman. She began to walk towards him, dragging the sobbing child behind her.

Fear seized hold of him: he had to get away from her! She began slowly moving towards him, her sharp, deliberate footsteps reverberating through the deathly silence of the cave. He struggled to push his body backwards along the cold, slimy ground, grasping, pushing back until he could retreat no more. He collapsed onto the ground, his body exhausted. There was nowhere to hide.

She was standing over him, now barely inches away, the menacing features of her face still shrouded. She began to reach down with a pallid, long-fingered hand and as she did, locks of long red hair fell in dangling curls from beneath the veil...His eyes closed shut not to open again, as the cavern was swallowed up in the darkness.

Several hours would pass by the time David recovered consciousness. His head and neck bore painful witness to his fall. Though his memories of the woman and child were still chillingly clear, he could not be sure if what he had experienced was anything more than an illusion. The confusion lingered as he lay on his back on the hard ground, his forearm resting on his forehead. He was slow to comprehend that although the cave was still dark, he could actually see. Somewhere nearby, there had to be an opening to the outside; light was reflecting off the moist walls of the cave. The daytime had come; it had to be early morning. He rolled over and made his way to his feet and then out to the main cavern.

The stale grotto air was now increasingly displaced by the salt smell of the sea. Each forward step he took found the stagnant echo of the grotto pools gradually replaced by the more vital sounds of running water, as the excess runoff of the pools was combining to form an underground stream. He followed the course of the stream until another familiar, more vibrant sound began to be heard; his spirit began to lighten. The sounds that now filled his ears were unmistakably those of the wind-blown wash of the tides. He climbed out of a rocky cove and his tired eyes beheld a welcomed sight: the shimmering yellow-white sands of the seashore. He breathed a long sigh of relief as he walked out onto the beach and felt the warm, shifting sands beneath his feet. The caves did indeed lead down to the sea.

# CHAPTER 9

David lumbered the long mile from the beach to the house in a virtual daze, shielding his eyes from the bright morning sun. By the time he arrived back at the house, the past night in the caverns was remembered more like a bad dream. But to be sure of himself or more precisely, of his sanity, he had to return to the cellar; it was the only way to prove to himself that what happened had actually happened.

He managed to crawl into the house through an open window in the kitchen, grateful he didn't have to break in. From halfway down the cellar stairs he could see the vault door still ajar. He paused to wonder how he could have squeezed through such a narrow opening. For a multitude of reasons, he decided that he would keep the discovery to himself, at least for the time being. He put his shoulder and weight to the door and pushed until it was flush with the wall again. That accomplished, he began to consider the significance of the previous night's discovery. Certain of the tales he'd heard were apparently true; the caverns would have been perfect for hoarding smuggled goods, not that he'd found any evidence of the same. But if those stories were at least partly based in fact, then what of the rest?

The portrait of Hannah caught his eye as he approached the living room. Instantly rekindled was the vision of the specter in the caves; he shuddered as the sheer, brutish malevolence of the woman's presence was recalled. The falling locks of red hair said unmistakably who the apparition was, and the thought of seeing her so soon again was something he found unnerving. His first instinct was to continue up to his room but he couldn't, not just yet.

But his male ego kicked in; the thought of actually being afraid of a painted image was something he could not accept. Thus, he turned and walked into the living room determined to confront his fears, his eyes focusing on everything but Hannah's portrait as he walked across the room. He could feel the harsh stare of her eyes watching him, reveling in his foolishness. He put his hand out and grasped the mantle beneath the picture; summoning his courage, he looked up.

Face to face, the woman in the painting's stare was not so formidable a thing. In fact, her clear eyes and entrancing smile caused him to fall lost hopelessly in doubts. The face he now saw was filled with the dynamism of a woman who had lived and loved life. This woman was as far from the wretched phantom he had seen in his dream as light was from darkness. And, he concluded, that was what his vision in the caves must have been also: a dream—a nightmare shaped by the horror stories he had heard so many of. That was all it could have been. He had allowed himself get lost in the lurid spectacle of the tourist hype surrounding Hannah's life and times. Getting back to the safety and comfort of the house had rejuvenated the more skeptical side of his nature.

As David entered his bedroom, he glanced over at the clock on his nightstand. Emphasized in large red numerals was the relative lateness of the morning hour.

"Ten o'clock! I've been gone the whole night—Shit!…I was supposed to go that church with Connie this morning."

He fumbled as he began to take off his clothes and practically fell onto his bed; he was too tired to stand any longer. He rolled over and lay staring at the telephone, too afraid to call her; before he knew it, he was asleep. When he awakened, the nightstand clock's red numerals told another story: three more hours had passed. It was now early in the afternoon. There was no point to calling her now. She was one of those women who didn't appreciate being stood up, and was far too stubborn to call him to ask what happened.

"…Even if I told her," he thought, "she wouldn't believe me. Who in their right mind would?"

But David couldn't leave such matters in such an unsettled state. He showered and dressed, and drove over to Constance's second floor apartment armed with an apology-sized bouquet of flowers in tow. Constance lived atop a neighborhood grocery store, the shelves of which were meagerly stocked with products mostly unfamiliar to the eyes of an American. Like most small businesses in Monmouth, the store served as a local gathering place for folks to stop, pass time and indulge in gossip, that most hallowed of human democratic institutions. David was keenly aware of their attention as he walked by the open storefront; grist was added to the rumor mill as he entered the side door that lead to the upper floor.

He knocked twice. Connie came to the door wearing an oversized white t-shirt and a pleasant smile that quickly soured to a frown when she saw who her visitor was. David adroitly blocked the door with his foot before she could slam it shut and thrust the bouquet of flowers quickly in through the opening. An impassioned barrage of words flew back and forth in a brisk exchange of views on simple courtesies and showing the proper respect. David ended the discourse with: 'at least let me at least tell you what happened!'

Connie snatched the flowers from David's grasp and stepped back, allowing him to come in; he stood by the doorway surveying the small room from there. The apartment's flat-white painted walls were bare of decorations, except for a wooden crucifix set to one side of an oversized bed. On that bed, curled up in a ball between two lace-edged pillows, was the fattest gray tabby David had ever seen; he reached quickly into his pocket for a handkerchief.

"I guess that must be Sumo…"

Constance answered his attempt to begin a conversation with a scowl that nonetheless he took for an affirmation.

"You weren't kidding, he's a big one. I can see why old man Tovey gave him away", he said, turning to Constance with a quip: "That one cat probably eats the food of three."

"Are you saying my cat is fat?"

"Me? Hell no Connie, he's just big-boned."

"It's not like you haven't been here before," she replied shaking her head. "I'll put him in the bathroom."

David composed himself, and immediately launched into his apology as she returned: "Look, I really am sorry. Lemme explain what happened last night."

"Last night?" came the retort. "Talk quick man! The meter's running and your dime is almost up."

"Okay, now Connie you would not believe—You know, since we're talking about courtesies, you could at least look at me."

She deigned to comply, spinning around on her heels. "Okay, so now I'm looking at you."

David managed to get out the news of his discovery the previous night in the wine cellar, of the staircase down to the caves, of the passageway through the caverns to the sea, describing his descent as 'a real live journey to the center of the Earth'. Reluctantly, he went on to tell her of the rest of his other experience that night. The account faltered as he was unsure how to couch his description: was it truly a supernatural experience…of a sort, or a dream?

Constance's indifference towards him did not appear to be immediately swayed by the eeriness of the story. She walked over to the bed and began to stroke Sumo under his receptive white-whiskered chin, considering whether she would remain angry or not.

"Caves under the estate…Now, that might explain a lot of things I suppose. I remember hearing stories of ghosts haunting the gardens at that place when I was a child. Maybe," she said with a widening smile, "the voices belonged to people, not ghosts. Maybe even then, those crazy people were holding their ceremonies at Buxton, but not *in* the house…"

"But in the caves *under* the house," he added, finishing her sentence. "Would you like to see the caverns?"

"Sure…Why not later today?"

"Good!" He clapped his hands together. Then he realized that Constance had glossed over something else in what she had said.

"…You said: 'even then'."

"I suppose I did."

"Are you telling me that these rituals are *still* going on there?"

She answered his question, passing along rumors of strange ceremonies held on moonlit nights in the area, including the hill of the stone circle. "Don't know about rituals, but I've heard of bonfires burning up on Fromesbury Hill. I tell you man, if I ever saw such a thing, I'd steer a wide course around it. I mean," she arched her eyebrows and raised her voice in the patois of the island, "who knows what crazy things those people be doing."

"You sound as if you know who 'those people' are."

"David, don't you? You're the smart one doing all the reading…The Stone Circle Society of course. Who else could it be?"

The prospect that the Society may still be actively holding ceremonies had not occurred to him, and was an idea he found quite intriguing. But why was the current Society so secretive about its activities? According to the accounts he'd read of their activities, the original Victorians had conducted their affairs openly in almost a garden social club atmosphere. He was certain that if the Society did still exist, then the Old Guard families were the people he should be talking to, and the Tovey's quite naturally came to mind. With a bit of cajoling and pleading, he persuaded Constance to take him over to Hatherleigh on her next visit so that he might chew the fat with Rhonda again.

However, as they talked further, Constance started to grow uncomfortable with the idea and changed her mind. She suggested that he talk with Brendan first, since Brendan had been friends with the old girl far longer than she had. She picked up the telephone at David's urging and called Brendan.

At first Brendan scoffed at the whole idea, but in the course of the discussion he relented and admitted to David that he had his own suspicions about the Society's being active. David demanded to know why he hadn't told him any of this before.

"...the folks here are an eccentric bunch Davie," came a tired reply. "I don't have to tell you that. Now you've got to understand, a lot of things have changed here on the island the last decade or so. They feel like there're losing control and well, to tell the truth, they've gotten pretty defensive about things. You'd only be wasting your time. They won't say a word, not to an outsider."

"I'm not sure I'm understanding this. Brendan," he asked, trying to suppress the exasperation in his voice, "are you telling me to back off?"

"No way, man! I'm just tryin' to clue you in to what you might be up against. These people don't easily share aspects of their private lives with just anyone, and especially not strangers. But, if you're really set on this, let me see what I can do. Let me see what I can find out."

David put down the telephone receiver unsure of whether he could really trust him to follow through. Brendan had sounded almost protective of people he had once claimed to dislike. Or perhaps it was a case of not biting the hand that fed you, since after all, these same people were Brendan's clients and customers. Whatever the case, David was uncertain as to just how much more Brendan knew that he wasn't saying.

"So are you happy now?" asked Constance, the old mischievous sparkle back in her eyes. It was a look that captivated David's heart whenever she looked at him that way.

"...Not quite. You said you'd heard about bonfires up on Fromesbury. Was it from Brendan?"

"No," laughed Connie after a second, "it most certainly was not. Whatever are you thinking?"

"Nothing at all. It's just that a lot of this is falling into place a little too easily."

"And what's wrong with that?" she asked.

"You're right. I guess I shouldn't complain. I should appreciate the fact that Brendan's committed to helping. Hey," he continued without hesitation, "how about we have dinner tonight?"

"What?"

"Dinner, tonight. Like you and me."

"Ah…Tonight is not so good, I have plans. And before you ask another question, I'm going out with Warren."

"Warren Stevenson?…But I thought you and the Doc weren't friends anymore."

"David!" she shouted, plainly vexed at having to explain herself. "Where do you get these things from? When did I ever say anything like that? Anyway, whoever I may choose to go out with is strictly my business, thank you very much!"

David was stunned and quickly apologized, acknowledging whom she went out with was very definitely her own business. Constance for her part immediately regretted shouting at him. She walked up and gave him a hug from behind, resting her head on his shoulder; she felt somewhat gratified by his open admission of feelings for her.

"David, you are truly a nice man and a good person, and I really do like you. But I think I told you, I'm not ready for anything 'serious' right now," she squeezed him tightly at that moment to prevent him from turning and making a response. "Please understand, and try being patient with me."

He said nothing; it was time to leave. What she had said, in so many words, was that she did not now and probably never would share the same depth of feelings as he had for her. The word 'patient' struck him especially hard, and would stay long in his mind. He slowly closed his eyes. It was a sentiment he had heard before in his life, a sentiment that left him with tremendous feelings of emptiness.

David left the apartment with a forced smile as he tried to salvage as much as he could of his wounded pride. He came down the stairs oblivious this time to the gathered gossips in the store. As he got to the Benz he stopped; he was in no mood to go back to the house.

Someone had once told him that 'a lesson lived is a lesson learned'. But he vaguely remembered that same person also ending the discussion with a reminder that in the final analysis, we are all responsible for our own happiness. Before long, he found himself outside Bill Redditch's inn and was surprised to find the place closed; he had forgotten it was Sunday. He walked over to the alley beside the building to check the dockside entrance and was gratified to find Bill there stacking beer bottle crates filled with empties. Although it was the Sabbath, Billy explained that these kind of things still needed to be done. He turned around to see his friend's long face; it didn't take long to discover why.

Though he had warned David about getting involved with Constance in the first place, Billy avoided a lecture of the obvious. Instead, he took his friend on a philosophical voyage of the mind, relating the folk story of a poor fisherman who had long had his eye on catching a particular splendid blue marlin he called the 'Big Blue'.

"Wait a minute," interrupted David, "but haven't I heard this one somewhere before?"

"No," chided Billy. "Let me finish the story, man."

The tale went on. The Fisherman would get up early in the morning and sail out day after day, barely able to make a living for himself and his family with his meager catch. Then one afternoon, just as he was pulling in his sparsely filled nets for the last time before turning for home, he saw a huge fish jump high out of the water: it was a magnificent blue marlin!

The large long fin on its back bellowed as it caught the ocean winds, its wet skin glistening almost black as the fish flexed in mid-air: the sight was magnificent! It stirred his soul, and had so filled him with awe that it affected his life from that day on. Every day he would keep a keen watch out for Big Blue; catching that fish would mean a new life for him and his family. But much more than money, that fish would be the prize that would be the high point of his life on the sea. But it was not to be. Try as he might to catch that fish, searching the far off horizons day after day, he never saw that fish again.

David, who had been listening in silence to the story, tried then to draw a parallel to the situation with Constance. But Billy laughed at his blase, fumbling interpretation. David was flabbergasted, and demanded to know what the story was supposed to mean. Billy's explanation was quite simple.

That the Fisherman never saw Big Blue again was true, but the marlin had profoundly affected his life. The desire to catch that fish gave him an added reason to get up every morning. The fish gave him a purpose, a goal in life. It gave him daily a renewed pride in being just who he was: a plain old Fisherman.

David waited for him to continue. "…That's it?"

"Yes sir! That's the end of the story."

"I don't get the connection to me."

"Did I say that the story had a connection to you?"

"Well, no. But what was the point, why tell me the story at all?"

"To get you mind off that gal," he slapped David on the back, "and get you to stop feeling sorry for you damn self."

David nodded his head in understanding, turning the cast of the frown he wore upside down to an acknowledging grin. "Tell me Bill, you ever heard of a fella named Hemingway?"

"Sure I do, Stanley Hemenway in Falmouthtown. Where you know him from?"

"Stanley? I don't know him. I meant the American—*Aw*, just forget it."

"Alright, if you have nothing better to do, you can give me a hand with these crates."

Later that evening, Constance made the visit to Buxton Hall as agreed to take a first hand look at David's subterranean discovery. Things between them were a little uncomfortable at first, as neither felt comfortable making eye contact. But the situation quickly resolved itself as Constance revealed she had broken her date as "not a good idea". After the exchange of a smile and a hug, it was as if nothing had ever happened.

"Did you remember to bring a flashlight?" he asked.

"Yes," she answered reaching into her handbag. "It's right here."

"Good! You know, you folks could use a couple of 24-hour convenience-type stores down here. I couldn't find a one that was open."

"The simple truth of the matter is that you people don't plan ahead. That's why there're so many convenience stores up there."

"Okay," he answered, "we can debate the inclinations of American society to immediate gratification another time."

David led her through the house to the kitchen, but had to wait to reveal his discovery as Constance paused to search the refrigerator for some sparkling water. Once that craving was satisfied, she allowed herself to be ushered down the cellar stairs. David leaned in and pushed the vault door open.

"This is absolutely amazing!" she whispered in wide-eyed astonishment, cautiously staring into the dark space.

"Yeah, kinda reminds you of the movies you saw as a kid at the Saturday morning matinees. Normally, after opening a door you let the lady go first but I'm sure you won't mind if I go through this time."

"By all means," she laughed, "please lead the way."

Leaving a step-stool propped in the doorway, a hasty concession to Constance's last second attack of claustrophobia, they entered the antechamber that led on to the caverns below. There, in front of them was the old candelabrum, standing where it had been left for untold years; on the vault's bare floor was the ring that had provided access to the caves. David positioned his companion in front of the center alcove on the rear wall and returned to the center of the room to twist the ring. They were soon cautiously descending the stone stairway down into the dark caverns below.

"You believe me about the vision too, don't you?" he asked.

"David, I have no reason *not* to believe you," she replied, trying to be as supportive as possible.

Nevertheless, that was as far as Constance was willing to go into the caves; David's story was proven to her satisfaction. The return to the wine cellar began, this time going back the way they had come rather than following David's original, more perilous trek out through the underground caverns. Just before they reached the vault door, Constance grabbed David's arm and had him redirect the flashlight towards the vault floor.

"What's wrong?" he asked.

"I thought saw something shiny…on the floor."

"It's probably just the ring." He continued on towards the vault entrance.

"Well do you mind if I look?" she insisted, slightly irked by his dismissive attitude. After a few moments, she called a wandering David over: "Come take a look at this."

"It's just a big piece of iron," he replied.

"Have you seen Rhonda's silver collection?"

"Yup, Brendan took me on a tour of the house."

"Okay, so will you look at this. It's a lot like one of those neck bracelets she has up there. You know, like the one's the Celtic tribesmen used to wear."

"You mean the torcs? I didn't notice…"

"David, look how it's shaped, especially the big rounded bulbs at the opening." She took her car keys from her pocket and began enlarging the scratches on the ring. "It's painted black. I think your torc here's made of silver."

David managed to pry it loose from the retainer; they took it with them upstairs to the kitchen. In the better light however, they came to a slightly different conclusion. The ring indeed appeared to be a Celtic torc, but it was not silver; the color of the metal was a deep, rich yellow. It was a ring of solid gold, fashioned in the strangest of forms. David was perplexed; he remembered seeing similar designs or embellishments somewhere before. Finally, it dawned on him that the base of the sundial in the garden was covered in similar designs and, as near as he could reckon, the sundial sat directly over the caves.

Of course, it could all be coincidental, but the odds where overwhelmingly against chance. Constance had to restrain David's now bounding enthusiasm; it was really too late to go out to the grove. The sundial would still be there in the morning.

Other questions abounded: was the torc a key to an even greater treasure hidden somewhere in the caves? He began to wonder if the legend of Hannah was something of a ruse, concocted to keep people away from the house and hunting for treasure. They sat in the kitchen a few hours more, speculating upon speculations, until the time came for Constance to leave. She left David alone to contemplate the mystery and significance of all that they had discovered.

But the mystery of the night's new discovery was not the paramount question in David's mind. There was the enigmatic Constance herself. He was a little troubled by how easily she had broken off her date with Warren. Then another little fact struck him. Billy Redditch had admitted casually that he was Warren's uncle. He had told Billy earlier that day about his quarrel with Constance, and like magic, she showed up at his door: all was forgiven. Was it coincidence? Brendan had mentioned that the good doctor was a member of the GAMMBYs. He wondered what, if anything was the significance of it all? He was tired and wasn't too sure who he could trust anymore. Sleep came easily to him that night, aided by the contents of an amber bottle of imported rye.

# CHAPTER 10

Brendan was true to his word. He followed through with his promise, inviting David over to his studio on Wednesday that week to talk about observing Stone Circle Society meeting.

"Like I said," began Brendan, "I did my best to get Rhonda to sit down and talk with you, but she refuses to admit that the Society even exists anymore. In fact, she was grinning from ear to ear like one of her cats, pretty amused by the whole thing."

"So where does that leave us? I thought you said you'd set something up?"

"Hold on, I'm getting to it. Now, as it happens, I know a little more about what goes on hereabouts than the old girl gives me credit for."

Brendan explained how an unnamed source revealed that the Society was going to meet at Rhonda's estate quite soon. He outlined a plan whereby he and David would 'sneak' into Hatherleigh to observe the secret gathering.

"And you're sure you can get us into the house?" David questioned.

"As sure as I can be. Look, my 'contact' told me that whenever they have these get-togethers, they give the household help the night off."

David chuckled: "Guess they don't want any witnesses around."

"No, I suppose not...Look Davie, the Tovey's live in another zone. They don't believe that anyone around here would have the nerve to break into their place, and they definitely don't believe in alarm systems—too high tech. And anyway," he smirked, "they have the grounds patrolled by that squadron of attack kitties!"

"Yeah," David let out a half-hearted laugh. "How could I forget about the cats? So when's it to be?"

"Maybe this weekend, maybe next. I'll let you know when I know. My friend says that the meetings are tied to the phases of the moon."

"Lunar cycles…I guess that makes sense. Speaking about the moon, that reminds me. I made a very interesting discovery the other night, something I hope maybe you could shed some light on."

The chance discovery of the caves below the house was revealed; but the news did not appear to come as much of a surprise to Brendan. Both he and Francis actually knew about the caverns; they were a part of the lesser-known folklore of Buxton Hall.

"Everyone knows the rumors about old Samuel Claymore bein' involved in smuggling. The existence of the caves was once a well-guarded secret, for the obvious reasons. But secrets don't last long around here. In fact, the previous owners of the house used to run guided tours through the caves, until some fool woman was almost killed strayin' off on her own. Frank decided to keep them closed for exactly that reason: the caves are dangerous. I hope you're not thinkin' about going down there again, especially not alone."

David responded immediately with a deliberate lie: "Oh, no way! I get claustrophobic in a shower stall."

Brendan however, while seeming satisfied with his response, still continued to emphasize the dangers of the caves.

"There's something else," continued David. "I took Connie down there on Sunday…because I had to share the discovery with someone. But when we were coming back out through the vault, we found this on the floor."

He reached into his pocket and produced the torc, wrapped in a large, white handkerchief. Brendan's eyes almost popped out of his head when he saw what was uncovered; he eagerly took the ring and examined it carefully.

"Where'd you find it?" Brendan asked.

"On the vault floor. It opened a panel in a recess at the back wall. I thought it was just a retaining ring or something. Connie's the one that actually found it."

Brendan visibly struggled to remember the layout of the vault. "You said it was on the floor?"

"So you've been down there?"

"Yes, I told you. But it must've been two or three years ago now. I don't remember any recesses in the wall, or anythin' on the floor for that matter."

"There are three recessed alcoves in the back of the vault," David emphasized, "right behind the old candelabrum."

"A candelabrum? What did it look like?" he asked excitedly.

The subsequent description and his means of access to the caverns led Brendan quickly to conclude that there must be two distinct entrances to the caverns in the wine cellar. Brendan began anew to emphasize the hazardous nature of the caves, but the tone of David's reply indicated a crisis of credibility.

"Okay, I appreciate your trying to save me from myself, but all this makes me wonder: what if the danger from the caves has been deliberately overplayed over the years? What if this little torc here, is only the tip of the iceberg? Suppose there's a whole treasure trove of trinkets like this, hidden away down there from old Samuel's day. I read an account the other day that alluded to a collection of ancient artifacts. Why not a collection of Celtic riches, bigger and older than Rhonda's silver collection?"

"Okay David, sounds all very nice. But I hate to burst your bubble. Those caves were scoured from stem-to-stern back in the 'Twenties. Remember what I said 'bout the tours? I think someone was brought in to survey the caves plottin' out routes. I seen an old brochure with a map that was printed up to advertise the tours upstairs in the library."

"Maybe so. But you didn't know about my vault or the candelabrum, and you certainly didn't know about this." He picked up the torc and held it in Brendan's face. "Exhibit One," he concluded.

Brendan slowly moved David's hand: "I can't argue with you there."

"Exhibit Two is in the grove at Buxton: the sundial. I think the markings on the sundial are very similar to these on the torc. Now, the grove sits more or less above the caves, right?"

"Perhaps."

"Okay, now what if the markings are a map, maybe to old Samuel's personal treasure trove. Smuggling and avoiding His Majesty's revenue collectors could not have been a very healthy career."

"I think you're letting your imagination roam a little too much now…"

"But it all seems to fit."

"If that's all you've got Davie, I'm afraid I'm going to have to burst your bubble again. I'm reasonably sure that the sundial was one of Hannah's acquisitions. The Buxtons by then were totally legit. What I think we have here is a solitary relic, probably related to her activities with the Society."

Brendan's logical, informed analysis took the wind out of David's treasure hunting aspirations. He sat looking at the torc, deciding what to believe. Brendan again seemed just a tad too much in the know. For every question or angle he took, Brendan was there with just the right answer.

"What are you goin' to do with that?" asked Brendan about the torc.

"I guess legally, it belongs to Francis. It's his house now. I'll ask Jeanna to put it away for safe keeping."

"Sounds like the right thing to do. But don't scratch off anymore of that paint, you could damage it."

"Okay Brendan. I would love to stay but I've got to be going now."

"Seein' our Constance tonight?"

"Hey buddy, you had your chance," joked David. "She's all mine now." He got up from the table, putting the torc back in his pocket.

"Correction Davie, she's her own woman. But I guess you've found that out already."

"Yeah," he hesitated, feeling too insecure about his feelings and status with the lady in question to dally on the subject. "I'll be waiting to hear from you on when the Society's supposed to meet."

Hoping to take advantage of the long summer days, David persuaded Constance to come out to look at the sundial in the grove after work one afternoon. She showed up at the door of Buxton Hall still wearing what he referred to as her 'shop-girl' look: a white blouse and blue plaid skirt fastened at the side with a silver buckle. They took a short scenic walk down to the grove; David carrying a bag he said contained wax-crayons and paper with which to make a rubbing of the designs on the sundial's raised base. He informed her along the way that he had already compared the pattern with that on the torc, and regretfully concluded there was no discernible pattern to the designs.

"If that's so, why are we still going down there?"

"Because I want you to see it. I think it's made of bronze and the weathering over the years has made it a thing of beauty. And, with you being a beautiful woman yourself…"

"Oh," she sighed, "here we go again. Now David, really, you're going to have to get off this visual kick you're on."

"But I meant what I said. Beauty appreciates beauty." He stopped. "Take a look…Well, what do you think of it?"

She began to study the sundial, impressed by the ornate detail of the workmanship, walking all the way around the dial before she spoke again. "David, this is really unusual. I hate to admit it, but you were right."

As Constance studied the sundial, David in turn studied her. His eyes gladly following the relaxed curve of her leg upward, lingering a moment on her well-formed rear. In the depths of his admiration, he understood why Brendan chose to make her the subject of one of his sculptures. If he himself were an artist, he would have thought that her turned-up nose and small, full mouth were her most perfect features, noting to himself that the rest of the package wasn't bad either. In his mind, he justified his close attention by concluding that his fascination with the woman was as much aesthetic as it was sexual.

As she leaned forward to stroke the arched pinnacle of the gnomon, he shook free from his fanciful musings long enough to call out a warning: "Better take care, the point on that thing is sharper than it looks."

David felt gratified by her interest in the sundial. From the bag he carried, he pulled out a folded blanket for them to sit on, a bottle of red wine, and some sandwiches neatly wrapped up in tin foil. Constance stared hard back at him, rebuking him for the charade even though she'd already guessed there was no paper or crayons in the bag.

"Hey," he declared in plaintive innocence, "I thought you might be hungry after a long boring day at the office. I've got some crackers in here, and fruit too. Jeanna was nice enough to make some sandwiches. I picked out the wine."

"Well, I am kind of hungry," she said, allowing her annoyance to pass.

"Great! So let's—*Aw* hell, I knew I forgot something."

"What?"

"Cups. I was going to bring some paper cups."

"Red wine in paper cups? No David, I don't think so. I can wait 'til we get back to the house."

"You're sure now? We could share the bottle?"

"David, this blouse you so like to make fun of cost me almost a hundred and fifty dollars."

"One hundred and fifty dollars…American? For a blouse?"

"That is what I said. I do not need to get wine stains all over it."

"Damn, Connie…If it comes to that," he cleared his throat, "I'll lick the wine off the blouse myself. And you don't even have to take it off."

Constance smiled, surprised by his boldness. "Somehow," she said, "I should have seen that one coming. Boy, you better put your tongue back in your head and give me one of those sandwiches."

They sat down, and after a moment began to discuss how he had found the sundial after chancing upon the Buxton family crypt. He offered to take her to see that too, but she very definitely declined. Constance then asked him about his vision in the caves. He decided then to reveal to her the details of his earlier dream, of the tall veiled woman. She listened intently as he spoke.

"That is scary. You know David, you really should have told me about it earlier. I believe dreams can have messages and purpose."

"What?"

"Seriously, I'd talk with Mahernum if I were you. Remember, she has a gift. She might be able to help sort things out for you."

"And what would I need to have 'sorted out'?"

"The *meaning* of your dreams, David. Suppose, just for argument's sake, they're something else? I think she could help, whatever the situation."

He looked back at her with a strained, hesitant expression.

"Something seems to be going on with you and the house. Has anything else happened?" she probed.

"…No Connie," it was his turn to shake his head, "nothing I haven't already told you about."

"Okay. I had to ask," she replied. "Don't get upset."

"I'm not. Okay, enough of the Buxton family for now. I'll run up to the house and get some wine glasses…"

The minutes passed into hours, and the hours henceforth into days until it was late on a Tuesday afternoon. David arrived back at Buxton tired. Having spent most of the day out in the less than hospitable tropical sun with Billy Redditch, he was now ready to put his feet up and relax. He walked down the hallway to the kitchen and pushed open the door. To his surprise, Jeanna was seated at the far end of the kitchen table sharing the newspaper with a not too unfamiliar guest.

"Brendan!" he exclaimed in surprise. "I didn't see your car out front."

"Well that's kinda an odd way to say 'hello'."

"Sorry, I just didn't expect to see you here. I didn't see your—"

"Yeah, I know. You didn't see my car out front. Well hell Davie, I know my place. I used the servant's entrance and parked 'Old Yella' out back."

"Now why you have to talk that way?" interrupted Jeanna. "Those days they long gone."

"Think so, huh?" teased Brendan as he got up and helped himself to a bottle of beer from the refrigerator. "Jeanna, you know different. Things haven't changed that much yet."

She could not hide her amusement as she got up to gather the scattered sections of the newspaper to present to David.

"Man, it's about time you got back. Where you been?" asked Brendan.

"Been?" he replied, taking a seat at the table. "I've been fishing with Bill Redditch."

"My," he turned again to Jeanna, "he's been fishing. Leading the life of the idle rich, eh?"

They both shared a laugh at David's expense; but he was not amused.

"Remind me," David spoke to Jeanna from beneath a furrowed brow, "to leave you a list of people that are *not* welcome at this house when I'm away."

"Jeez…Now don't he sound like the rest of them 'round here," Brendan said, his voice tinged with sarcasm. "Mrs. Hendrie, can you please refresh my poor, ailing memory: how long has it been since Squire Llewellyn here bought the estate?"

"All right you boys, just cool it!" Jeanna stepped forward with her hands half-raised, just as she might stand between two children quarreling in a school playground. "…Thank you. Now, if you gentlemen will excuse me."

Both men realized just how foolish the situation had gotten and offered embarrassed apologies to her. David resumed his original mission, himself retrieving a short-necked bottle from the refrigerator before returning to the kitchen table.

"Man," began Brendan, "I've been here waitin' for a couple of hours now. The show is on for tonight!"

"…That's not much notice."

"I only just got word myself. The Society is meeting up at Hatherleigh after eight-thirty. I tried to call as soon as I heard."

David looked down at his watch: "It's almost eight now, that doesn't leave us much time."

"This is probably the only chance we'll get to see the Society in all its glory. Man, if you're serious about doing this, we'd better get moving."

"Of course I'm serious! I don't go breaking into houses every day."

Brendan chose not to answer; he looked down at his watch.

David got up from the table and asked another question: "Tell me, what do you think will happen? I mean, is it going to be like some kind of island *Trilateral Commission?*"

"Tri-what what?"

David explained the reference was to a secret group of old-money industrialists and other wealthy types back in the United States. "They allegedly orchestrate or influence every major national decision, like choosing who our elected leaders will be. You know most of the black people here believe that the whites will never completely give up control of island affairs."

"Maybe it's true, maybe it ain't," commented Brendan as he checked the time again. "Now, as much as I'm enjoying the delightful conversation, if we don't get our asses in gear, we may as well call it a night."

David changed into a gray t-shirt and blue jeans, apologizing for not having anything black to wear. Brendan muttered something about 'watching too much television' before he pushed David ahead of him on the way out to the jeep.

The drive over to Hatherleigh began quietly. The sun had just set, leaving the Coast Road in a growing darkness. David looked out onto the seascape and saw an iridescent band of red-orange sky that sat just above the horizon. He was reminded just how small the island of Grand Kirkmuir was. A few miles away, on the other side of that horizon was home. At that moment, it all seemed so very close and yet very far away at the same time. His mind began to drift off on that point of philosophy.

Suddenly a large car with big, oversized headlamps on high beam flashed around a corner. David held his hands out on the dashboard braced for a collision, but the car sped by quickly, leaving the jeep shuddering in its wake. Brendan leaned on his horn and cursed at them for not dimming their lights but calmed quickly. He told David that even with the apparent recklessness with which the Kirkmuirians drove, the accident rate was still far lower than that back in the 'States. Based on his own experience, David found that supposed fact more than a little hard to believe, but he kept his opinion to himself as he saw a curious sight on the road ahead. A line of sea crabs was crossing the road, glowing almost bright white in the jeep's headlamps.

"Must be dozens of them," remarked David.

"Yup, maybe even hundreds…"

"Hey, aren't you going to slow down—"

His question was answered immediately as Brendan drove straight through the line, the shells of the crabs crushing sharply beneath the car's wheels.

"What?" Brendan glanced over at his passenger's pained expression. "You didn't think I was gonna stop did you?"

David now was the one staring silently ahead, preoccupied with his own thoughts. Brendan waited a few minutes before he informed David that he had told Mrs. Hendrie to take the night off: "That okay with you?"

"Yeah, sure. I really don't need her there the whole night."

"Good. Anyway, it's too late to change things now. We're here."

Brendan left the main road, driving down what appeared to be an infrequently used access road for the estate. Leaving the car parked under the concealing branches of a tree, they walked a few hundred yards under the clear night sky to a six foot high brick wall which surrounded the inner grounds; it didn't prove much of an obstacle. From behind a line of trees on the other side the wall, they could see that the light of tall oil-burning torches stuck in the ground illuminated the back of the house. Tables were set up outside in buffet fashion, with various dishes left out under protective coverings; but there were no signs of any people.

"Well," commented Brendan as he took the measure of the situation, "looks like we'll have to go inside to where the party is." He slapped David on the back.

"Wait up. What if the doors are locked?" asked David.

"Just let me worry about that. A locked door does not necessarily a barrier make."

Even through the mottled shadows, David could see a roguish gleam building in Brendan's eyes: "You're enjoying this, aren't you?"

"My friend, somethin' I learned a ways back was to try to enjoy everything I do in life." He reached over and patted David on the back. "You could try to do the same."

"I'll keep that in mind," he replied. "Well, I guess we'd better find a way inside."

"Sure Davie. Let the fun begin."

Brendan led the way up to the house, motioning for David to remain hidden until he had checked things out. A few moments later, he waved for David to follow: the patio doors were open.

The main dining room was empty. David stood looking around; he thought it strange for a 'secret society' to have tables set up outside in the open, when they could have hid in the curtained seclusion of the dining room. Brendan meanwhile was peering out onto a dark main hallway, and noticed what sounded like music coming from the direction of the old chapel. They moved quickly and silently down the hallway, stopping outside the chapel door. They could hear music coming from the other side of the door.

"This doesn't do us a whole lot of good," David lamented. "What are we going to do: knock and announce ourselves?"

"There you go givin' up again. Chill out, man…Now, there is a way in, but you are goin' to have to put the brakes to a little problem you have."

Behind them, he reminded David, was the room that had been adapted into the ultimate housecat's habitat. The work on the restoration of the chapel was still going on, and the construction had left covered openings in the wall between the cat's room and the chapel. Again, Brendan's familiarity with the interior details of the house proved useful. After a moment's hesitation, he agreed to the plan; he could put up with a few wretched cats for a worthwhile cause.

David's mind began to wander. Everywhere, the island was a mélange of outmoded, staid colonial institutions and dynamic, evolving forces for change. He began to think of how he could angle the story to do the most good for the Kirkmuirians and, quite naturally, himself. A *Pulitzer*, he mused, indeed might not be too far-fetched a possibility. A jab from Brendan's elbow returned him sharply to reality and they entered the doorway to every housecat's nine heavens.

The room was as dark as the night outside, with the only illumination coming from cracks in the wall on the left side of the room. David entered the room fully expecting to be set upon by the diminutive felines; past experience convinced him that cats could actually sense his fear of them. But such was not the case. As he stepped carefully towards the gray slivers of light, David found himself besieged instead by branches from a tangle of unseen vegetation. He stopped where he was, deciding to wait a few moments for his eyes to adjust further. By that time, Brendan showed up to guide him by penlight to a gap in the wall and then left to find a vantage point of his own. From there, David would be able to observe the goings on in the next room.

He found himself staring in on something he wasn't quite expecting; an elaborate, full-scale costumed ceremony was underway. The meandering flames of perhaps half-a-hundred well-placed candles lit up the chapel's cold stone arches in flickering hues of black and gray. David knew that the original members of the Society were interested in ancient Druidic traditions, but he had kind of anticipated an evolution of the modern group into something more along the lines of a quasi-political association: in short, he expected to see a board meeting. This costumed re-enactment by the contemporary members of the Society came as a total surprise.

There were about fifteen people present, barely twenty feet away, dressed in hooded white or yellow robes, all standing in a group near the chapel altar. From the way the robes hung closely on their wearers, it appeared that they were wearing little else underneath the garments. David angled to get a better look at the participant's faces. Although they were almost directly in front of him, he could not see any of them clearly and regretted not venturing out to the front of Hatherleigh to at least jot down a few license plate numbers.

He pressed closer to the opening to look towards the front of the Chapel. Packed along the near wall were bare tin cans of what looked like paint and other building materials, so much in fact, that he counted himself fortunate to be able to see anything at all. At the altar stood a lone hooded individual attired in a flowing white robe; this was obviously the leader of the group. A closer look affirmed it was a woman. She was holding a long-bladed sword with both hands held slightly above her head, enthusiastically chanting cryptic passages from a huge book set upright on the altar table. Occasionally, the others would echo her chants in apparent well-rehearsed unison. At first he couldn't understand any of what was being said; the music was too loud. Then it dawned on him, from the almost lyrical cadence of their words, that they weren't speaking English. If what he was witnessing was their version of an archaic Druid rite, then it made sense that the liturgy was being conducted in a Celtic tongue.

David became even more mesmerized; his focus changed instantly. Gone was the simple, high-minded approach he had been considering to the story. The story he now envisioned would be a study in the similarities and contrasts of the groups on the island, a story that could delve into how blind self-interest served no one's interest. In his short stay there, he had heard disparaging remarks cast in closed reference to the 'superstitious, infantile nature' of the blacks on Grand Kirkmuir when rationalizations were made of why the wheel of change was turning so slowly. Looking out onto the candlelit scene, upon the pagan rites being so meticulously followed before his eyes, he could only speculate on how many of those same people were here tonight.

In his preoccupation with the ceremony, David failed to notice the arrival of a small, curious presence at his feet. One of the cats boldly decided to check out this visitor to its domain, and had been sniffing at his legs and feet. Then, as if it had felt slighted by not receiving the accustomed attention, it decided to get closer, arching its back as it jumped up onto a brace of the panel through which David was looking. But the cat missed its perch, and fell into David claws first!

David shrieked in surprise at this painful and unexpected arrival and jumped back in shock, knocking free a brace of the wall...A terrible chain reaction ensued, initiating a sequence he was powerless to prevent. The panel where David been stationed fell forward into the chapel with a loud crash!

His first reaction was to retreat into the darkness of the cat room and hope he hadn't been seen...But almost in the same instant that he took a step backward, a small fire ignited—the panel had knocked several candles into a loose pile of cover cloths. He froze in his tracks, torn between an instinctive need to escape and thoughts of doing something about the fire. In the split second he hesitated over what to do, the pile of cloth practically exploded!

—Another larger explosion followed: flames shot out in every direction! Shouts and screams born of fear and confusion filled the air; the flames were spreading everywhere. People stampeded towards the chapel door, some throwing off the robes they wore as they ran by in panic.

David jumped into the chapel. He grabbed up a cloth and began swatting frantically at the flames, but the fires were burning all around him. A hand came out of nowhere and grabbed his shirt.

"What the *hell* are you doin'?" a voice screamed.

David turned around: it was Brendan; he had his forearm up covering his face.

"Drop it!" he ordered, ripping the smoldering robe out of David's hands and flinging it onto the ground. "Let's get out of here!"

Just as he began to retreat with Brendan back into the cat room, David heard a scream and looked back. At the altar, he saw an auburn-haired woman hysterically tearing at the white robe she was wearing: she was on fire! David wrenched his arm free from Brendan's grasp and ran back towards the conflagration. A section of the ceiling collapsed before him in a violent rush of flames, the heat pushing him back. In an instant, the woman was lost behind a furious wall of smoke and fire. Brendan came up and tackled him from behind, seizing him in a lock about the head and shoulders.

"Let me go! I saw a woman back there. I think it was Rhonda!"

Brendan paused for an instant to stare back with tear-filled eyes through the flames: "There's no one there!" He began to cough uncontrollably.

"I saw her!" David cried out, still struggling to free himself.

Brendan spun him around and shouted at the top of his voice. "If she was back there, she's dead!" He shook David so hard his head snapped back: "Do you hear me…Dead! Let's get the hell outta here before we are!"

The drive back to Buxton was long indeed. No words were spoken almost until the estate came into view. Brendan then launched into what was probably a well-considered soliloquy of what David should and should not do. Dejectedly, David brought up the question of notifying the authorities, a notion that was quickly and brusquely cast aside.

The jeep stopped abruptly at the service entrance of the house and David was discharged with an angry, frustrated warning: "Get yourself a drink…And for Christ's sake, say *nothin'* to no one!"

# CHAPTER 11

Bright morning rays from the rising Caribbean sun reached in through the study's easterly windows, first shaking then wrenching David free from the jaws of a troubled sleep. It was now the morning after. He found himself stretched out on the living room sofa, his clothes wringing wet with perspiration, one of his arms pinned awkwardly beneath him. How he had gotten there he couldn't recall.

On the floor by his head, an empty glass lay idly on its side amidst a long, dark telltale stain on the Persian carpet. Barely a yard away was a liquor bottle similarly disposed; the tale thus told of where the night had gone. Yet despite the relative discomfort of his position, he could not bring himself to move; his eyes roamed across the room and fixed upon the slow ticking hands of the clock on the coffee table. It was a little after six in the morning: some eight, long hours had passed since he had left Hatherleigh. He closed his eyes and shuddered with the realization that memories of the night gone by would not depart as easily.

He rolled off the sofa and pushed himself up to his feet. Before he could take a step he was struck by the onslaught of a pounding headache—the parting legacy of the bottle on the floor. Hunched over, his eyes barely open, he made his way up to his room the same way he had first learned to walk as a child, step by step. Once there, he crawled onto the bed and lay sprawled on his back, looking up at the bare white ceiling. Word of the events at Hatherleigh was by now spread across the northern part of the island; of that he had no doubt.

Again, the grisly sight of Rhonda frantically tearing at her burning clothes replayed in his mind, the smoke and flames engulfing her as the chapel's ceiling collapsed. There was nothing he could have done to save her...Nothing. He was more or less convinced of that. But lurking deep in his heart was the conviction that he alone was to blame for the woman's death. He suffered in the torment of that guilt: if he hadn't pushed Brendan to take him over to Hatherleigh, she might still be alive.

He was not left long to wallow in the vagaries of self-pity. A sudden, hammering knock on the bedroom door shook David to the core, causing him to almost roll off the bed onto the floor. His vocal chords were virtually paralyzed with fear...

"David!" came a shout. "Hey man, you in there?"

It took a moment, but he realized it was Brendan's voice, bellowing from the other side of the door. David wondered how he had gotten inside the house, and more importantly, whether he was alone.

Still he said nothing. Not too unexpected images of a betrayal to the local police began to form in his tortured imagination. He sat frozen, propped up on the bed, waiting for whatever future the Fates had woven for him. He watched the antique brass knob turn, and the door crack open. Brendan slowly entered the room; he was very much alone.

"Were you asleep? Didn't you hear me?"

The reply was voiced quietly with another question: "How'd you get in the house?"

"Francis gave me a key to keep, in case of an emergency."

David relaxed, rolling back onto the bed; he had forgotten about Brendan's long-standing friendship with the house's owner.

"You don't look so great," observed Brendan.

"How do you expect me to look?"

"I thought you would've gotten cleaned up."

"Brendan, I'm not at all well right now."

"You mean you've got a hangover. I saw the bottle on the floor downstairs...Man, I told you to get a drink, *not* try and drown yourself."

"I was trying to forget about last night."

"Ah yes, last night. Well, you can relax. I have some good news for you. It's Rhonda...She's alive."

David stared at him incredulously.

"I said Rhonda Tovey is alive and well!"

"Are you sure, is she at a hospital?"

"No, she's perfectly fine, no injuries or nothin'. I spoke to her myself this morning."

"But how can that be? I saw her," he stood up, "I know what I saw!"

"Whoa! Calm down fella." He made David sit back down on the bed. "I spoke to her myself this morning over at Hatherleigh. She was lookin' over the damage."

"But…I saw a woman back there. I saw the same tinted hair."

Brendan shrugged his shoulders, and then reassured David that he had indeed seen and spoken, face-to-face with Rhonda.

After a moment of wild-eyed confusion, David fired back: "Then it had to be someone else!"

Brendan looked back unfaltering but silent in his resolve.

"Then you tell me, who else around here has hair like that?"

"Well *er*, no one I can think of right off."

"So what are you saying: that I imagined the whole thing?"

"Hey, things got kinda crazy last night. Maybe whoever you think you saw got out—"

"*Think* I saw?"

"Yes, I mean…Damn! I don't know what I mean. But maybe this woman got out okay."

"Brendan, I *saw* her clothes burning. I *saw* the ceiling collapse. She was trapped back there."

"And *I* saw the police there, and the fire department. They didn't come out with any body bags."

David was on the edge of exasperation. "Well maybe they just haven't found her yet!"

"The place wasn't damaged that badly. I know it looked bad when we left, but the fire pretty much stayed in the chapel area. Rhonda said a couple of the cats are missing, but that's about it. There're already about fixin' the place back up."

David suddenly felt very tired; he lay back on the bed. Truthfully, he just didn't know what to think anymore.

Brendan saw the exhaustion and confusion registered on David's face, and decided it was time to go. He promised that he would go back to Hatherleigh later that day and check again, if that would make David feel better. Agreement came without argument with a simple nod of the head.

Despite his mood being buoyed by the welcomed news that Rhonda was alive, David was understandably troubled by the implications. What was happening to him? The dreams, the eerie vision in the caves, the woman trapped by flames at Hatherleigh, he wondered: had he really seen any of these things? To his credit, he realized that he was presently in no condition to make judgements on anything, let alone his own sanity.

After a long hot shower, he decided to fix himself a late breakfast. He had barely stepped out of his room when he was startled by a loud noise upstairs on the third floor; it sounded like a door slamming shut. As far as he knew, he was alone in the house. He stared up the stairs momentarily before concluding an open window was the likely cause. But the footsteps heard late one recent night came to mind, as did Norma's vivid stories of strange happenings in the house. While he was sure that an errant gust of the Caribbean breeze was the more plausible explanation, he couldn't help but wonder.

He looked towards the top of the stairs, uncertain if now was the right time to confront the creature of his nightmares. Spirits and the like weren't supposed to appear in the daylight, he thought. All of his other 'experiences', for better or for worse, had come in the latter hours of the day, and usually at times when he was at less than his best. Now, however, he was awake and totally sober.

Encouraged by the argument of his own reasoning he continued up the stairs. He was being stupid, allowing a wind-blown door to set him on edge. He reached the top of the stairs. Before him, at the far end of the hall, were the private living quarters of his host, Francis Hurrell. To his left was the library, the door was slightly ajar. His intent was to check if the library's windows were closed securely, but all that changed suddenly as he heard the screeching sound of a chair being moved on the bare wooden floor. So much for ghosts and hobgoblins; someone had broken into the house!

Ignoring common sense and his own safety, David decided to confront the intruder, picking up a silver candlestick holder from a hall table. He crept over to the near wall and readied himself to catch the burglar in the act.

He pushed the door open with a challenging shout, his war club raised at the ready. But no one was there. He looked around; the windows were closed and fastened, the furniture all seemed to be in place. He lowered the candlestick to his side, wondering if he had come into the right room, and was about to leave when he noticed a dark shape from the corner of his eye. There was someone else in the room, hiding behind the opened door. It was the oldest trick in the book, he thought; it was not going to work this time.

Instantly, he slammed the door hard as far back as it could go, leaning into it with all his weight! The door crashed into the wall, the impact sending David reeling onto the floor. He scrambled for the candlestick and turned around as quickly as he could. But his haste was for nothing; there was no one behind the door. He got up off the floor feeling pretty foolish, and was checking the wall for damage when he heard rapid footsteps in the hallway.

Somehow, the burglar had gotten out! He raced out to the corridor and over to the stairs, but saw no one. He leaned over the stair railing and looked down to the first floor; again, there was no sign that anyone else had been in the house. He straightened up and took a deep breath, realizing that he was running around like a chicken without a head; there was nothing left to do but put the candlestick back where it belonged. Clearly, he was imagining things. As he leaned on the banister to go downstairs, a woman's tittering laughter made him spin around.

"Damn you!" he shouted. "What do you want from me?"

He stood staring down the hallway not daring to breathe; waiting for an answer that he knew would never come. It had to be Hannah! He was sure of it; she was enjoying the pleasure of tormenting him with this little game of 'hide and seek'. Relegated to the back of his mind was a more distasteful alternative concerning the questionable state of his sanity. Instead, he decided to get out of Buxton Hall and away from the house's suffocating legacy; a long drive out in the countryside would do him good.

For whatever reason, his journey took him to the outskirts of Betheltown, to where Mother Foster and her followers had their encampment. David left the car and wandered practically unnoticed through the noise and bustle of the local market crowd, until he caught sight of a small, very active figure. It was Mahernum; she was wearing the same old battered straw hat that was, in his mind at least, her signature. Almost at the same moment she turned and saw him, waving for him to come over.

It was then that he began to recall the bizarre conversation he'd had with her not so long ago. Most vivid in his mind was the warning she had given him, a warning which he had almost forgotten, a warning that had made absolutely no sense until now. Before she could utter a greeting, he literally pulled her away from the crowd of people and launched a barrage of questions her way. Mahernum begged him to calm down before she could answer anything.

"You knew that the fire would happen! I remember now: you said there would be a fire, stoked high by lies and deceit. I'm *sure* that's what you said."

"Mr. Llewellyn—"

"David! My name is David…"

"Okay, *David*. Please, try and compose yourself. Let's go inside the trailer, get out of this hot sun and have some tea. Then tell me everything that has happened to you."

# CHAPTER 12

Mahernum listened with great interest as David told her of the Stone Circle Society, and of the gathering at Hatherleigh on the night of the fire; she didn't even know that the organization existed. It seemed that as soon as he began to talk to her, a great burden was lifted from him; he soon calmed. The two sat at a small metal table at the rear of the trailer, sipping hot tea out of plain white stoneware mugs; a louvered glass window provided a view of the goings' on outside. That the Society was dedicated to the preservation of ancient Celtic tradition was something she surprisingly accepted, commenting to David that all people should be proud of the cultural heritage of their ancestors.

"There's a whole lot more going on than just the 'preservation' of a heritage," he contended.

Mahernum readily agreed: "Yes, those people have a whole lot on their minds. But David, you look tired."

"…I didn't sleep well last night."

"You're welcome to use the settee here. It's big and comfortable. It will do you good to be away from that house for a while."

David easily took Mahernum's offer, while fatigue did the rest. Several hours passed before he awakened. But this was not to be the restful sleep his mind and body needed. The tragic visit to Hatherleigh was repeated in the throes of a nightmarish dream. It was the fire all over again: the smoke, the heat, the confusion of bodies rushing to escape, the terrible screams of the woman as her clothes caught afire. He vividly remembered and focused on the terror on the woman's face, feeling anew the anguish of helplessness and guilt. His agonized shouts caused Mahernum to rush to his side; she roused him quickly.

Once David had settled back down, she took on almost a maternal air in demanding to be told everything. He opened up to her, revealing the circumstances and details of his recent experiences. But were these genuine supernatural encounters or simply dreams? He began a self-diagnosis, telling her of a theory that he had once heard about visions and hauntings, how intense human emotions can unleash a kind of energy that can become trapped in a place, appearing now and then like photographic still or moving images. Perhaps his dreams and encounters were the energies and impressions of events passed. Though he couldn't or wouldn't make the final leap to a conclusion himself, Mahernum was sure that she knew the answer. Her dark eyes began to sparkle excitedly as she spoke.

"David, dreams *are* reality. If they weren't, we wouldn't be talking about them now. They bring messages to us about our lives that we're either too busy or too blind to see. The solution is in what we do with these messages. I believe that these visions are a warning of evil. But it's not too late." She cradled his hands in hers. "If I am to help you, you must do as I say. You must be willing to accept the Lord's salvation. You must trust me. You must be ready to listen. What I will ask you to do, you may not understand…You may even dismiss it as 'island foolishness'. But it's no mere coincidence that you came here David, the good Lord sent you to me. I have been called upon to help save you!"

She now had his total attention. But the rapid change in the woman's demeanor had David a little concerned; he began to wonder what this woman was really about. Mahernum was certainly far from what he might have considered normal, but normality out here had quite a different feel. And this plainly, was not a normal situation. In the end, it was her absolute self-confidence that helped influence his decision.

"What do you want me to do?" he asked.

"I want you to listen to me, and accept what I tell you. I know you David Llewellyn, I know the kind of man that you are. I know how difficult it was for you to tell me all you have."

He replied affirmatively.

"I want you to come back here tomorrow evening," she continued. "I will prepare a bath that will help protect you from Evil, a baptism to cleanse your troubled soul. I will immerse you in the glory of the Holy Spirit. If I am to help you, you must trust my methods. It will take most of the day for me to prepare. And David, I don't want you to tell a single person that you're coming."

As he returned on the road to Buxton Hall, the allusions Mahernum had made to baptism and the Holy Ghost remained in his thoughts. Although he wasn't really what one would call a religious man, the concept helped give him a needed comfort in his decision. After all, many in the Catholic Church back home advocated a return to more spiritual roots. How then was Mahernum any different? He suspected that his doubts of her had grown out of his own prejudices. Perhaps in the end, putting his trust in another human being was all that was needed to help restore his battered sense of self.

As he turned down the driveway to Buxton Hall, a small orange car parked in the driveway gave notice of a visitor to the old house. Constance met him at the front door; she embraced him in a big, warm, emotional hug. Her body pressed close to his felt good.

"Oh David, I was so worried. Are you alright? Why didn't you call me? Brendan told me everything that happened at Hatherleigh. The whole idea was foolish to begin with. He should never have taken you there."

"Well, I think I had a lot to do with that decision. But it's nice to know you care."

She looked up immediately and was about to admonish him for doubting her sincerity, but was stopped by the look of genuine fatigue in his face. Instead, she hugged him again and led him up to his room and made him get immediately into bed. After a kiss on the forehead, she left with a promise to return later.

As soon as she left the room, David began to drift off into sleep. He presently found himself walking by flashlight in the dark subterranean caves beneath the old house, listening to the percussive echoes of groundwater dripping onto the cavern floor. Ahead in the great hall of caverns, a dim light was flickering hypnotically, drawing him in closer into its heart. He stopped at the mouth of the hall and stared in at a totally unexpected sight.

In the middle of the chamber were two floor-length candelabra spilling light from dozens of candles, each one set on one side of a huge, ornately gilt metal vessel of some sort. The vessel appeared to be a grander version of the big silver bowls Rhonda had described as cauldrons in the museum room at Hatherleigh. But as he walked in closer to get a better look at the beaten motifs on the sides of the object, a figure emerged abruptly from the shadows in front of him. It was the tall woman from encounters past, still swathed in gray veil and gown. She began to walk slowly towards him; his heart began to fill instantly with dread.

But instead of continuing towards him, the woman stopped beside the vessel with her back towards him; he guessed somehow she must not have seen him.

She began to disrobe, carefully removing and folding her garments as she set them on the cave floor, until her thick red hair rolled down in curly locks to the middle of her pale white back. She then reached down for a silver basin on the floor, pouring a flittering snowfall of dried flowers and petals into the huge bowl. He strained through the darkness and his own fear to get a good look at her face, but her back was still to him. The woman then lifted herself into the bowl, and proceeded to bathe in the mixture of dried herbage and what he assumed was water, using what looked like a scallop shell to anoint herself from the bath. David noticed that the bath was leaving her pale white skin colored by the mixture. She leaned back, her hair hanging loosely over the edge of the vessel, and began to laugh softly. Although he was still afraid, curiosity drew him in closer. The water she was bathing in seemed almost red in color. At first, he assumed that the flowers had tinged the water, as might a dye. But as she raised her arms exultant in her joy, he knew the terrible truth. In the fluid running down her arms, though mottled by the detritus of petals, he could see that the 'water' of this bath was colored a hue of dark crimson. He stepped back in horror; he knew now that she was bathing in a cauldron filled with human blood…

David awakened feeling more shaken ever than before. In an attempt to clear his mind, he decided to watch whatever mindless entertainment was offered on the television. Since there was only the one channel, choice wasn't exactly a problem. Yet even as he sat trying to immerse himself in the intrigues of an American soap opera, he recalled a detail that he remarkably had missed. He was sure that the broken candelabrum he had seen in the wine cellar vault below that was identical to the one that stood outside the chapel at Hatherleigh. The shared, winding tree-like design convinced him that they were once a matched pair, but whether there was any significance beyond that fact he couldn't say. In any event, the candelabrum at Hatherleigh was almost certainly a casualty of the fire, thus probably rendering any further inquiry along those lines useless.

The telephone rang twice with the ring characteristic of an intercom call. It was Jeanna, announcing the return of his earlier visitor; a few minutes later he made his way downstairs to find Constance waiting. She seemed somewhat agitated, but his apologies for keeping her waiting were shunted aside. A decision had been made, a decision which David did not let on but he was very pleased to hear: she was returning to the U.S. almost immediately to pursue studies for a Law degree.

Constance explained that a job interview she'd had in Charlestowne, a job that supposedly held promise for a real career—turned out to be a dud. The final straw that tipped the balance was an argument she and Warren had gotten into. She had even been considering getting back together with Warren Stephenson; after all, he did seem to have changed. But earlier that day they had become embroiled in a confrontation over his involvement with the GAMMBY's, and her relationship with a certain white North American. David feigned shock at the disclosure, then asked her what the GAMMBY's were planning to do that she had found so disturbing.

"Well it's no secret. Most of the tension around here now revolves around the Blagdens Shoals property. Warren and his group are moving to scuttle any hopes that Mahernum and her people have to get financial help from the government."

"But Connie, isn't your father a member of Warren's group?"

"Yes, and they're both interested in only one thing: making money. They think that by shutting down Mahernum, they'll only have to contend with the Old Guard. And believe you me, they're pret-ty confident they've got the upper hand there."

"Why so?"

"Because of people like my father of course!" she exclaimed. "The GAMMBY's are in bed with the government."

"But what you're talking about sounds almost illegal."

"David," she began to shake her head, "this is not the good ole' U. S. of A., you know. No one is going to try and 'impeach' anyone over a little matter like this. The only people that will get hurt here are the poor! It all makes me sick to my stomach. And to top it off, that idiot Warren has the nerve to question my motives."

"Now you're losing me. You *are* for the little guy, right?"

"David," her eyes lit up, "I knew you would understand. He thinks I'm trying to get back at him and my father both by supporting Mahernum. And please don't ask me what he thinks of my friendship with the Tovey's. He has absolutely no use for Rhonda."

"I think I can safely say that the feelings are mutual. But what about your father? I've heard that he and Rhonda aren't exactly friends."

"Oh…Well, that was all a long time ago. Rhonda seems over it now. She once pulled me aside and said to me that the sins of father's don't fall on the daughters. I think that was very nice of her."

"I guess…And does your father consider their problems 'water under the bridge'?"

"I really don't know what he thinks. He can be pretty hard to deal with. The last time I asked, he said that he has absolutely no reason to talk to Rhonda. She invited him out to Hatherleigh when they had the Santiago bash. Did you know that?"

"Yes, Brendan filled me in. So why's Doc Warren upset about your relationship with me?"

"*Doc Warren*," she laughed, "I like that."

Constance went on to pump up then deflate David's ego as she repeated what had vexed friend Warren so, recounting her admiration of David's calm, caring manner. She also reiterated the fact that she still was not ready for a serious relationship.

David then chimed in with an idea he had been considering for a while. "Connie, my vacation's almost over. I was thinking: if you're going back over to the 'States, why don't you fly back with me?...New York's not that far from Baltimore. I could come down on the train, help you get settled in."

She considered his offer a moment longer, knowing full well what her answer would mean to him. She shrugged her shoulders and let loose a smile. "It sounds like a great idea!"

The directness of her smile meant a lot to him; but he was not allowed to enjoy the moment for long. Constance departed the house within minutes, declining his invitation to stay for Jeanna's curried chicken with rice and peas. David pulled up a chair and sat alone at the kitchen table but he was not unhappy, for he was considering how this night could mark a turning point in his life.

No sooner than he had begun the meal than did the telephone ring. It was Mahernum; she immediately began to enthusiastically relate the details of the ritual bath she was preparing. The details evoked a quite recent memory when mention was made of certain dried leaves and herbs as essential components of the bath. The vision of that other woman bathing in the cauldron filled with blood was all he could see. He could not help but wonder about the significance of his dream coming at the time that it did. And although he was reasonably sure that he had nothing to fear from Mahernum, he was not comfortable with the thought of placing himself in such a vulnerable position with anyone at this time.

"Mahernum," he interrupted. "Look, I really appreciate all the efforts you must have gone to, but—"

"But what? Is the time bad for you, maybe you want to come later? We must use the herbs while they're fresh."

"No, it's not a question of the time...To be perfectly honest Mahernum, I can't go along with this. You yourself said that I have to believe. And right now, to tell the truth, I don't believe this will do me any good."

A heavy sigh was heard on the other end of the line; her conversation lost much of its energy thereafter. She was plainly disappointed in David's decision. But she would not try to change his mind, for as she had said and he had just acknowledged, his belief was crucial. Mahernum begged him to heed her advice; she was preparing a small amulet she asked him to wear around his neck. Since she had plans to meet with Constance on the morrow, it was agreed that the amulet would be left with her.

As David put down the telephone receiver, he saw that Jeanna had been listening to the conversation. She preempted any discussion on his part by excusing herself from the room. He leaned back in his chair and watched her leave the room without saying another word. Two things became surprisingly clear to him from that short exchange. The first was the immense respect that Mahernum commanded with the ordinary folk, the second was their overwhelming belief of the people in the mysteries and powers of the spiritual world. It was only now that he gained a conscious appreciation of how very different his world was from theirs. Even in the stark materiality of the twentieth century, he was surprised at how real the spiritual world was to many of these people. He conceded that everyone needed to have something in his or her lives in which to believe, and it was Mahernum who provided many of these people with hope. Hope for a better day, hope for a better lot in life, hope for a better world in this the life they knew and struggled daily to survive.

# CHAPTER 13

All vacations come eventually to an end, but whether the experience was one that would be looked back upon with fondness or regret, is quite another matter. The time had at long last come for David to begin the preparations for the return trip home. He awakened that morning feeling physically better than he had in many a day, but as he lifted his head to look in the bathroom mirror, the face he saw was riddled with doubts.

Thoughts of leaving Grand Kirkmuir aroused deeply mixed feelings within him. On the one hand, he was returning to begin what amounted to a new life at home, since he felt that he had now the inside track to winning Constance; that was the only thing of real consequence or importance. But then there was the island itself. There was, to be sure, the overwhelming natural beauty of the place, the sight of which could leave no heart untouched. The prospect of trading the crystal blue waters of the Caribbean for the gray, harsh skyline of Manhattan held absolutely no appeal.

Such reservations however, were not the cause of the anguish building behind the image he saw reflected in the mirror. The face he saw carried many regrets in the furrowed burden of its brow, and guilt at the thought of departing the island at such a time. How could he go and leave so many questions unanswered? It seemed so very selfish on his part. Paramount in his mind was how the struggle for the development rights to the Shoals property would be resolved and the many, many implications thereof. But even if he stayed, he wondered if he as an outsider, really could do much to help Mahernum's cause be successful.

Even so, he wondered if any of what was going on was truly even his concern. And what of his dreams, or visions, or whatever they were; did the cause of them come from this world or the next? Or was this magical little island with its entangling, intoxicating mix of peoples and traditions, weaving a fine silken web to entrap and destroy his mind?

Then there was the enigma of the caverns below the old estate. Other than the accidental discovery of the gold torc, no evidence could be found that anything else of value existed in the caves, and recent events had dampened any treasure-hunting enthusiasm still lingering in his belly. But the clincher was the likelihood that anything he found in the house or grounds would belong legally to Francis, so reluctantly, he decided against risking life and limb down there again.

Despite the lingering qualms, David ventured out onto on the long back verandah of Buxton Hall to peruse a listing of the scheduled flights back to the U.S. mainland, planning the necessary details of his return. He had reached an uneasy accommodation with himself, recognizing the regrettable extent of his own limitations. After all, why did he think he could solve the problems of the world when he could not even deal with his own problems.

The ringing of the telephone brought him back into the house. His caller began with a greeting, then began to ask him how he was enjoying his stay on the island. It was a moment before David was able to identify the rapid-fire voice on the other end of the line as belonging to his absentee host.

"Francis Hurrell!"

"I certainly hope so. Hey guy, I'm down here over in Charlestowne on some unexpected business. I thought I'd call and see how things were going. Is Jeanna treating you well?"

"Sure! She puts me in my place regularly."

"Great…That sounds like the old girl. She came with the house, you know. She's sort of the caretaker of Buxton Hall's traditions."

"Yes, I found that out pretty quickly. You plan on coming out this way?"

"Can't say. Depends on how things go, you know. Did you meet Brendan Costello?"

"Oh yeah. Brendan came over and introduced himself in my first week here. We've kinda been hanging out ever since."

"Good. He's a great guy. I asked him to sort of take care of you down there."

"Brendan's been a good guide. He knows just about everyone and everything about this place."

"Splendid!"

"I guess," David smirked. He was amused by how just a little time back on the island affected Francis' manner of speech. "Hey Frank, you don't have to talk the Queen's English to me. I understand you a whole lot better when you talk plain old American."

"Oh! But it's so damned easy," he sighed. "If you stay down here much longer you'll be spouting the lingo yourself."

He acknowledged Francis's observation with a laugh. "Yeah, I guess so. But it won't happen this trip: playtime's over. I'm almost ready to head home, maybe as soon as this weekend. I was just going over the airline schedules before you called."

"But I thought—I was under the impression that you were staying until the middle of August?"

"That was the original plan, but things have changed," he said happily. "I'll be traveling back with someone from the island here. She has to register for school soon or miss this semester."

He then began to tell his host about meeting Constance, and how he felt she was a very special person. Francis, while expressing his delight in David's happiness, reminded him that he had been down that road a time or two before. David for his part politely assured him that he was well aware of the circumstances of life and the bumps relationships can take.

"…No offense meant," continued Francis. "Well, I have got to run now."

"Wait up Frank. You haven't said if you were going to drop by the house?"

"I doubt very much I'll have time. I still have a few urgent matters to attend to."

"That's too bad. I wanted to show you something I found here at the house."

"What do you mean *found*?" Francis asked.

"It was on the floor of a vault off the wine cellar. A torc, like the ones Rhonda Tovey has stashed up at Hatherleigh in that museum she keeps. Except this one looks like it's made of gold…"

"A *gold* torc, "queried Francis, "on the floor of the vault?"

David filled in most of the relevant details of his night in the cellar, and the discovery of an apparent second entrance to the caverns. Francis listened intently to all that was said.

"Now David, you must promise me you won't go down there again. Those caves can be downright dangerous! And the last thing I need right are any problems from someone getting hurt. When I bought the old place, my insurance company made me sign documents and take measures to secure the entrance to the caves. Do I have your word you won't go down there again?"

"Of course. But what about the torc? You don't sound too surprised that I found it."

"I've found a few interesting knick-knacks there myself in the attic, but nothing like that. But that's one of the beauties of older houses, the trinkets you can find. What did you do with it?"

"Jeanna put it in the study writing table for safe keeping. I can have her put it somewhere else if you'd like," offered David.

"Oh no, the writing desk is fine. Just leave it in there."

"I guess I'll be seeing you in New York?"

"…If not sooner. And David, there's just one last thing: would you mind doing me a small favor?"

"Sure, I guess that's in order since you're letting me use your house. What is it?"

"This is sort of awkward, but I don't want you to tell anyone that you've spoken to me."

David hesitated before answering, but agreed to Francis' wish without asking why. They said their good-byes. In the back of his mind there was mild surprise that Francis would not be visiting Monmouth, given his close relationship with Brendan. By not telling 'anyone', he guessed that Francis meant Brendan. Perhaps, he thought, there was some sort of surprise in the offing.

Anyway, whatever Francis's reason, it was not any of his business. David's vacation was practically over, and he was determined to enjoy whatever time he had left. A visit with Bill Redditch seemed in order; it had been a while since he'd seen him. David hoped to entice him out one last time on a fishing trip. Along the way, he decided that he would check in with Constance and coordinate his airline reservations with her.

He walked the long hot mile into town, remembering with a smile the first time he had made that walk on his first day on the island. As he entered the small store front office where Constance worked, she spun around her chair and waved a greeting. She was busily talking on the telephone, fielding some tourist's inquiry as to sightseeing on that side of the island. David made himself comfortable, thumbing through a pile of rolled up travel posters highlighting the historical side of a visit to Grand Kirkmuir. Constance was politely ending her promotional talk and was bidding farewell to the caller.

"So what brings you into town at this early hour?" she asked.

"Came in to see old Bill, and see how you were doing."

"I'm fine. I gave in my notice to the company this morning. They didn't say much."

"It wasn't like you were planning to make a career out of this anyway."

"No," she replied smiling. "Oh, I almost forgot. Last night, Mahernum gave me something to give you."

She briefly disappeared behind the counter as she bent low to dig something small out of her handbag. It was a small, square sackcloth pouch, stitched tightly with fishing net twine all around.

David took the pouch by one corner and held it up to the light. Seeing nothing, he shook and probed the pouch with his fingers.

"I guess this must be the amulet," he observed wryly. "It's not quite what I expected. What do you think is in here?"

"Herbs and stuff, I suppose," she replied.

"What am I supposed to do with it?"

"Mahernum said something about wearing it around your neck with this." She produced a length of fishing line intended for him to fashion a necklace.

"I see," he said frowning at the idea. "How about I just keep it safely in a pocket?"

"David, I don't know about that," she warned. "Mahernum told me you have to wear it around your neck."

He sniffed the bag; it had a strong, almost bitter scent: "Powerful stuff. The way this stuff smells, it's potent enough to protect me from everything," he joked, "including your pesky Kirkmuirian mosquitoes."

David slipped the pouch in a pocket as they began to detail the requirements of the trip stateside.

It was just past the midday hour at Hatherleigh where another meeting of sorts was taking place. Rhonda had summoned Brendan over to discuss her plans for an informal dinner party. The two of them sat alone in the morning room sipping hot tea from fine porcelain teacups, eating small cakes and crustless watercress sandwiches. Brendan was surprised that she would seek his advice in this matter.

"So what's the deal?" he asked. "Who's the party for?"

"Your friend Mr. Llewellyn, of course. It'll be a small gathering. Constance is invited too."

"Sound cozy: just the five of us. What's the real reason for the party?"

"Brendan, you already know the answer to that question." She reached down and pulled out an almanac from the shelf beneath the coffee table. She laid it down atop the table and tapped three times with her finger on the cover. "Consider the date and time."

Brendan thumbed through the almanac and found that the upcoming weekend saw the rising of a full moon.

"Oh do show a little enthusiasm," Rhonda continued. "It will be a beautiful full moon to preside over our ceremony."

"I thought your ceremony had to be held on the first night of August? You're a month early."

"…I am impressed. You've been reading?"

"Yeah, I've been known to pick up a book once and a while. Help me out Rhonda, what's the big rush?"

"Actually, there's no hurry. The books you've been reading aren't very well informed. The Feast of Lugnasad is held on the night of the mid-summer solstice. This ceremony must follow, on the night of the first full moon."

Brendan's expression went blank; he decided to take her at her word. "So you're gonna hold your ceremony the same night as the dinner party?"

"That is the general idea," she answered patiently.

"On the same night, at the same time…That will be interestin'. Rhonda, tell me: who will you have subbing for you this time?"

His cynical allusion to Ellen Wainwright irritated her, as it was intended to.

"Ahh Brendan," she released a titter of laughter, "you are the one for jokes. I do indeed plan to preside over the rites. Just leave the details to me, thank you."

She began to get up and winced a little in pain, holding her hand out for Brendan to assist her.

"What's wrong?"

"Nothing. Just a touch of arthritis."

"Maybe you should see a doctor."

"Oh no, I've been drinking chamomile tea. Natural remedies work best for such ailments."

"Well, herbal remedies are fine but all the same, you should get it checked out by someone professional."

"It's such a bother to drive over to Port William," she said as she sat down next to him.

"Why drive all the way over there? We've got us a good doctor right here in Monmouth."

"Who? If you mean Warren Stephenson, I'd rather suffer in excruciating agony than let that boy put his hands on me."

Brendan shuddered; her words were delivered with an uncharacteristically bitter contempt. "But Rhonda, from what I've heard said, he's pretty good. I hear he went to pretty good Medical school in the States. Graduated pretty high in his class I've been told."

"Perhaps that's so, but he's so arrogant." She turned to look directly into his eyes, and half-whispered: "He's completely forgotten his place. That boy is entirely too proud…And besides, if he really worth his salt, why is he practicing here and not in Charlestown? All the truly *good* doctors keep their practices in the city."

"Now Rhonda, you're startin' to sound like a snob."

"And what of it? I really cannot abide insolence in these people."

"…Connie isn't exactly a pushover, and you seem to like her."

"Oh I do, and she's William's friend. But the Stevenson boy is different. His uncle is that public house owner…Redbeard Redditch, remember?"

"He's called 'Redeye'."

"Whatever! You see my point," she huffed. "I mean, look at the boy's family: his parents lived together, unmarried, all those years. I hear they didn't legitimize their relationship until the boy was five years old. And his uncle keeps the local drunkards simply swimming in rum. Now do you see?"

"See what, Rhonda? What are you gettin' at?"

"The boy comes from a background totally bereft of good breeding. I tell you this: I refuse to allow myself to even be touched by him. Why, you've seen him: I'm sure," she concluded, "that there's not a single drop of white blood in his veins."

Brendan was astonished by her remark; he was puzzled by how outspoken she was today. "…Your husband sees him."

"And what good has it done? The poor old fool is as senile as he ever was. Oh, William simply doesn't understand. He's a soft touch as far as these people are concerned. Remember, I *grew up* here. They're a silly, superstitious lot! I know how they have to be managed. William's only been here…thirty years at most."

"Rhonda, a lot of things have changed in the last thirty years, even here"

"Yes and not one of them for the better! Mark my words, we have to maintain our position in this society, or they'll destroy everything we've ever built on this island."

Brendan simply stared back at her in an embarrassed, suppressed silence; something must've happened to set her off. He was thinking about how to couch his question when maid knocked on the door, bringing a fresh steaming pot of tea. The maid carefully set the tray down on the marble-inlaid table in front of them, speaking briefly with Rhonda before leaving the room.

"Now," she patted Brendan on the forearm, "let's not talk about that wretched Warren Stevenson any more." She smiled. "Would you like some more tea? Its Oolong mixed with Javanese Pekoe, my own special blend. The used tea leaves are excellent for the roses."

"What was that?"

"The tea leaves…They're very good for the roses. A retired Army officer whose regiment served in India passed the secret along to my mother. And roses *are* originally from India. Did you know that?"

Brendan was dumbfounded; he shook his head.

"You put used tea leaves on the earth around the plant's roots, and they'll thrive. So few people appreciate or understand very much about roses nowadays, I find they're rather like children. All they need is a little cultivation, love and patience, and in time, they will grow to flower magnificently."

"A little love and patience," repeated Brendan. He couldn't help but squirm at the irony. "I will try to remember that."

With the dinner list thus set for the upcoming weekend, Brendan put down his cup and moved eagerly on to discuss the details of his show in New York. The old woman walked over to an antique desk and produced an airline ticket to New York City, telling him to call an associate of hers the following week in Charlestowne to arrange for shipping certain of his pieces to the U.S. for a showing.

"I spoke with Francis in New York this morning. He tells me that the chance of a showing at one of the 'name' galleries in the City is not very good at the moment. It takes time to schedule these things, and truthfully, they're not taking too many chances with unknown artists."

Brendan was not pleased to hear this; he began to wriggle nervously in his seat.

"However," she continued, "he has a business relationship with the owner of a small gallery in Greenwich Village which may have an opening coming up. I'm sure we'll be able to work out all the technicalities by the end of next week. But there is an alternative if we can't come to an arrangement."

"Like what?"

"The best alternative," she sighed with impatience. "If we can't find a gallery, we'll open our own and invite the art world in to view your works. How does that sound to you?"

"…It sounds like we're in business!" Brendan clutched the ticket in his hands with a certain satisfaction, studying the imprinted details. "There's no departure date?" he asked.

"It's an open ticket, good for several months. You can fly up and meet begin to look at sites."

Brendan stood up, seemingly satisfied by the progress of things. He thanked her for all of her efforts on his behalf and gave her a quick hug and kiss on the cheek. They walked together arm-in-arm to the front door, where she waited as drove away. Rhonda then returned to the Morning Room to place a call to Charlestowne.

"Mr. Hurrell please…Tell him the call is from Mrs. Rhonda Tovey."

Brendan hurriedly to return to his studio, anxious to begin the process of choosing the pieces he would like to have displayed in the show. He knew that good reviews of his work in the New York market could lead to a string of major commissions, perhaps even international acclaim. It wasn't money for money's sake that he wanted this so much, but what it could bring. Such fame would allow him to name his own terms, and grant him independence from the whims and fancies of purported patrons of the arts like Rhonda, or even Francis. While he sometimes fancied his work as rivaling the classical pieces of his revered Michelangelo, he realized that the current market favored the works of those drawing their inspiration from the cubist forms of Picasso. He desperately wanted to vindicate his adherence to a style that many considered antiquated, and this show could provide such exoneration by its triumph.

He was behind the wheel of a forklift truck when Connie showed up unexpectedly. She slipped silently into the background upon her arrival in the storage area, settling into watching the man at his work. Now that the time had come to leave Grand Kirkmuir, she began to wonder if circumstances had been different, perhaps they might have developed a fuller relationship. From the sexual distance of their relationship had indeed been born an unselfish and very unique kind of love. Greater things in life, she lamented, had been known to come from less.

"There you go again, sneakin' in to spy on me," shouted Brendan playfully. "You know Connie, I think you're somethin' of a voyeur. I really do think you like to watch."

She laughed, shaking her head. "Boy, what a nice welcome."

"Oh you know I'm always glad to see you! Come here, I have somethin' to tell you."

"That's a coincidence" she replied. "I came over because I have something I want to talk with you about."

Constance began to inform him of her decision to return to school in the States, and her reasons for doing so. Brendan seemed to be taken by surprise. He told her that he had heard good things about her interview with the television station in Charlestown, and chances were better than good that a job offer would be forthcoming. Constance rebuffed his optimism as being misplaced, since she had no intention of accepting the position even if it was offered. Brendan could not understand why she was so contrary. The interview was supposed to have been nothing more than a formality; he pressed her for details of how the meeting had gone.

It turned out that the station producer was indeed in search of a 'fresh face' for his television show. He seemed quite honest in his evaluation of her background, noting that her lack of experience or education in broadcasting would require her undergoing something of an apprenticeship. He assured her however that under his tutelage, her prospects for a rapidly advancing career would be excellent.

"I couldn't have been any more thrilled," she said.

But he then destroyed any hopes she had built up before she could even draw another breath. He told her without flinching that if he was going to put in time after hours with her, that she would of course have to put in time after hours with him, if she understood his meaning.

Brendan was incensed. He couldn't believe that his contact would not have warned him of the type of person she'd be dealing with. He offered profound apologies for having submitted her to such an outrage.

"No Brendan…It's all water under the bridge now," she reflected.

"I am really very sorry. I'll make it up to you somehow, I promise."

"Okay, enough said on that. You always let me talk too much," she smiled. "What's this other good news you have to tell me?"

"It's great news. Things are definitely looking up, professionally speaking. I'm finalizin' details on a showing in New York City!"

"That is great!" Constance exclaimed, expressing her joy for her friend.

"The show will be smack in the middle of the Village, if my good Irish luck holds out."

"That means that you'll be able to come and visit me often."

"You couldn't keep me away," he smiled.

Constance this time was quietly exultant in her elation. This meant that the two men she cared most about, other than her father, would both be with her in America within easy visiting distance. She reached up and slowly pulled his head down towards hers, bringing their lips together in what began as an awkward but warming kiss. Instead of resisting and pushing her away, Brendan accepted the gift of affection. He gazed into her big dark eyes seemingly at a loss for words, creating within Connie an excruciating agony of doubt and embarrassment: perhaps she shouldn't have kissed him.

"Well," he spoke at last, "what did I do to deserve that?"

"You didn't like it?"

"I didn't say that."

"Then you did…like it."

"How could I not," he replied in a hushed voice. "I've said it before Connie, you're a beautiful woman."

His words caused a smile to return to her face.

"Thank you for the compliment," came a belated response.

"It's not idle flattery, Connie."

"Well, flattery or not, truth or not, a woman likes to hear things like that. Keep whispering sweet nothings in my ear and I'll follow you anywhere."

"Anywhere?"

"To the moon and back!"

"Then how about to Hatherleigh this Saturday night?"

"Huh?"

"This might be jumpin' the gun a bit," he continued, "seein' as Rhonda was goin' to make the invitations herself. The mistress of Hatherleigh is havin' a little dinner party Saturday night. You, me and Davie have all been invited."

# CHAPTER 14

With his eyes closed and mind contentedly bereft of any serious thought, David lay face down on the hot white sands of Coral Trees Cove basking in the sun, working on a suntan worthy of weeks spent in the tropics. A small, borrowed radio beside him broadcast the lilting voices and melodies of reggae poets gently over his body, the plaintive messages of the music passing all but unnoticed. In a few short days he would be returning to New York, his vacation finally over; but for now, he was content to be just where he was. Alone and apart from the rest of the world, taking life one slow moment at a time: this was how he had decided to spend his last few days on the island.

He flipped over onto his side and opened his eyes, looking down towards the sea; a large white seabird skipping in the foaming surf caught his attention with its seemingly erratic movement. It was a moment or two before David realized that the bird was actually in search of a meal. It stood in the surging wash of the waves, sometimes flapping airborne for an instant before submerging its beak in exploring the returning waters for an uncovered morsel. The sight of the bird searching for food caused David to reflect again on his own circumstances. Here he was, laying flat on his back, enjoying the benefits of a life spent most recently in the pursuit of pleasures; his basic needs of food and shelter were assured of. As for the bird, it was a true creature of Fate, living daily a struggle to eke out whatever mean existence it could. The argument began in his mind: wasn't that was the nature of things, the simple, unabashed order of life? He had made his own world, shaping his own future by making the best of the opportunities his life had brought him.

The surf rolled in again, leaving smooth the ever-changing sands of the shore in its wake. David took in a deep breath; the island was indeed a beautiful place. He remembered the story Constance told him of the Swiss expatriate Karl-Heinz, the builder of the Somerset House Hotel. That a man would leave everything he had ever known and move out here was understandable, especially if he did not need to work to make his living. Having money definitely made life easier in the world of men. He smiled to himself, content in the knowledge that he *wasn't* born a bird.

He sat up and put on his sunglasses back on as he stuffed his things into a backpack in preparation to leave. This wasn't working. He had been doing his very best to forget Mahernum and the causes she stood for without much success. The bird simply reminded him who he was; he was glad not to have been born poor on Grand Kirkmuir either. He decided to drop in on Constance to see if she needed any help with packing.

The weather report on the radio that morning had forecast a seasonal high temperature for the day. Thus, the midsummer heat was something he was mentally prepared for. But the walk into town seemed longer than it had ever been before, and extracted a toll. He arrived at Constance's building suffering, and was truly thankful for the shade of the stairway up to her apartment. He rested a moment, his back against the wall, catching his breath before knocking on the door.

"My god!" she exclaimed, shocked at the tortured appearance of her visitor. "What happened to you?"

"It's a long story. I'll be happy to share it with you after a glass of that ice-cold water you keep in the fridge."

She stood on the other side of the doorway staring at him with an expression akin to a sneer on her face, a little put-off that he would come to see her in such a condition.

"*Er* Connie, can I come in?"

"Oh yes…Sorry, I don't know what came over me. Here," she took his backpack, "you'd better sit down before you drop."

Connie hurried over to the refrigerator, returning with a cold pitcher of water and a glass: "Drink it slow, now."

She waited for him to gulp down half of a second glass before she asked him again what had happened to prompt this unexpected visit.

"Lotta stuff," commented David. He was looking at a stack of cardboard boxes set neatly in a corner of the room with Sumo nonchalantly curled up atop them. "That is still the fattest cat I've ever seen. He makes a good paperweight."

"David," she protested, "will you leave my poor cat alone."

"Okay. But seriously, have you decided what you're going to do with him?"

"*Do with him?*…Yes David. William told me to bring him up to Hatherleigh. They lost two of their cats in the fire. They were lucky more of the poor little things weren't hurt."

David felt a twinge at the mention of the fire. "Lucky for you," he nodded his head. "So, it's back to 'cat heaven' at Hatherleigh for old Sumo."

"Unless I can find someone else who can give him a good home. Anyway, he'll be reunited with his mommy."

"That's nice," he smirked. He finished his water and gave the glass back to Constance. "Why are you staring at me?"

"I was wondering if you're wearing that amulet Mahernum made for you. She wanted you to wear it around your neck."

"Ah…I've been on the beach swimming and sunning most of the morning, you know."

"David, you didn't lose it?"

"Of course not, it's here in my bag." He began to get up. "You want me to show it to you?"

"No, I should have known. You have absolutely no intention of wearing it."

There was no reason to deny her assessment of the situation. Instead, he broke out in a smile and began to tell her of how he had miraculously regained his perspective on life, and decided to help Mahernum in any way he could given the time he had left on the island. This change of heart was received coolly by Constance. She matter-of-factly expressed her gladness that he had broken free of his 'mood of denial'.

Nevertheless, she informed David that the rumor-mill had a decision made on the Shoals property before the week was out. The news left David temporarily with a hollow feeling in the pit of his stomach, but he came up with a suggestion that Connie agreed was worth bringing to Mahernum's attention. He recalled how Rhonda had mentioned the inevitability of the 'march of change'. His idea was to quickly organize a real march on the island's capital, a march culminating in a camp-out in front of the building where the negotiations were being held.

"…Call it the *People's March on Charlestowne* or something. Let the lawyers, the bankers and the government's negotiators see the faces of the human beings that their decision will impact most. Let the big-shot politicians meet their constituents! Now, if that doesn't shake'em up, nothing will."

"And we can get the media in on this. Great! I really like it." She lit up as she began to buy into the idea. "You know, it's hokey enough that it just might work!"

"*Uh*, thanks…"

"Come on," she said, grabbing up her car keys from the table. "Let's go."

He rose somewhat reluctantly to his feet. "Where to?"

"Betheltown of course! Come on David," she ordered, taking his arm, "time's short. Mahernum is going to need all the help she can get this thing organized."

"But it's going to take days to get this together."

"David, I'm almost out the door. Are you coming?"

Preparations for a gathering of a different kind were underway barely five miles up the Coast Road. The afternoon found Rhonda Tovey zealous in her role as 'madam overseer', watching from below as a crew of painters was adding the finishing touches to the repairs in the hallway at Hatherleigh.

"You up there, make sure you apply the paint evenly, and keep the strokes going in one direction."

Her comment was directed at a small fellow painting the ceiling whilst laying flat on his back on a portable scaffold. The painter looked down and respectfully acknowledged his understanding of her wishes.

"Now Rhonda, the men are professionals." The voice of temperance belonged to William Tovey; his wife's admonishment to the workmen caused him to pause.

He had been returning from the garden with a large potted plant in tow on a trolley. "They've done good work for us in the past. I believe they can get along quite nicely without our help."

Rhonda turned around with a cross expression on her face: she hated to be contradicted, especially in front of the help. But her own upbringing was such that she would not disagree with her husband nor cause any kind of commotion or spectacle in public. Whatever irritation she may have felt quickly disappeared as she saw what her husband had on the cart.

"William, where are you taking that thing?"

"To the Cheshire Room. The dracaena on the north wall was destroyed by the fire."

"But dear, don't you remember? We brought another plant in to replace the dracaena just yesterday."

"Yesterday?" he repeated in surprise. "Are you sure?"

"Yes, William. Don't you remember? We drove over to Waterford and bought that dwarf palm you liked." She stared deep into William's stone gray eyes but saw not even the slightest hint of recollection. "Believe me, you'll see it just as soon as you open the door."

"Yesterday?…In Waterford?" His hand anxiously stroked through his hair as he tried his best to remember. "You mean Tom Parkinson's nursery?"

"No," she spoke almost in a whisper, "I believe Barry Osgood owns the place. Remember? The retired major from the Guards…"

William's lower lip trembled then stiffened as he drew in a quick breath; he couldn't recall even leaving the house. He left the cart and walked slowly over to the Cheshire room door and opened it carefully. To not even his surprise, a dwarf palm spread out dark green fronds near the center of the room's north wall. He then reached down and stroked a young cat that had rushed up to greet him, before carefully closing the door. He returned to the cart with his head lowered, and proceeded to take the plant back out to the gardens without acknowledging Rhonda's presence.

But she was not upset by the brusqueness of his departure, for she understood only too well the effect that his infirmity had on his pride. This was yet another reminder to her of his advanced age, and the unsettling realization that he was nearing the end of his days.

The solemnity of her thoughts was interrupted as a visitor was announced. A tall, thin man came around from the foyer; he was dressed formally in a summer suit and bow tie, and was still wearing sunglasses. A deep leather saddlebag hung over his shoulder. His very blond hair was thinning on top, and was cut so short that it resembled a fine coat of down.

"It's so good to see you again," he said. "You look as charming as ever."

"Thank you, Francis. I really wasn't expecting you until tomorrow."

"I couldn't stay in Charlestown any longer when I heard about the torc."

Rhonda smiled an obviously false smile, and then led him by the arm to a small room at the end of the second floor staircase; she wanted to get him away from the obtrusive presence of the workmen.

"I've brought some things you might find interesting…Rhonda, you're staring at me."

"I'm sorry," she said while still examining the newly lean lines of his face. "You look as if you've lost a little weight."

He caught himself before he laughed out loud at her typically uptight restraint, and confirmed that he had indeed lost weight, some twenty pounds in the last eight months.

"Twenty pounds? You might want to see a doctor when you get back. There's no one around here I could recommend, even if my life depended on it."

Francis knew full well that her jibe was directed at Warren Stevenson. "Actually, I've been to a doctor. He ran a bunch of tests but couldn't tell me anything definite. A friend recommended I try a fruit-based organic diet, which quite honestly may as well have been roots and berries for all the satisfaction it brought to the stomach. But we are what we eat."

For a brief moment she considered making a comment about Francis' high-priced lifestyle, but chose to resist the impulse. Instead, she chose to inform him of a little research project she had commissioned in the 'States that concerned a mutual acquaintance. She had hired a private investigator to check into the background of one Brendan Joseph Costello of Millers Falls, New Hampshire. He reported back to her that no such person or family lived there, or had lived there since at least the decade preceding the turn of the century.

Francis was visibly surprised by the news. "So, he's using a false name. He's probably hiding from the law…And that more than suits our purposes, wouldn't you say?"

"All the better," she agreed. "Now Francis, there aren't going to be any surprises, are there? Your relationship with Brendan isn't going to get in the way, is it?"

"Of course not," came back the answer without hesitation. I've been preparing for this for a very long time now."

Rhonda took him at his word. With these more peripheral issues apparently settled, the agenda continued on to matters of more immediate importance.

"Well then Francis, what did you bring to show me that's so important?"

He reached into the bag and pulled out a flat box made of black lacquered wood, about twelve or so inches long by four wide then set it down on a table and slid off the top. The contents of the box were wrapped up in a shimmering white silk. He removed the cloth carefully revealing a broad-bladed gold knife of an ancient design. Rhonda studied the decorated blade with great interest, and recognized the knife as a reproduction of a ceremonial Celtic knife found in a Saxon chieftain's barrow in England.

Francis smiled, impressed by her expertise. He happily corrected her on one point however: "It's not a reproduction."

"…I won't ask you how you came by it."

The knife was not the only item of interest in the bag. Francis also produced a translation of a Roman author's description of Celtic rituals, which drew only disdain from Rhonda. She stated emphatically that her knowledge of the traditions handed down to her were far more meaningful and accurate. Her unabashed scorn for the document ignited a fierce debate between the two.

"A manuscript! Did Hannah Taylor need a manuscript, answer me that?"

"We don't know. She may very well have—"

"Oh stop it! People like you think that the answers to everything are written down on paper. Well Francis, let me tell you this: the written page yellows and decays into dust. It is the spoken word that resonates with the gods, and assures that the Druid priesthood will endure forever."

"But Rhonda, I don't think I have to tell you that oral traditions can change as they're passed down from one generation to the next. The author of this manuscript was there, standing in the damp, cold of a forest clearing, two thousand years ago! He was an eyewitness to a ritual that we are almost blindly trying to reenact. What I have here in my hand describes the *real* McCoy."

"Perhaps he was there. And so what? Let me remind *you* that your 'eyewitness' was a Roman. How could he even hope to understand the true meaning and significance of what he saw?"

"Meaning? For crying out loud, the man was there!" He slammed the manuscript down on the table and slid it towards her. "The meaning is not what's important here. The protocols of the ritual are what's important. This is an authentic transcription of what was done, step by bloody step, of the entire ritual leading up to the sacrifices. And get this—the use of a torc is described."

"So, meaning isn't at all important? Oh please excuse me Francis, I'm forgetting that you're the one who gave up on Christianity because your 'college studies' of religion made you an agnostic."

"Now, that's not quite true." His hand stroked the top of his head, causing the hairs to bristle in its wake. "All I ever said was that the story of the death and resurrection of Christ had parallels in other African and Middle-Eastern cultures. My research couldn't find any real evidence that the Christ of the Scriptures actually lived and died, the way we are taught to believe he did."

"Evidence? And the evidence you want has to come from books and manuscripts like this I suppose." She reached down and pushed the manuscript on the table back towards him. "No more argument! The rite will be performed according to the spoken tradition, not some Roman's scrawlings. This ceremony will be conducted *my* way, or not at all."

Her summary declaration irked Francis; he picked up the manuscript and began to stuff it back into his bag but stopped. "Look, Rhonda...I have something to tell you."

She stared angrily back at him. "Well, what is it?"

"Now, this is not very easy for me to say, but the doctors I spoke to," he took a breath, "they've told me my illness is terminal. Chances are, I may not live out the year."

Rhonda seemed hardly surprised by the admission. Without the slightest hint of compassion in her voice, she continued. "But you've known that for a while, haven't you?"

He raised his head but said nothing.

"You knew that before you went back to New York, didn't you? I mean, why else would you want to risk involvement in something like this?"

"Look," he fired back impatiently, "I need this ceremony to go off perfectly. Don't you understand?" he pleaded, the desperation building behind his voice: "this may be my *last* hope."

"Your last hope," she repeated. "Well, perhaps mine too. I tell you this: I'm not at all ready to succumb to a life of old age infirmity. I mean, look at what's happening to William. My God, the man barely knows what's been happening from one moment to the next!"

"At least you've gotten to live to a decent age. I'm not even fifty. Don't you see? Finding that torc is a sign. Rhonda, please...do me this favor."

"So now you believe in Providence...Oh very well," she relented, "I will look at your Roman's manuscript. But don't grovel. Do try to hold on to some vestige of your manhood."

Francis ignored her backhanded remark and eagerly took the manuscript from the bag again, spreading the pages out across the table. Rhonda picked up the first page and held it up to the light; she shook her head. "I'll have to get my glasses. This thing is written in English, isn't it?"

"I've had a new translation made from the original to ensure the accuracy of the ceremony. By the way, where's the torc now?"

"Still in your study desk drawer, under lock and key."

"But I thought you were going to take it into safe keeping?"

"I was. But really, I only wanted to see it. And anyway, why take the risk of your guest finding it missing? The police could be called in and things could get very inconvenient. It's safe enough where it is."

"Okay Rhonda, I see your point. Can we get on with this? There isn't much time to get it right!"

# CHAPTER 15

The speed with which Mahernum marshaled her supporters was something that David found to be truly amazing. Within hours, the word spread through the countryside and people were swarming like ants to Betheltown for the march on Parliament Hill. Mother Foster's backers were apparently not only amongst the downtrodden for later, two rented trailer-trucks arrived laden with supplies for the march and the marchers both, donated by a generous but anonymous donor.

And that was not the only surprise. When asked before about her reputation as a miracle worker, Mahernum would only smile and say people sometimes needed miracles to believe. But the little woman must've had at least one up her sleeve, as somehow she arranged to have a special train run take her band of followers across the island to Charlestowne the next morning. They would eventually be dropped off a few short miles outside the capital, and commence the march from there. They would make stops across the island at the old plantation loading docks. Constance could not miss the irony in this, as this train would now ferry the hopes of people whose ancestor's forced toil had made plantation owner's wealthy.

Captains were appointed for the many tasks that needed to be accomplished, and soon the camp was loud with the shouts and cries of the frantic effort that lay before them. Not even the untimely demise of daylight would affect the level of the activity, as bonfires were lit and planned and impromptu speeches were made to drive the level of ebullience to a zenith. Nevertheless, the night ahead would be long in passing, for all knew well the stakes that were involved.

Morning did come, sending warm rays of light out to rouse and empty Betheltown of a fair portion of its inhabitants. With only the clothes he had on his back, David joined the singing 'thin black line', as they now called themselves, on the journey to the train station. Constance had driven ahead to the capital the night before, ferrying several of the other organizers to critical intersections, and had taken on the task of informing the local police of the marchers' coming.

Still chanting and singing favored local hymns, the marchers boarded open rail cars designed for high, overflowing piles of sugar cane as orderly and quickly as they could. Every man, woman or child carried whatever amenities they needed, for no refreshments would be served along the way and no hotels with soft, comfortable beds awaited the end of this journey.

David stood for much of the five hour ride, peering through gaps in the railcar's worn wooden sideboards, seeing places he otherwise may never have had the unfortunate opportunity to see. The journey took them through the desperately poor villages of the Hill Country, places that no tourist would ever deliberately see, hamlets so bleak that the rude settlements at Bel Rios seemed luxurious by comparison: these people were the truly forgotten. These were the people left behind as their kith and kin went to the Betheltowns of this world in search of a better life.

David also saw other depressing sights along the way that he hadn't expected. Hidden behind a thin green mask of tropical vegetation were several abandoned strip mines that appeared out of nowhere like large, gaping wounds in the flesh of the Earth. The trees and bushes had all been bulldozed and scraped clear, leaving the once bauxite-rich red soil, barren and open to the mountain air. Dotted here and there were stagnant black lakes of water that gave life to nothing. Back home in America, David thought how mining companies would be legally obligated to restore such sites. But here, the rape of the land had been complete. Abused and discarded, the shamelessness of the crime was absolute; yet there was little if any talk of punishment or redress in the halls of Kirkmuirian government. The almighty dollar had spoken. Time and Nature were left to work whatever magic they could to heal the scarred landscape.

The marchers disembarked at a weigh station outside of the capital as planned, traveling the next segment on foot. The decision had been made to set up camp at a rough public soccer field complex outside of Charlestown, with makeshift covers of plastic tarpaulins to provide shelter from the as yet still hospitable elements. Several more anonymously rented trucks arrived with donations of further provisions for the tired and the hungry. Mother Foster took time to tour the campsite, giving words of praise and encouragement to her flock. The smile they all saw was genuine, for she was truly proud of them; they had accomplished in two days what she may have even thought was impossible. The word was that almost thirty thousand people would be converging on the city to stand up for their dignity and rights as human beings, doing for themselves what many had been content to let others do before. She believed now more than ever in the righteousness and ultimate success of her cause, refusing to accept the possibility of anything less in her heart.

Constance rejoined the marchers and was happy to find David after search a while. She had made a quick dash back to Monmouth for a change of clothing and other creature comforts for both David and herself having completed some public relations chores. After a last organizational meeting to go over the plans for the rally in front of the Parliament buildings, the two decided to take a late night stroll around the bonfires before turning in. They were surrounded by a crowd of enthusiastic, mostly smiling faces, comprised surprisingly enough from folks drawn from many different walks of life.

"…And to think, all this is because of you," beamed an admiring Constance.

"I couldn't take credit for all of this. Sure, the original idea may have been mine, but these folk would never have turned out for me. And look at that," he pointed over to some city workers still unloading portable toilets and shower stalls. "That little lady really has some pull. I mean, everyone has cooperated. The police, the local governments…I don't think anyone has asked for so much as a permit, or thrown up any red tape to stop this thing."

"You're right about that. Mahernum's name certainly does carry a lot of weight. But I think that the suddenness of everything really worked in our favor too. The opposition didn't have enough time to get organized."

"And what a shame it is too. Score one for our side!"

They settled in to rest beneath the dark canopy of a star-spotted night, with David becoming increasingly unmindful of his surroundings as he stared at the woman in the sleeping bag across from him. She was, in his eyes, the consummate vision of loveliness, sleeping childlike so with her petite mouth agape. He had never been much of one for prolonged outdoor activities like camping, but one look across the way was enough to convince him that his travail the last day or so was indeed worthwhile. He congratulated himself on his inspiration for the protest, pleased to see one of his hare-brained ideas actually paying off.

Eventually however, his thoughts turned to the logistical details of the march, as he began to wonder how Mahernum was able to get the use of the railway. The questions began to add up and really gnaw at him after a while; he couldn't get to sleep. He rolled over and saw that the little woman was still up talking with a few people, and decided to wander over and ask the question. After all, where had the trucks and all the other contributions come from? Perhaps it was a little like looking a gift horse in the mouth, but he was kind of curious.

"...I'm sort of surprised you didn't ask sooner," was Mahernum's spry response.

"I saw that you were busy, and I was a little preoccupied myself...with everything."

"Yes, Constance can be quite engaging. Anyway," she continued quickly to avoid embarrassing him, "Winston Churchill once made a statement which I find to be very appropriate to this situation. He said that he would make a deal with the devil himself if it would help him get what he wanted. We *must* win this debate. We must be victorious for the sake of the people. I did what I had to do. I called Mrs. Rhonda Tovey, and asked for her help."

"You called Rhonda? Wow, that's one for the books...But if you were going to call a Tovey, you would've called William. He seems far more reasonable."

"Yes, I heard he's a fair man. But in a situation like this, I felt it was best to go straight to the horse's mouth. I know that if I went to her husband first, she might've found a way to stop us. So I appealed to her sense of—"

"Not justice..."

"Man, let me finish. I talked with her woman-to-woman, to propose an arrangement."

"You made a deal with her."

"Well," she stuck out her lower lip, "that's as good a word as any...Maybe I prefer 'bargain'."

"How could you do that?" David appealed to the heavens for understanding.

"I really didn't have much of a choice. How else could we move so many people so quickly? The vote is set for this Friday, just two days from now. We have to make them understand, or as you yourself said, make them see the faces of the people that this vote will affect."

He was silent on that point.

"Do you understand now?" she continued her appeal.

"I guess I do. But tell me, in every 'arrangement', as you put it, there's something in it for both sides. What did you have to promise her? I know she didn't help out of the goodness of her heart."

"Well, God does work in mysterious ways."

"Mahernum..."

"Don't worry so, boy. Believe or not, I've worked with her before. Maybe not on anything this grand, but I didn't have to give up much."

"What do you mean?"

"The word is out on more than a decision being imminent. The sources I have say that the Old Guard's proposal is not in the picture. It's between the Bankers and us. Rhonda knows that too."

"I think I'm beginning to understand."

"Yes," she explained. "I *know* what motivates that woman. I've known people like her all my life. Having power is nice, but there's nothing she fears or respects more than money. The GAMMBY's have plen-ty of that, we don't. Believe me boy, she had a hard choice. Better the devil that you think you can control, than the devil that can control you."

"Chose the lesser of two evils from her point of view. But that way, she doesn't win."

"She doesn't lose everything either. It's human nature to relish the role of spoiler, I counted on that. Now then David, it is long past late. We have a *lot* to do in the morning."

Thus saying, she packed him off back to his bed. With each step that he took, developing in his mind was a clearly different picture of who this little woman was: Mahernum the politician; Mahernum, the leader; and not least of all, Mahernum, the pragmatist. This person was nothing at all like the mystical woman of cast-eyed trances and mystical charms whom he had come to know of late; there was no word to describe her other than 'extraordinary'. In truth, David began to think that this woman was possessed of perhaps the most complex personality he had ever encountered.

The timely but discordant crowing of several roosters called the gathered multitude to rise *en masse* in the morning, thus beginning the March on Charlestowne in earnest. David felt almost as if he had been transported in time. Surely, this must have been how the U.S. Civil Rights marches in the 'Sixties must have been. Constance agreed, with one notable exception. The American marches were mostly through hordes of bitterly hostile onlookers, whereas here, the crowds not only cheered, but many abandoned whatever they had been doing to join in. This slightly annoyed her, since she didn't want the importance of their message and reason for being in the city to be lost in the carnival atmosphere the event appeared to be taking on.

Though they were no more than two hundred at the beginning in Betheltown, their numbers swelled with each passing hour, growing into the forecasted tens of thousands by the time the old and new buildings of the Capital came into view. The route chosen by the organizers took them by some of the more picturesque areas of the city, including the old Spanish fortress at the promontory of San Sebastian, thus drawing the maximum attention possible. The police, though evident by their uniformed presence, stayed mostly in the background; only occasionally did they halt the marchers to allow vehicles to trickle through their lines. The marchers had been informed that an agreement had been reached between the local authorities and Mahernum's associates in the capital to not unnecessarily tie up traffic. However, the agreement did not extend as far as access was concerned to Parliament Square.

Barricades had been set up to channel the boisterous marchers into a park on the grounds below the seat of Grand Kirkmuir's government where a platform had been erected for the delivery of speeches and allow the news media to cover the event. Awaiting their arrival on the stage was a mixed group of sympathetic and perhaps opportunistic politicians. David and Constance found for themselves a strategic shaded perch on the stairs leading down into the park from which to listen and watch. From there, they noticed a squadron of riot-equipped and mounted police hidden away from the sight of the crowd, standing at the ready should things get out of hand. Constance considered their presence to be completely unnecessary, but allowed the government the right to security and caution on the Parliament grounds.

"…for all they know," she added only semi-sarcastically, "this little gathering may be the signal for people all over the island to rise up and throw the buggers out!"

"Hey don't joke. Stranger things have been known to happen."

Nevertheless, the proceedings got underway peaceably enough, with an invocation given by the Anglican Archbishop of Charlestowne which plead the entreaty several times: 'Lord, hear our prayer'. Speech after speech was delivered by politicians and activists in ringing support of the marcher's position, each greeted in turn by the ever-increasing volume of the crowd's appreciation. But undoubtedly, the emotional peak of the afternoon was reached as their leader Mahernum arose from her chair, as she was introduced by the simple mention of her name. A resounding cheer rose up from the crowd as she came to the microphone to address the throng wearing her signature straw hat. After expressing her thanks to God for the dual bounties of good weather and a friendly welcome to the capital, her remarks were concise and to the point, loudly detailing what they wanted and her group's plans for the development of the Shoals property.

It was perhaps midway through the speech that David's eyes left the stage, drawn into ebullient surging sea of overwhelmingly black and brown faces. He remembered Constance's explanation of why the people in Betheltown remained amidst the less than favorable conditions there simply on the hope of something better. He saw those hopes now expanding into vivid expectations, and wondered how many of those dreams could actually be fulfilled. His philosophical musings were interrupted as Constance grabbed and rudely shook his arm.

"What's up?"

"David, look! It's that boy who attacked us in Bel Rios! Down there in the crowd, by the water fountain."

"You mean the guy with the scarred arm. What was his name, Seely?"

"Yes! Look," she pointed, "down there!"

Sure enough, it was he. Carlton Seely was not someone David would easily forget. He stood not fifty yards away on the steps of the fountain, his attention squarely focused on Mahernum. A chill ran down David's spine. He didn't like it; he was sure the man was up to no good. He glanced back towards the riot police; it wouldn't take much to get them charging in there. Instantly, he began to perceive a dangerous plot in his mind. Although he could not see any of Seely's old accomplices nearby, David was sure that they were down there somewhere, milling in the crowd. They must have been brought in by one of the opposition groups to cause trouble. He bridled with anger at the prospect; someone could get seriously hurt! Mahernum's enemies would not allow her victory to come unsullied. Surely, he thought, here in front of the cameras and with the full attention of the nation, this would be their last, desperate chance for affecting the outcome of Friday's vote.

And he was certain that he knew who might stoop to such a thing without a care for those who could get hurt. What better way for Rhonda and her cronies to show how 'unready' these people were for a project as large as developing the Shoals, despite her aiding the march. He decided that he could not stand by and just let this happen; he would do something while he still had the chance.

Dispatching Constance to alert a police constable near the stage, he made his way down the steps, circling behind the fountain where Seely was standing. But what to do next? If he attempted to confront the man, all hell could break loose: what would the crowd see except a white man fighting with a black man, and with what possible consequence? The altruistic purpose of the rally could be quickly subverted. Even if the crowd stayed out of the confrontation, there was the question of whether he could physically overpower or even hold Seely long enough for help to arrive. Perhaps, he thought, now was as good a time as any to let discretion be the better part of valor and wait for Constance to bring help.

But time and the opportunity to consider alternatives were not David's allies. For some inexplicable reason, Seely turned around and stared directly at David. He too recognized an antagonist from that night in the Hill country; his eyes bore a cold, deadly serious expression. Before David knew what to do, Seely began to make his way effortlessly through the massed bodies between them. David breathed in deep and held his breath; now it seemed like a foolish decision to have gone down there alone.

He began to move backward through the crowd, deciding to try drawing Seely with him towards the police. Mahernum's impassioned words from the dais merged with the crowd's many voices into an imperceptible droning in his ears. Seely followed behind, a hand raised in the air. David hurried down to where he thought he had sent Constance for the police, but she wasn't there. For an instant, he froze. Suddenly, he felt a hand on his shoulder and turned around: it was Seely, standing there with a smirk on his face.

"Man, where you runnin' to?"

"…I'm not running anywhere," David replied, as he anxiously hoped to delay a confrontation until help arrived.

"You no hear me calling you? I want to talk."

"Talk? Sure, let's talk."

"Man, what's the matter with you? Chill, I'm not gonna hurt you. I want to talk. I *want* to apologize."

"There's nothing wrong with me," he fired back before realizing what Seely had said. "What was that?"

"I said, I want to apologize. That night, I was drinking with me friends. We didn't mean to hurt anybody. Things, they just get a little outta hand."

"Oh sure. We just overreacted."

"Look man, I'm sorry. Things just got outta hand. We was just gonna have a little fun, hassle you a little, and then let you go 'bout you business."

"A little fun?"

"Look, I feel real bad 'bout what happen."

"Okay, if that's so, why didn't you turn yourself in to the police?"

"I did."

"What?"

"I did. Two weeks gone now. I got tired of bein' away from me family. They need me."

"Two weeks ago?" David knew the natural progression of things was a wee bit slower on the island, but if Seely was telling him the truth, he assumed the police would have gotten in touch with him by now. "Let's say I believe you, why are you here…at the March?"

Seely explained how he and his friends were going to hear Mahernum speak that night back in Bel Rios. When the meeting was cancelled, with nothing else going on, they began to drink and got a little drunk. The rest was history, but he claimed to be a devoted follower of Mahernum. He conceded how she may not claim him as a member of her flock, but hoped that obtaining David's forgiveness would somehow help assuage his own conscience on the matter. He held out his good hand in a gesture of friendship, repeating his apology as he did.

David was confounded by the sudden change of events from what he had expected. How should he gauge the motivations of the man? Perhaps Seely's only motivation was to get him to drop the charges, but something inside him wanted to believe that the man was telling the truth. He reached across and shook Carlton's right hand instead. The two men looked at each other: one with a feeling of redemption in his heart, the other, simply, with a feeling of relief.

"You better get out of here now," advised David. "I sent my friend to get the police."

Carlton felt that he no longer needed to run. But David warned him that given the general ill feelings about the Shoals property, any incident involving the police might easily be misunderstood by the crowd; and as he himself had said, things have a way of getting out of hand. The advice was reluctantly taken.

As he returned to the stairs, a frantic Constance greeted David. When she was unable to find David, she naturally began to fear the worst may have happened. The story he told her she initially found hard to accept, but conceded that perhaps it was in the best interests of all concerned to let Seely go. Feeling very much relieved with how the situation had resolved itself, they returned to their perch on the steps to take in the remainder of the day's historic events.

# CHAPTER 16

A fateful Friday arrived. Rather than remain in Charlestowne to watch the parliamentary proceedings to run their course, David and Constance elected to return to Monmouth Bay and observe the happenings from there. Each had their reasons for the decision, both spoken and unspoken. Constance cited work commitments, saying that she wasn't able to properly close up affairs at the office before leaving for school. What she would not say was that she didn't want her father to see her cavorting with the enemy should Mahernum's side now gain what seemed like an undeniable victory. No matter what she may have said in the past publicly about their relationship, she was still 'daddy's little girl', and still very respectful of his feelings. David, for his part, while reasonably certain of that victory, was nonetheless more of a realist. He didn't want to stay around should the GAMBBy's call in all the political favors he was equally sure they may be owed. He wanted to remember Mahernum's followers as they were, enthusiastic and confident of the chances for victory, in perhaps his last such memory of them. He had resolved however, to remain by the radio as the tally of the vote was broadcast.

    When the hour of reckoning came at last, David chose to be alone. He sat listening to the radio in the study at Buxton with a brandy bottle beside him, ready either to lift a glass in a toast to belated justice, or else drink to the demise of the establishment and its profligate lineage of self-perpetuating institutions. Presiding over his watch was the portrait of Hannah Taylor. Seeing the ever-radiant confidence of her smile, he wondered anew about the stories about her, given his recent experiences. If Rhonda Tovey, the grand dame of the Old Guard, could go against everything she outwardly stood for and aid Mahernum's cause, even if only in spite, that showed no one was beyond hope.

The radio announcer broke into regular programming with a feed from the close of the debate in Parliament. The Speaker of the House called the role and the vote was recorded as being for Option 'A', 'B' or 'C'. After almost an hour, the final count had Option 'C' winning on a simple majority of eight slim votes. David raised his glass with a smile and shouted: "Yes!"

They had pulled off the practically impossible. Within moments, the telephone rang as Constance called her voice singing with excitement. He invited her over so that they could pop open a bottle of Francis's finest champagne but she declined. She was still waist-deep in boxes and paperwork; they could always celebrate the victory after the dinner party at Hatherleigh that night.

Thus feeling gratified with how events were finally ending up, David went ahead and confirmed arrangements for his departure on Sunday afternoon. Since Constance was unavailable, he chose to spend a few of his last uncommitted hours on the island in the company of Bill Redditch at his pub.

David sat at the end of the bar, staring out from the comfortable shade of the bar onto the open vista of deep blue waves and sky. As was their habit, he and Redeye were engaged in idle speculation, talking about nothing in particular. Their ramblings were interrupted as Billy's nephew came into the pub and approached.

"Mind if I join you?" asked Warren.

"How you doin'?" greeted Billy.

"Just fine Uncle," came the reply; but he wasn't smiling.

"Have a seat," added David as he pulled out and patted a barstool. "Off duty?"

"As the only doctor for thirty miles around, I'm never off duty. My nurse knows where to find me." He chose to remain standing.

"Guess you won't be drinking with us then?" joked David.

"You're right, on that small matter at least."

David finally caught on that their visitor was bothered by something.

"Doc, you gotta learn to relax, lighten up."

"Why?" came back a less than friendly response. "I'm quite happy with the color of my skin."

"Now Doc, you know I didn't mean it that way."

"Warren, what's wrong with you?" In jumped Billy. "You know the man was just tryin' to get you to relax."

"Uncle, I'm going to have a talk with this man before he leaves our country. Would you mind?"

Billy took the hint, excusing himself. David lowered his head and slouched forward onto the bar top; he was reasonably sure that he knew what was about to come. Warren finally sat down.

"I heard you helped that madwoman Mahernum Foster organize that foolish demonstration."

"Hey! She may be a little theatrical, but I can assure you, she's far from mad."

"A matter of opinion," replied Warren with a sneer.

"That 'foolish demonstration' as you put it, was far from foolish. Or haven't you heard who won?"

Warren shook his head. "I think that they'll find that winning the vote is only the beginning of their problems. Managing a project of that size is very difficult, perhaps it's even beyond their...abilities."

"What is this, sour grapes?" asked David.

"You know I'm stating fact."

"But at least she's trying to reach out to help folks here that need help. All you people were doing was trying to make money for yourselves!"

"I don't know how you come by your information, but I can tell you that nothing could be further from the truth. You're supposed to be a journalist—I would have thought you would have checked your facts a little more closely! Our proposal had provisions included that would have benefited those very same people you claim to care about."

"But there's the big difference. While you and your business partners make a show and *say* you care, Mahernum really does!"

"Mr. Llewellyn," he sighed, "I'm not here to play at semantics. When exactly are you leaving our island?"

"...This Sunday. I have an afternoon flight to Miami."

"And Constance?"

"I think you already know she'll be on the same flight. But hey fella, if she hasn't told you that herself, then it's not my job to let you know her business."

Warren at this point looked as though he was going to blow his tightly controlled lid, but he managed to suppress his seething emotions. He took off his glasses and began vigorously rubbing the lenses with a handkerchief.

"Mr. Llewellyn, I happen to love that woman very much. Can you say the same?"

David didn't hesitate to reply: "Warren, I think I can say that I love her every bit as much as you claim to. But more than that, I hope and believe that in time, she will love me as much as I love her."

"Love? You think you *love* her? You've been in this country for a few short weeks…and you *think* you've fallen in love? What do you know of our people, our traditions? I offer her a good life, here amongst her own people."

"Oh come on, she's told me what you've offered her. You want her to be the little barefoot woman who's home to cook your meals and raise your children."

"What's so wrong with that?"

"Doc, if you can't answer that question, after all the years you've known her, then she's right: you don't know her! She wants to be her own woman. She wants to accomplish something by herself, on her own merits."

"Oh, is that was she's told you?"

"Yes, and I'm sure it's exactly what she's told you."

"Well Mr. Llewellyn, that's the voice of the child Constance you've been listening to. You're right, I have known the woman for years. I know her better that she knows herself. I know that she doesn't have a clue about what she wants to do with her life. All you've heard is the voice of the child, rebelling against everything she knows, everyone she knows, and everything she is. It's a phase she's going through. When she is ready, I will be there to give her life direction."

"You think so, huh?"

"I *know* so," he said calmly. Warren put his glasses back on and stepped back. "I will be here, waiting for her when she realizes what's truly important in her life. I will be here when she returns home. I will be in her life long after you're a memory. And believe me, Mr. Llewellyn, that day will come…very soon. Have a pleasant journey home."

Having had his say, he got up and left the pub. Billy waited a moment before he returned with two clean glasses that he promptly filled; he couldn't help but overhear some of what was said.

"Bill, the Tourist Board isn't going to like this."

"Like what?"

"He didn't even invite me to come back to the island."

Billy laughed half-heartedly as he reached across the bar to grab David's shoulder. Despite the obvious attempt at humor, Billy saw that his friend was clearly troubled by what had been said.

David remained at the bar until it was time to return to Buxton to dress for the going-away dinner party. He had arranged for Constance to drop by and pick him up around six, and they would go together as a couple to Hatherleigh. In the back of his mind, he hoped and expected that this would be the first of many such outings to come. He gave no credence in these thoughts to any consideration of what Warren had said. Her immediate and long-term future, he was sure, was inextricably linked to his.

Constance arrived at Buxton Hall a little after six, looking as spectacular as ever in David's eyes. She was wearing a short, strapless white dress, remembering as she did that David had only Brendan's borrowed white dinner jacket to wear.

"This way," she added, "we'll look coordinated."

"You can make anything look good," came a compliment, "even an overweight thing like me."

"Oh stop it. There's nothing wrong with you that diet and a little exercise won't cure." She rubbed his stomach. "Ready to go?"

"Yes, but first, I have something for you…"

He produced a small, gift-wrapped box about six inches long. Inside was a glimmering diamond tennis bracelet he described as 'a gift of friendship, whose brilliance matched the sparkle in her beautiful brown eyes'. The present had the desired effect, Constance was overwhelmed; she fell into his arms as they embraced in a long and tender kiss. As he fastened the bracelet around her wrist, she leaned forward whispering warmly in his ear: let the Tovey's have their old, droll party without them. They were going to celebrate Mahernum's victory anyway, but why not have their own party, just the two of them, right here in Buxton Hall tonight? Her invitation was what he had wanted to hear for a long time, but since this get-together was to be in their honor, no matter how reluctantly, they were still obligated to go.

"Okay David, if that's what you *really* want. Let me touch up my makeup before we leave."

Constance made her way down the corridor to the first floor guest bathrooms. As she stood admiring the way the bracelet lay so nicely on her wrist, a dark shape reflected in the mirror surprised her. She turned around, but she was alone. For the briefest of moments, she thought she had seen a woman behind her. Jeanna wore a black dress often, almost as a uniform. She thought Jeanna had come in, but then she remembered David telling her that Jeanna didn't usually work late on Saturdays. Anyway, she closed the door and put the matter out of her mind and finished freshening her make-up. She turned to leave but was in for another surprise: the bathroom door wouldn't open.

"Okay David," she called out, "now's not the time to play. Open the door, we'll be late."

After what seemed like an eternity of waiting, she began to bang on the door with her hand. When that effort proved futile, she took the metal top off an ornamental tissue box holder and banged loudly on the door with that. A minute later she gave up and sat down on the commode lid; she didn't want to work up a sweat. She sat for perhaps another five minutes before David finally arrived, knocking on the door.

"Connie? Are you still in there?"

"Of course I'm in here!" She got up and walked over to the door; she tried the door handle again. This time it opened without a problem. "…Oh very funny."

"What do you mean?" asked David.

"Why'd you lock me in the bathroom?"

"What?…I did no such thing, I couldn't have. See, there's no lock out here."

She made a point of looking. "I was stuck in there. The door wouldn't open. Didn't you hear me making all that noise? I was shouting and banging on the door!"

"…I didn't hear a thing."

"Where were you?" she asked.

"I've been down the hall the whole time, waiting for you."

"And you didn't hear me?"

"No, I swear Connie: I didn't hear a thing. But hey, that's hardly surprising, this door's pretty solid. Maybe it absorbed the sound. I only came down here to hurry you along. We haven't got much time."

"You don't think I know that?"

Before he could answer her, an eerie, uncomfortable feeling overcame him. Strange things were beginning to happen in the house, once again.

"David, what's wrong? You've got the oddest expression on your face."

"Nothing, nothing's wrong. Look, let's get out of here. We're already late."

The incident at the house was quickly forgotten once they were underway, their thoughts turning fully to the night ahead.

"It'll be almost strange to see Rhonda again," began David, "seeing how she actually helped Mahernum to win the vote, that is. Do you think we should…thank her?"

"I don't know. Maybe we shouldn't say anything at all. I think she might prefer it that way."

"*Noblesse oblige*, I guess. We wouldn't want to embarrass them," he continued sarcastically, "or make them feel uncomfortable."

"Oh David, I wish you would stop that. They're basically good people. You've made up your mind that they're ogres, out to control everything including the island's supply of coffee beans."

"Now you're making it sound like I'm the one with a problem."

"You don't trust them, do you?" she asked.

"I have no reason to. But tell me more, I didn't know about the coffee deal. Are they trying to corner the coffee market?"

"You're not serious…"

"No," he laughed. "Just exercising my warped sense of humor."

David rested his arm on the back of Connie's seat as they drove. The march on the capital and the little incident at the house were quickly forgotten as giggles and innuendo filled the air. Possibilities for the night to come filled David's imagination. But first, they had to get through the dreaded ordeal of Rhonda's dinner party.

The lady of the house herself met them at the entrance to the great home; strangely enough, she explained that she had given most of the servants the night off. As David stepped into the foyer, a shudder of remembrance caused him to pause a moment; this was the first time he had been at Hatherleigh since the night of the fire. Though thinly camouflaged, the smell of fresh paint still lingered in the hallways, and was the only evidence that anything out of the ordinary had happened there at all. It all served mightily to rekindle his memories of the fire, awakening some partially forgotten feelings.

Rhonda did not allow him to tarry long in the past with his thoughts; she took his arm and led the way down the corridor to the first floor library. She informed her guests that cocktails were planned first, with a little surprise to follow. Most of what was being said however, passed right over David's head. He turned to stare down the other end of the hallway towards the Chapel one last time before they entered the library, and the door closed behind them.

"Mr. Llewellyn," began Rhonda, "you know everyone here."

Brendan, who had been talking with William Tovey, called out a greeting to them both: "Connie, David, good to see you! I was beginning to worry you guys might've changed your minds about comin' out."

"Brendan," replied Constance coyly, "how could we do that? This gathering is in David's honor after all." She tapped David with her elbow.

"Uh…Yeah, we really appreciate your going to all this trouble. There's no way we'd miss it. Mr. Tovey," he called over to his host, "good to see you again."

William returned an awkward greeting, appearing not to remember David. He nodded his head then quickly turned to Constance, complimenting her on looking 'absolutely marvelous'. Rhonda picked up on the sentiment, as she voiced her admiration of Constance's dress.

"It must be something you picked up in America," she said. "I haven't seen anything quite so interesting in the stores here locally."

Constance confessed that a friend had sewn the dress from a photograph she had provided from a high fashion magazine. Rhonda professed to be very much impressed by the workmanship, and made Constance promise an introduction to the seamstress.

"Excuse me ladies," interrupted Brendan, "but since I'm playing barkeep for the night, what'll it be?"

"You first dear," prompted Rhonda, "you're my guest."

"Thank you." She turned to Brendan: "Can you mix me up a martini?"

"In a partyin' mood, huh? Good...but why don't you try some of this." He went behind the bar and took a metal pitcher from a small refrigerator. "It's a punch made according to an Old Irish recipe."

He proudly poured out several glasses of a dark beverage, garnishing each with a slice of lemon.

"To tell the truth, I had to modify the recipe a little bit because of trouble I had findin' good Irish whiskies hereabouts. So I took into account our Caribbean locale, and flavored it with ginger and three different rums," he said handing the glasses to William, Constance and David. The offering was gladly accepted. "But the end effect, I think, will be much the same. I know you're gonna love it!"

Constance was about to try some of the exotic concoction when she noticed there was someone without a glass. "Rhonda, you're not going to try some?"

"Perhaps later. Rum can be such an indelicate beverage. It simply doesn't agree with my constitution. I'll stay with my Madeira, thank you."

"What's that?" queried David.

"Madeira? It's a fortified wine some of we older folk enjoy," she replied slowly.

"Oh...Well, Mrs. Tovey, you don't know what you're missing," David commented after downing a third of his glass. "This stuff is pretty good."

The alcohol in the beverage began to quickly do its work as the assembled guests began to cheerfully settle into the fine art of polite dinner conversation.

"So will you miss our little island?" asked Rhonda.

"Most certainly," replied David. "But I'm still working on that piece I mentioned about my vacation here, and the recent history of the island."

"Oh, that sounds interesting," she exclaimed. "Hopefully, it will bring attention to the wonderful history and lifestyle we have here."

"That's just what I hope too."

Just then, someone knocked loudly on the library door.

"Ah!" smiled Rhonda. "That must be my surprise."

With a full glass of sherry balanced precariously in hand, she hurried almost gliding over on tiptoes over to the door. "Come in, please. It's so nice of you to join us."

In walked Francis Gordon Hurrell, formally attired in white dinner jacket and silk scarf, black tie; he had a long, unlit cigarette in hand. Rhonda took his arm as she walked him in.

"I believe you know everyone. Here's my surprise everyone! I heard he was in Charlestowne and decided to invite him over."

"So *that's* why you didn't want me to tell Brendan!" exclaimed David. "Good to see you."

In an instant, Francis became the center of the room's attention as they all came over to greet him; everyone that was, save for Brendan. He was astonished at the sight of his friend. The two men had not seen each other for several months; Francis's newly lean appearance came as something of a shock to him. Brendan made his way over slowly.

"Francis," he began, "it's been a while." He was unsure of what to say with everyone standing around; he extended his hand in welcome. "It's good to see you, man."

"Yes," was his quiet reply. "Good to see you too."

"Gentlemen," Rhonda took both men by the arm. "Let's not forget there're others here tonight. We all would love to hear what new theatrical project the world-renowned Francis Hurrell is planning to bring to the stage."

"Yes," agreed William. "Tell us what's new in the world of the stage."

"Oh by the way," interrupted Rhonda, "William's real estate group has added the construction of an outdoor center for the performing arts, as part of a development proposal. Enlisting the support of someone with your credentials would be quite the feather in our caps!"

"Yes, that's right," added William, sounding a little unsure of himself. "We'd like to get your thoughts on the idea."

It was then that Rhonda noticed the sparkling bracelet on Constance's wrist and left no doubt of her admiration of it. When Constance described it as a 'token of friendship' from David, all eyes turned to him for such was the quality of the gift. His brief and unsuccessful attempts to deflect their mostly unspoken speculation left nothing but smiling faces all around.

The mood for the evening was thus set. It was a little after eight o'clock when the announcement was made for dinner. Rhonda gathered together her guests and herded them through a set of double doors to the adjoining dining room.

David walked in and was immediately surprised by the room's sheer size and furnished elegance. The grandeur of an age long passed was evoked; the polished cherry wood dining table alone was large enough to accommodate a dozen or more people.

Rhonda seated everyone at the table in a fairly predictable pattern: David was seated next to Rhonda, with Constance diagonally across the table next to William Tovey; Brendan was next to David, a few spaces down. The gaunt-faced Francis sat on Rhonda's right. Dinner was brought in almost immediately and served by the house's remaining servants with almost a military precision. Rhonda informed her guests that the night's menu was to be American in style as a hearty green salad was brought in to begin the meal. David expressed his pleasure at the sight, stating that he had not even seen a romaine lettuce since he'd left home. He sat back in his chair, quietly taking it all in, feeling very gratified and impressed that they had gone to all this trouble. In fact, his enthrallment was such that Francis felt it necessary to prompt him to join in on the conversation.

The main course was also much to David's liking, as his hosts had a magnificent roast of beef as the entree. Most of his meals during his stay on the island had been either white meat or the catch of the day from the Caribbean, which was okay since he could stand to lose some weight. But a nice juicy steak with all the fixin's was something he had found himself fantasizing about. He was beginning to believe that the Toveys must have read a personal dossier on him, for the meal was also accompanied by one of his favorite wines, a vintage, robust Red Burgundy; it couldn't have been any better if he had died and gone to Heaven.

The only blemish on the magnificent repast were some odd-tasting bread rolls that Rhonda proudly proclaimed as coming from an old family recipe of her own. She got up from her chair when the rolls were brought in and personally handed them out with a pair of silver serving tongs to each of her guests. David couldn't decide if it was the savory herbal flavor or something else, but the bread definitely left an aftertaste. He wasn't the only one to notice, as other faces expressed surprise at the taste. None of this escaped the hostess's attention. Rhonda explained that the herbs used came from a time before sugar was common in Europe, and consequently the rolls were probably healthier for them.

Nevertheless, the drinks continued to flow freely. After two brimming glasses, David began to refuse more of the punch; it was going straight to his head.

"...I really must be out of it," he let out a slurred observation. "My head is spinning. I can usually hold my liquor a lot better than this. Mrs. Tovey, I really cannot have another drink."

"Oh nonsense," she replied. "You're amongst friends. If it comes to it, we'll either put you up here or I'll have Kennedy drive you home."

"I think he'll have to take me home too," added Connie, her eyes barely open. "I feel like I could curl up and go to sleep in the middle of the floor."

"Do you want to lie down?" asked Rhonda. "There's a couch in the next room."

"You know," Constance replied, "that really sounds like a good idea." She stumbled as she got up. Brendan hastened to lend his assistance and within moments, she was gone to the world.

David looked on, barely able to keep his eyes from closing. At the other end of the table, he was able to make out the figure of William Tovey. The old man was still sitting upright in the chair, but his head was bowed, his jaw almost resting open on his chest.

"Mr. Tovey, are you okay?" he tried to ask the question.

David arose unsteadily from his chair intent on finding out for himself but couldn't make it another step; his hand reached back for the table. Again, help was there. "Hey man," he asked Brendan, "where'd you come from?"

"Relax Davie," was the reassuring reply. "You'll feel better after a short nap."

"*Uh*, yeah. Maybe…a nap will help." He began to prattle forth apologies meant for anyone that was listening. "Wow…I'm sorry. I've never gotten drunk so easily before. I'll be fine…"

"Is he out yet?" Rhonda asked Brendan as she bent over her husband, loosening his tie.

"Looks that way. How's Mr. Tovey doin' over there?"

"He's unconsciousness," she replied, dutifully checking his respiration and his pulse.

"I gave him half the dosage I gave these two," assured Brendan.

"I know, but he's takes several medications regularly. I want to make sure there's no harmful interaction."

Brendan moved from David to check Constance again; she stared long into her face before announcing that they were both out cold.

"Excellent. I'll have Kennedy bring the car around. Brendan: why don't you call Ethel to clear the table after we get them in the car. Remember to mention that we're taking your friends home, that they've had a little too much to drink."

"Whatever you say."

"She's right." Francis finally spoke up. "We've got to start establishing the story line now. I've arranged for an entry to be placed on a hotel registry down the coast in Falmouth."

"How's that?" Brendan inquired.

"They'll be checked into and out of the hotel register as soon as I make a telephone call," replied Francis. "As far as the world is concerned, they went from here to spend their last night on the island together in a romantic rendezvous."

Their last night: Brendan hesitated, feeling decidedly uncomfortable with Francis's choice of words. But he kept his silence. He chose to take Rhonda at her word that no harm would come to David or Constance. After all, wasn't this attempt to recreate an old Celtic ceremony not much more than a parlor game for them?

He looked on. To be sure, Rhonda and Francis had acquired some very interesting artifacts but they were pieces of metal, trinkets just the same. And yet, across the room were two very serious people, who revealed not the slightest hint of levity in their purpose. The moon, which had risen pale and bright above the horizon, was now shining in through the dining room windows. Time was of the essence. What Brendan had once indulged as little more than an old woman's fancy, now was beginning to take on a whole new, quite serious light.

# CHAPTER 17

Two vehicles made a guarded return trip to Buxton Hall. Kennedy drove his mistress and the three sedated sleepers in the Bentley limousine; Francis planned to follow a discrete distance behind with Brendan in a rented Range Rover. As he was getting into the car, Brendan noticed the white, woolen robes and other paraphernalia that would be used in the ceremony, and some other closed cardboard boxes in the back of the car.

"What's in those?" asked Brendan.

"Some pieces from Rhonda's private collection. They'll add a touch of authenticity to the ceremony. Most of these artifacts are well over a thousand years old."

"I guess they'll qualify as real antiques. But what's the pole back there for?"

"I really couldn't say," replied Francis. "This show is all Rhonda's production. I'm just following her lead."

"Did she tell you about the gold torc David found at Buxton?"

"Ah yes, that. You know, I must've been down in those caverns a dozen times, and I've never even seen so much as a bug crawling around."

"Guess it must be the dumb luck of a tourist," affirmed Brendan.

"Most definitely. I mean, who would ever have thought that there'd be another entrance to the caves in the wine cellar? We'll have to go down one day and take a good look around."

"Could be interestin'."

An uneasy silence overcame the two. Occasional glances passed a series of unasked questions from Brendan, questions for which Francis had long been preparing and practicing his answers. The stalemate continued until the driveway lights of Buxton Hall came into view.

"So Frank," came the long-delayed question, "how long have you guys been plannin' this?"

"Now keep calm…"

"Keep calm he says!" scoffed Brendan.

"There's nothing at all to worry about."

"That's easy for you to say."

"Brendan, really. No one is trying to hide anything from you."

"Then why didn't you fill me in? When did you decide to come to town?" He stopped the car abruptly halfway the driveway up to the house. "What're you and Rhonda really plannin' for tonight?"

"Brendan, just relax guy." He turned completely in his seat to face him. "You're absolutely right. We should have kept you better informed." He reached over and began to encouragingly massage Brendan's shoulder and neck. "Forgive me."

"It would be nice to know what's going on," replied Brendan. "That's all."

"Yes, I should've told you I was coming. I'm sorry."

The apology was quietly accepted.

"Great! Now we've got to get moving," he said looking out the window at the moon. "It's time to set up for the ceremony."

They followed the course of the road around to the rear of the estate and walked from there down to the grove, lugging the boxes and assorted paraphernalia the rest of the way. The wind was beginning to pick up noticeably, causing a commotion to build in the branches of the trees. Ahead of them, in the clearing near the old sundial, they could see Rhonda's man Kennedy building a huge bonfire.

"Why are they setting up there?" inquired Brendan, looking visibly agitated.

"We want to create as authentic a setting as possible. Many groves were sacred to the Celts. Being in harmony with Nature was vital to every aspect of their lives."

"Yeah," Brendan grunted in reply. "Harmony…"

As they drew in closer, they saw what anyone surely would have taken as a strange sight. Laying very still, face up on the grass were the unconscious bodies of David and Constance. Nearby, William Tovey was sitting propped up against a tree, his head still drooped in unconsciousness; his jacket, tie and shoes had been removed. Not far away, Rhonda was throwing off her clothes into a pile as she hurriedly put on her costume as the 'High Priestess' for the rite; she turned her head as she saw their approach.

"Hurry you two! Take off their clothes, and bind their hands and feet," she ordered, pointing to Constance and David. "Do it quickly now, we haven't got much time!"

"Why tie them up?" Brendan issued a challenge to Rhonda.

"For their own good. We need to draw a little of their blood," answered Francis stepping in. "We don't want them waking up and thrashing around. They might hurt themselves."

Brendan reluctantly complied. The somber task was scarcely accomplished when Kennedy came hulking over. Rhonda whispered animated directions to him. He complied, positioning the unclad bodies face down with feet touching and heads apart, such that their bodies formed a 'v' pointing to the sundial. He then returned to William to finish undressing him. With the fire now crackling bright as it burned, Brendan noticed a small red and white ice chest that seemed very conspicuous by its presence. While he stood wondering what might be in the chest, Francis began to shed his own clothes and get into his costume. Before Brendan could say another word, Rhonda came up from behind him and grabbed his arm. Her transformation was complete: she was now dressed in full regalia. The long white robe she wore was secured at one shoulder by a large, gleaming silver ornamental brooch. A woven crown of fresh flowers adorned her head. Her hair was brushed back in a twirl, held in place by an ancient ivory comb.

"Isn't it a beautiful night," she raised her eyes to the dark sky above in exultation. "Listen to the whispering voices of the wind. Can't you feel it?…The gods of old are with us again, awakened from their long, blissful sleep. Do you hear them Brendan: can you hear their voices?"

"Oh yes…I can hear them," he replied, deciding to humor the old woman. He looked back to Constance and David on the ground and saw Francis kneeling over them, pouring something thick that glistened like oil or honey over their bodies. He then began to help Kennedy empty large bags filled with flower petals, throwing them high into the air; the entire area around the sundial was quickly covered. The night had been full of surprises thus far; Brendan didn't know what quite to expect next.

"Have you ever seen a moon so full and bright before?" exclaimed Rhonda, waving her arms wildly in her ecstatic ramblings.

"Not in a long while," replied Brendan, "it's an eerie sight."

"Eerie?…Nonsense! It's a magnificent omen of good tiding," she smiled, nodding her head. "Tonight will be a success."

While Francis was busied laying everything out for the ceremony, Brendan stood staring in amazement at how his friend was now dressed. He had witnessed the Society's ceremonies before, but they had never gone so far in their attempt to capture the look and feel of the age; the night was definitely taking on an air of the bizarre. Francis had smeared a blue substance on his face and bared chest, and daubed his head with some kind of thick, white mixture that made the little hair he had stand up on end. He was wearing a loin cloth with trouser-like leggings secured by thongs of leather, while around his neck was a short cape of tanned leather, fastened by another, very ornate brooch. He summoned Brendan over and gave him a bundle of similar clothing that was hesitantly accepted; it was time for him to get into the appropriate attire.

Francis then began to light the first of three torches from the bonfire, setting one each in the ground near the head of David and Constance. The third torch was set at the far side of the sundial.

"Kennedy!"

Rhonda called him over. He had been carefully sharpening both ends of the wooden pole they had brought with a machete. The two spoke briefly; he stepped over the now petal-painted bodies and stood at the sundial. He then squatted low as if bracing himself for an almighty effort, and began to turn the sundial on its base. The strain of the labor was heard from both man and machine, as the dial began slide off its pedestal. A few seconds later, as the dial cleared the base, Francis brought a torch over to reveal a huge bowl-shaped object in the deep, dark depression below. Francis handed the torch to Brendan, then leaned over and rapped the side of the bowl with his knuckles in several places; a heavy, metallic ring resounded each time.

"…Appears to be still completely intact."

Brendan stood in amazed, wide-eyed silence.

"The Cauldron of Bran," announced Rhonda gleefully. "Hannah Taylor's most prized possession."

"But," stammered Brendan, "that's just a story…The Cauldron of Bran is a *myth*. You can't think that old tub down there's the real thing?"

"I most certainly do! Ah, you should see it in the light of day," she smiled. "Even tarnished by the passing of uncounted years, the quality of the craftsmanship is simply astounding."

"Oh come on now, it's probably a fake made up by some old Victorian shyster!"

"No," Francis contradicted. "I think not. I had it checked out myself. It's made of an ancient silver alloy formula, and the panels on the sides are inlaid with gold. The style of the workmanship and the motifs used are clearly from a very early Celtic period."

"Okay, okay…So maybe the thing is old enough, but it *can't* be real. Don't you people understand: Bran's Cauldron was just a *legend*."

Francis simply sighed and shook his head. He returned to his task of filling the cauldron with another huge sack of the same flower blossoms, and another sack of largely unrecognizable roots and herbs. Brendan looked over towards the bonfire and saw that Kennedy had placed two boxes on the grass. One was large, the other a smaller wooden box which the big man opened by sliding off the top. He moved closer, curious to see what they were. The flames from the fire leapt wildly towards the night sky, revealing in the dancing light the contents of the boxes. The large box contained a mallet and what looked like ancient hand tools, the other, the golden torc that David had discovered.

"This was Hannah's other prized possession," Francis said as he held up the torc. "I believe this to be the fabled collar of the hero Cu Bodicaa. It's verified by my scroll. The shape and markings on the torc are identical to those described by the Roman soldier and historian, Marcus Caecilius. It has the power to restore speech to the Awakened."

The Awakened? Brendan felt suddenly a sickness building in the pit of his stomach; he didn't want to even ask what Francis was talking about. But then, Francis produced another object from the boxes, something that changed the night forever.

"Now hold on!" he shouted. "You don't need a knife like that to take a little blood." He turned to Rhonda angrily. "You promised me no one would get hurt!"

"And no one will be hurt," she replied, raising her eyebrows.

"Then what the Hell do you need that thing for? Okay Rhonda, this has gone far enough!"

Brendan started towards her, but suddenly one of his legs cramped and gave out; he collapsed to one knee, then both. He couldn't stand up.

"At last!" triumphed Rhonda, jubilantly watching his difficulties. "I was beginning to wonder if I'd put enough of it in his food."

As soon as the words left her lips, Brendan realized that he had been betrayed. The next instant, a rope was wrapped tight around his throat; he was being dragged him backward!...It had to be Kennedy. The rope was knotted and pressed in right against his Adam's apple; he was choking. He couldn't fight back. His body felt inexplicably weak, his lower limbs were losing all sense of feeling. He couldn't utter a sound; he was sure that he was going to die.

"Your pain will not last long," assured a wide-eyed Rhonda. "The bread rolls I gave you tonight had a very special ingredient: a preparation called *Cymell Hun*. It's a very ancient formulation I've tempered with linden and sage. Eventually, it causes complete paralysis of the central nervous system."

Francis turned and walked a few steps away, unable to watch.

"Kennedy, not there!" screeched Rhonda. "Take him over by the cauldron. Finish the job there."

"Wait! I'm not finished setting up yet," interrupted Francis. He hurried over to the small ice chest and took out something like a ball wrapped up in multiple layers of clear plastic. It was a few moments before Brendan's eyes could focus again; Kennedy held him like a rag doll, helpless in the hold of the garrote. His eyes began to tear from sorrow when he realized what Francis had cruelly taken from the chest.

"Ah yes," began Rhonda with an unmistakable sense of triumph in her voice. "I see that you recognize the lady. But I think perhaps, you've seen her looking a lot better."

It was Ellen Wainwright's disembodied head; the long, chestnut-brown hair hanging down from Francis's hand confirmed the shame. He proceeded to mount it unceremoniously on the sharpened pole, which he then pushed into the soft ground.

"I know you liked her Brendan," continued Francis, "but it's important to have such a witness to the ceremony. She was a member of the Society, she would have understood. It is by her sacrifice that the ancient gods will return from their sleep, and honor us with their presence tonight. It is through her eyes that the gods will bear witness to this great homage we do them, and grant us our wishes tonight."

"It's in his Roman's manuscript," added Rhonda in a condescending remark. "Your death, dear Brendan, will not be for nothing. The three of you will be sacrificed, so that the three of us may have health and youth restored to us."

She looked down at the bound duo on the ground and saw that David was beginning to stir, and ordered Francis to make sure he was securely tied. David was indeed beginning to awaken prematurely from the sedative. But he had been given the same poison administered to Brendan and even if fully conscious and untied would not have been able to do much. The confirmation came from Francis: David would not get free.

"It's too late for him anyway. Too late for any of them. Constance, well dear, it is indeed a pity; you weren't bad company. But I will have a fitting revenge on your father. You should all be happy your sacrifice will have meaning. Now come on Francis, let's get on with it!"

While David's vision was blurred, there was nothing wrong with his hearing. He had been listening to what was going on as he slowly regained his consciousness, but only now did he begin to comprehend that these people were bent on murder! He tried to move but the ropes were too tight. His head was reeling, his mouth was dry; he couldn't understand why he felt so weak. He lay panting on the ground, trying in vain to roll over, struggling now just to catch a breath

Francis nervously took the gilt-handled ceremonial dagger and held its point skyward, uttering in old Briton the beginnings of a final consecration. He then took a horn filled with water, carefully pouring it along the fine, sharpened edge of the black iron blade. Rhonda looked over to Kennedy, preparing to give the signal to end Brendan's life. He pulled taut the ends of the rope, ready to give the garrote a final twist. Francis returned with the heated blade and held the edge ready.

"His death must come in three ways: by poison, by the rope, by the knife," Rhonda declared. "Are you ready Francis?"

She received an affirmative nod, and raised her hands skyward to the moon. "I call upon the spirits of the earth and sky, I call upon the spirits of the wind and sea: Bear witness, I beseech thee, to this our humble sacrifice and find it worthy. Restore to us the vitality of youth now gone. Great spirits, we bid thee to listen to our words. Grant us now, by blood three times shed, the gift and full bounty of life and health." With that last entreaty, she pronounced a terse, final sentence on Brendan: "Cut his throat."

"Remember Brendan," Francis stuttered, "…remember always that I loved you."

This professed declaration of love angered Brendan; all he could think of was the betrayal of his friendship. He fixed on Francis's cold blue eyes and fanned that anger instantly into an all-consuming fury. The rope suddenly tightened, choking off his air. It was now or never…He let out a grunt of rage and pushed backward with all his might, sending both himself and Kennedy tumbling backwards over David's prone body. They crashed onto the sundial!

Kennedy began to gasp and gurgle as his lungs filled with his own blood: the point of the sundial was buried deep in his back. His hold on the rope relaxed.

Freed from the grip of death, Brendan fell to ground, his fingers frantically loosening the rope around his neck.

"You goddamn fools," Brendan gasped. "You don't know what the Hell you're doing!"

"You've killed Kennedy!" Rhonda stood aghast.

"Shut up you old hag!" yelled Brendan hoarsely. "The ritual can only be performed at the time of the *Lugn Asad*. It's weeks away. You two are amazing. You do the homework…even find the cauldron, and screw up the simplest detail. You almost had it, Francis…But harmony with the natural world is only one part of the rites of the *Dubh Gwrach*."

"What?" asked Francis.

"I know the rites of the *Dubh Gwrach*: the Black Witch…and the secret of life everlasting. You'll need more than a blood sacrifice to draw upon the power of the Cauldron."

"Life everlasting…"

"He's lying!" interrupted Rhonda. "He doesn't know anything!"

Brendan sat back against the sundial's pedestal, laughing briefly before breaking into a bout of coughing. "Does the name Siann Mack mean anything to you?" He didn't wait for an answer. "Well, you're lookin' at him."

Rhonda and Francis were dumbstruck by the revelation.

But abruptly, Brendan's expression changed as his body was racked suddenly with pain. Almost frantically, he attempted in vain to stand but he couldn't get his legs working underneath him. "You fools…Get me to a hospital! Your ceremony here's a farce. It ain't gonna work. All you'll do is kill those two…and create a big, bloody mess here. You've seen the photograph of Karl Heinz in town. Well people, you're looking at him too! Help me get me to a hospital. I'll show you how to conduct the ceremony…And show you how to do it right!"

Rhonda was the first to react: "He's lying Francis…He's making the whole thing up to stop us. Finish him."

But Francis would have none of that. "No Rhonda…Look at that face. *It is him!* He is Karl Heinz Wilhemenius."

"Shut up!" shouted Rhonda. "You're desperate enough to believe anything."

"Look at him Rhonda. He always knew just a little too much about Rhonda…About the legend."

All of a sudden, Brendan collapsed. He lay helpless on the ground like a fish long plucked from water, unable to move. "Too late," he gasped. "It's too late for me…I killed the children. I killed all those kids to get the ceremony right. I killed a lot of people so that I could live forever with *her*. Then she went and died on me. I couldn't bring her back…Now, you're gonna take my life, hoping to cure your ills…And," he laughed, "you ain't even doing it right."

"He's babbling. Francis, finish him off!" shouted Rhonda. "Cut his throat!"

Francis readied the knife. With trembling hands, he lifted Brendan's head and placed the sharp edge against his throat. Slowly, he brought the knife back, and then dropped it on the ground. "No Rhonda," refused Francis. "I can't do this!" He knelt over his friend, cradling Brendan in his arms. "He could be telling the truth…"

"What are you saying?" she asked in disbelief.

"Brendan's right. This has gone far enough," he replied shaking his head. "Rhonda, it's over."

"I knew it!" she shouted back. "You weakling! You coward! I knew I couldn't depend on you."

"That's enough! We are not going through with this."

"No," she whispered to herself. "I will *not* let you destroy our last chance."

She walked over to pick up a mallet, concealing it behind her. As Francis leaned forward, consoling Brendan with his regrets, she rushed forward, striking him as hard as she could on the side of the head; he fell forward in a heap across Brendan's legs.

"I don't need you," she cried out. "I can do this all myself!"

She snatched up the knife and held it pointing up to the night sky, calling out in a Celtic tongue for some ancient deity to grant her wishes. Clutching the handle of the knife with both hands, she brought the blade crashing down into Brendan's chest, screaming her delight when she had done so.

Rhonda got quickly to her feet, her neck, chin and robe splattered with blood, and rolled Francis's unconscious body off Brendan. She summoned every ounce of her strength to drag her sacrifice by the arms over to the cauldron.

"Don't worry William," she said, straining to speak. "The gods have granted me the might to do what I must do. You will soon have the vitality and pride of your youth restored to you…I swear it!"

She fell to her knees as she struggled to push and position the bleeding body so that the blood flowing from his wound would fall into the cauldron. But the blood was still flowing too slowly for her purposes; she decided to cut his throat and lift his torso to hasten the stream. The same fate would then befall the other two, as she intended to fill the cauldron in readiness for the ritual bath in blood.

As Rhonda reached to pick up the knife to complete the task, she halted halfway through the motion; there was someone else in the grove. She raised her head slowly, convinced that there was someone watching from the shadows of the tree line. Sure enough, she was able to make out the solitary figure of a tall woman in a long dress.

"Who's there?" she shouted. "Come out, I said! I know you're there. Show yourself!"

She picked up the knife carefully, gripping the long handle firmly; no one would stop her now! She walked then charged forward ready to kill, but stopped abruptly short of the tree line; she knew who the woman was.

"You! It must be…It is you."

The woman held out her left hand.

"What is it?…You want the dagger? Take it, it's yours!"

Rhonda handed the knife to the woman as if it were an offering.

"You're here to help me, aren't you? You've come back to help me finish the ceremony, haven't you?"

The woman slowly shook her head.

"Then, why have you come?"

The woman transferred the dagger to her right hand, and then very deliberately, began to raise it high.

"No! You can't…"

Rhonda turned to run but only take a few steps; she clutched her chest in pain and fell face first to the ground. Her heart was pounding furiously, erratically; the pain was like huge, sharpened claws ripping at her chest from the inside. She cried out in fear as she realized she was having a seizure. She began to crawl back on her stomach towards the bonfire, the pain growing greater with every terrifying moment.

The soft grass and earth welled up in her face, filling her nose and mouth as she now struggled desperately to get away. The specter was somewhere behind her, coming for her, bent on taking her life. But it was too late, her time had come. In the end, she could not escape from herself.

The tall woman dropped the knife on the ground by Rhonda's side, then moved in silence across the grassy heath, pausing here and there, searching the stilled faces of the fallen. It was only then that David became aware of the strange woman's unexpected presence in the grove. He struggled to lift his head to see who the stranger was but could not, and so followed her progress as best he could. The woman's quest seemed to come to an end as she reached Brendan's body, a few feet away. She knelt down by the corpse and began to shed tears of sorrow, sobbing her regrets in mumbled words that David could not fully understand. But the loss that was mourned was not that of Brendan Costello, for the name that was so sorrowfully spoken, was not his.

The woman's weeping caused David to open his eyes again. He managed to move his head a little, but he was still unable to see very much more of her than a shadow. He seemed to sense that she meant him no harm, and fought to form his lips to shape words seeking the woman's help; she must have heard his plea, for within moments she was by his side. She knelt down on the grass beside him, and began to stroke his hair tenderly. He tried again to raise his eyes to see who this was that had come to his aid, but a hood concealed most of the woman's face. Speaking in a soft, still quavering voice, she told him to rest, saying that help was on the way. She told him that she would have to go now, but promised to return and see him when he was well again. As she prepared to rise to her feet, locks of long red hair fell dangling from beneath the hood; the bonfire suddenly flared, bringing to light the gentle, elegant features of a face he knew well. The timeless, reassuring beauty of her smile would be his last memory of that night.

There was a witness to aftermath of the ceremony, but only from afar. Jeanna had been given the night off, but returned to the house that night with her husband to get a bag of groceries she had left behind. While he sat out in the car, she noticed what appeared to be the glow of bonfire burning in the grove from the kitchen window and called the local police. A constable arrived very quickly. The three of them began to walk down towards the grove, fearful and uncertain of what they might encounter out there. They all had heard of such things before, and were reasonably sure they knew what was going on; the big black limousine parked on the back road only confirmed their suspicions.

Nevertheless, they were totally unprepared for the ghoulish scene of carnage they were confronted with. At first, they thought everyone was dead: bodies were strewn all over the place. Jeanna recoiled in revulsion when she saw Kennedy's upright figure bloodily impaled on the sundial, then screamed loud in horror at the terrible sight of Ellen Wainwright's head stuck up on the pole.

The constable sent both her and her husband back to the house to call for more help; nothing he had experienced in his many years on the police force had prepared him for this. He could not even imagine what these people had been doing to be dressed the way they were. In absolute disbelief, he began to count aloud the number of corpses then added one more to the tally, as he looked reluctantly again upon the disembodied head.

Only after a moment did he move from where he stood; he was afraid of disturbing the integrity of the crime scene. He began to look around, apprehensively searching the ominous darkness of the bushes and the trees. He was uncertain about what had happened, or who the perpetrator or perpetrators might be, and more importantly, where they were now. But he quickly gathered his wits and pressed forward to check the bodies to see if any were alive.

He was surprised to find that only two were dead for sure. A young man with a bloody knife wound in his chest did not seem to have much of a chance, but nevertheless, he carefully removed the knotted rope from Brendan's neck. He could only guess at what had happened to him. By that time, Jeanna's husband had returned to the grove. After a quick check of the others, he sent him rushing back to the house to call for an ambulance: three others were alive.

Within minutes, the back of the house was lit up by the rotating red and blue lights of police and ambulance vehicles, as the bonfire began to slowly burn itself out. Warren Stephenson had been called in and was able to revive William Tovey. He was convinced that Constance and David had been poisoned; their very survival depended on getting them to a hospital in Falmouth in a hurry. An emergency helicopter was sent for. As for Francis, his poor health only served to amplify the severity of his head injury; his chances were pessimistic at best.

As the helicopter took off, the swirling wash of air from its rotors sent leaves from the trees flying out in all directions. The police immediately set about the earnest task of their investigation. Laying covered up on the ground were three dead bodies; each life had apparently met a violent end.

One of the police officers found a tightly sealed plastic package in one of the sacks filled with flower petals. Upon opening it, he discovered a crystalline, white powder that was almost certainly cocaine. There was more than enough going on here to warrant a call to the central government; a major criminal investigation would have to be undertaken. Given who was involved in the mayhem, the implications spoke of a conspiracy that might be international in scope.

Although William Tovey was revived, he could tell them nothing; he sat on the ground, staring over at the covered body of his wife in a muted, muddled state of shock and disbelief. It was quite apparent to everyone there that the full truth of what had happened in the grove that night might well never be known.

# CHAPTER 18

David did survive that night, but he lay slipping in and out of consciousness in a hospital bed in the Falmouth General Hospital for several days. He eventually regained full consciousness to find catheters set in one of his arms; a plastic tube was uncomfortably fed down his nose into his stomach. When he was able to think clearly, foremost in his thoughts were the whereabouts of Constance. The hospital workers were permitted to ease his mind and tell him that she was alive and expected to fully recover, but that was all; he guessed that the police had become involved. At one time, when his door was swung fully open, he saw a uniformed police officer stationed on guard: for his protection, he was informed. He somehow doubted that story.

It was another two days before he was allowed to learn the fate of the others. The attending physician judged him well enough to remove the tube and begin eating normally again; the return to normality extended to other matters. He was told that an investigator from the government's Home Security Office wanted to speak with him; a time was arranged. Despite assurances that he had nothing to worry about, David was very concerned, for he knew that they were the equivalent of the FBI back home, and the investigation was not something to be taken lightly.

From the investigator, David learned fully of the tragic aftermath of the farewell dinner party. Mrs. Rhonda Tovey was dead. The same was true of Milton LeRoy Kennedy, her chauffeur, and their described 'associate' Brendan Costello. The disclosure of Brendan's death visibly shook David; the investigator paused a moment to allow him to come to grips with the news. From there, he continued, the story got even stranger. Some person or persons unknown had broken into the mortuary and stolen Brendan's body before an autopsy could be performed. The question was asked but not answered; David knew nothing that could reveal who or why the body had been stolen. That, explained the policeman, was the reason why there was a guard stationed at his door.

And then there was the extraordinary circumstance of Mr. Francis Gordon Hurrell. He had died in the hospital after succumbing to complications from his illness and injury, but only after making an incredible "deathbed confession". The validity of certain details of that confession was what the authorities wanted to confirm. David stated up front that he probably would be of little help, as he had virtually no recollection of the events of that night. But the investigator insisted that he at least hear the story, hoping that he would recall some helpful detail. He next told David of the manner of Rhonda's death, of how she appeared to be vainly trying to escape from someone. The revelation sparked an ember in David's mind, as he recalled a fragmentary memory of the woman that appeared vision-like to calm and comfort him. He would say nothing to the detective of her.

Francis told the police where they could find a journal that would tell all. Before he died, he named some obscure person in the New York Theater world as the heir to his estate, since Brendan had preceded him in death. The journal described the details of Francis' entry into the conspiracy. He had learned a year or two earlier that his illness would cost him his life, but only after draining his body of its vitality, and with it, much of his desire to survive. His writings admitted knowing that he had discovered his illness years earlier than he had previously acknowledged. He had bought the old house at Buxton Hall only after hearing the remarkable tale of Hannah Taylor from a friend who had been vacationing on the Island. His journal told of his sheer desperation. Though some might call it grabbing at straws in the wind, he hoped to discover Hannah's secret of youth eternal with the single-minded goal of beating the odds doctors had given against his long-term survival.

After searching and researching every inch of Buxton Hall, its grounds and Hannah's legend, he quite by accident discovered the mechanics whereby the sundial in the grove hid what he took for the Cauldron of Bran. The Cauldron was renowned in Celtic mythology as being empowered with the ability to restore life to the dead, though without speech. He debated the idea for a long time, but the thought of living the rest of his life as a virtual zombie held little appeal. Things dramatically changed after he met his neighbor, Mrs. Rhonda Tovey. Her collection of ancient Celtic silver pieces and her superior knowledge of the period convinced him to confide his discovery in her.

Rhonda was delighted, and wasted no time in divulging to him the existence of the Society of the Stone Circle, and a lesser known side of the fable of Bran's Cauldron. It was said that when a certain ceremony was performed and a golden neck torc was used in a sacred blood rite, all infirmities of the living would be cured and the aging process halted. Indeed, she even suggested that repetition of the ceremony could remove and reverse years of aging from the old. Thus, Rhonda's motivation. They put together the saga of Hannah and the discovery of the Cauldron in the grove with the ancient Celtic legend. The tales of the disappeared children in Hannah's day served to cement the confidence of both.

They resolved to find out all they could about the ancient ritual, with the goal of re-enacting the ceremony down to the smallest possible detail. Thus, the participants, or sacrifices, were to be of Celtic blood or heritage. On his return to New York, Francis acknowledged that he had a singular goal in mind: a search for a suitable victim to sacrifice. Sacrifice was mentioned, for the blood sacrifice of human beings was called for by the legend. New York City, it has been said and he was sure, had amongst its inhabitants people from throughout the world, all with their own philanthropic or political groups. Francis found David's name in the roll of honorees of the Cymric League, a social organization of persons of Welsh or Brythonic Gaelic descent, and set about getting to know him. David Llewellyn fit the bill perfectly, for he was single and free of any other close, permanent relationships. That was where Constance came in.

The next revelations were hard for David to accept. According to Francis, Constance was the 'honey" to be used to attract David. She was instructed to keep David engaged and distracted, but wasn't given full knowledge of the plan. The same was originally true of Brendan, but things grew increasingly complicated there for Francis. Other happenings on the island began to take control of events as the controversy over Blagdens Shoals erupted. They were still looking for the third sacrificial victim in New York, when the impending government takeover of the estate evoked bitter memories in Rhonda. She and husband William were instrumental in the formation of the Old Guard, but her agenda apparently differed from the other members of the association. She was goaded into action because of the much-ballyhooed inclusion of Constance's father in the group set up by the Greater Antilles Merchant's Bank to develop the Shoals property. Her hatred of Norman Lorrha now saw an outlet in a chance for revenge. Not only would she take away his beloved daughter, but she would ruin the man's reputation by despoiling his daughter's memory in the cloud of an illegal drug scandal. That part of the scheme could not have been easier. After all, was not one of her very closest friends currently serving time in a U.S. prison for drug possession?

The journal was proof of Francis' dying confession, and served to clear the others of illegal drug and conspiracy charges. David, Constance and even Brendan: all, it seemed, were pawns in an insane and deadly scheme begotten in the minds of two very desperate people.

David attempted to find out the price extracted by both Brendan and Constance for what despite all else, he now saw as his betrayal. The detective was unable to answer that question. He told David that the confession had cleared him from criminal charges, but the rest of the investigation was continuing. As he prepared to leave the room, he couldn't help but notice the dejected expression of the man laying on the bed and out of pity, decided to do what he could to lift his spirits. He reminded David, that all else considered he was extremely fortunate to still be alive.

"Thank goodness for small favors," was David's reaction to his supposedly good fortune.

He watched the detective leave, and then rolled over in his bed symbolically turning his back to the world. He had expected that knowing the truth would have lifted the burden of betrayal, but far from relief, he was left feeling very much alone. The voiceless silence that ensued in the room caused him to sink further into his blue melancholy mood. He was feeling down on life and on all types of relationships, but mostly he was down on himself. He lay in bed for hours without moving, nibbling insincerely on the soft foods the nurses brought in for his recovering stomach. Occasionally, the once-cherished image of Constance's smiling face would creep into his consciousness, only to be chased away by the stinging indignation of a man feeling he had been used and lied to. But gradually, the memories of that night in the grove began to return.

Later that same day, the sullen quiet of the room was broken by the arrival of a visitor. At first, David refused to see anyone, but the nurse chided him, telling him that he was going to see this person whether he liked the idea or not. He would be glad that he did.

Into the room walked a wide-eyed but slightly subdued Mahernum Foster, bearing in her small arms a 'get-well' gift in a plain brown cardboard box. She set the box aside momentarily as she leaned over to greet David with a gentle hug. He hugged her back, glad at last to see the face of a true friend.

"It's good to see you too," she said as she gently pushed the hair back off his forehead. "How are you feeling?"

"Oh, lousy in a word. I've been poisoned and stabbed in the back."

"Stabbed? I didn't see—I mean, they didn't say anything about a knife wound."

"I'm sorry, Mahernum. I didn't mean it that way. I was speaking about…Connie and Brendan."

"Oh, I see," she said pulling up a chair. "Did you *er*, hear about Brendan?"

"If you mean do I know that he's dead…Yes. And I've also heard about the theft of the body."

"Oh. Well, those people must be mad. What would they want with that poor boy's body? It's a shame he ended up that way. I've known Brendan almost since he came to Grand Kirkmuir, must be four or five years now. He was at heart, a good man."

"A good man? Mahernum, he set me up. He pretended to be my friend. He set me up to get killed! He got exactly what he deserved."

"Now you can't mean that."

"I as sure as hell do! Boy, am I stupid; I should have known. They've been shepherding me around, manipulating my every movement ever since I came to this godforsaken island!"

"Hush!" she ordered, physically preventing him from sitting up. "Doctor's orders: you're not to get overexcited."

"Then let's not talk about them."

"Not even about Constance? I just came from her room. She was asking about you."

"So what? Look, I don't want to hear her name again."

"Oh, it's like that is it?"

"Like what? Mahernum: she was in on this! She was a part of this…this jackass plot from the beginning. And you want to hear the funny part of it? I fell for her hook, line and sinker! I would've done anything for that woman…Anything."

He repeated the sentiment again as his anger melted the wall of reserve that previously had welled up tears of self-pity. Mahernum consoled him as best she could.

"Yes, let it out, boy. Shed those tears and let them heal your heart."

He was embarrassed to the point of blushing to have shed real tears in that way and struggled to regain his outward composure.

"I'll bet she had some good laughs at my expense! I told her things…I unburdened my soul to her, and she was in on the plot to kill me."

"Now David, that's not so. She told me that she knew nothing of their true plans!"

"Of course, she'd deny anything to stay out of prison."

"Now stop that, immediately! Just in case you'd forgotten, Constance is also a patient in this hospital, that crazy old woman tried to kill her too."

"Oh we only have her word for that."

"No David, that's not so. I was there."

"What? I thought you said—"

"That's right, David. I said was there…"

She had indeed been at the grove that night. Mahernum began to explain why. After hearing David's increasingly vivid descriptions of his encounters with the tall woman, she admittedly became very much intrigued with the story. She remembered an old woman named Sophia Martin in the Hill Country, who had lived in the Buxton parish as a child. She would make the claim, to anyone that cared to listen, of having a special knowledge of Hannah's legend but no one really paid her much notice.

On a recent journey up to the Hill country, Mahernum decided to seek out and ask this woman what she might know of Hannah Taylor, but couldn't find her. However, the old woman heard that Mahernum was looking for her and went to Charlestown to hear her speak. They eventually met, and Mahernum was treated to a tale of an Obeah Priestess named Cajuil. Sophie said that her own grandmother, who swore that she had witnessed everything as a child, told the story to her.

Cajuil was a tall woman, fine of features with jade-green eyes and skin as black as the night. She mysteriously appeared one night in the deep forest during the festival time of the high-god Huru Kan. She came boldly into the midst of the gathering dressed all in white, riding on a ghostly white mare. No one had ever seen this woman before; her arrival caused a hush to fall upon everyone, the chanting and the dancing ceased. She slid down off the horse and strode up to the sacred fires, boldly proclaiming herself as the living daughter of Huru Kan, demanding the loyalty and obedience of all. The high priest stepped forward, angered by the gall of the woman. Carrying the ceremonial machete that was the symbol of his authority, he began to slowly approach Cajuil, hurling threats and blasphemies her way. Everyone was afraid. He intended to kill this woman that threatened to usurp his rule. But as he got to the altar, the fire roared up out of the pit: Cajuil pointed at him and screamed out a curse. The man fell down dead where he stood!

No one ever challenged Cajuil after that; no one dared. She picked up the machete and held it high for all to see, and then disappeared into the night on that white horse. She was only seen thereafter on the sacred festival nights, and ruled thereafter supreme.

"But what does all this have to do with your being there at the grove that night?"

"*Shh*! David, have patience. All things in time. But first, you must understand the whole story."

One night, in the frenzied celebration of an offering to the gods, Cajuil took the blood of a chicken from the altar and smeared it all over the white headscarf she wore on her head. Calling together the faithful, she announced that they were about to bear witness to a miracle. Thus saying, she pulled off the headscarf and threw it onto the ground revealing to all a full head of long, fiery red hair. Cajuil walked down from the altar to the accompaniment of silence; she threw her head back and let out a shrieking laugh. She declared that the great god Huru Kan had turned her hair red, to signify to all her lineage as his daughter: she was the living blood of the sacrifice. The throng immediately began to shout their adoration. She was in their eyes, Huru Kan, born again into the world of men, reincarnated as a woman.

But there were others of Huru Kan's priesthood who were not at all convinced of her legitimacy. She was an interloper who had used a few spectacular tricks to confuse the people; they conspired to end her reign. The next time she appeared, they were ready for her. Cajuil rode hard after she left the ceremony but horses leave tracks, and hers were followed; the trail led up to the old stables behind Buxton Hall. It was then clear to all who she really was. The scarf Cajuil had left behind was examined; a long black mark was left at the hairline. The smell confirmed that it was the residue was of burned cork.

"Burned cork…Makeup?" asked David.

"Apparently so."

"Hannah?"

"That's what they said," confirmed Mahernum. "That might certainly explain part of the legend. You remember the claim that said that she 'took off' her skin at night."

"But, the story's just…too crazy."

"What do you mean?"

He pushed himself up. "Look Mahernum, she had everything she could possibly want. Why would she get involved in *voodoo* rituals? For the thrill?"

"I can't answer for the way people think or act. Maybe you've answered your own question."

"Well, if that story is even half true, it calls into question most all of the tales I've heard about Hannah Taylor."

"It also raises questions about her death."

"What do you mean?"

"We can get into that later. But I was going to tell you about why I was in the grove that night."

"Ah, I'd almost forgotten."

"I was coming over to see you that night, to thank you for all you'd done the last few days, and to tell you the story of Cajuil. I saw the bonfire at the back of the house and I was going to join you, until I saw everyone except Rhonda, laying on the ground. Lord Jesus," she shook her head. "At first, I thought you all were dead! I started to run to get the police. I was almost out of the grove when I heard a woman scream: it had to be Rhonda. I went back part way. I saw Rhonda laying on the ground, she wasn't moving."

"And that was all you saw?"

"No.... There was something else."

"Or some*one* else. Did you did you see her?"

"...I can't swear to it, but I thought I saw someone else out there. For a moment, I thought I saw a woman walking into the trees."

"Hannah," sighed David in vindication.

"Maybe so," Mahernum added with a smile. "Hannah or Cajuil."

"You know, she came over to me when I was on the ground. Mahernum, I saw her face, she touched my head and spoke to me."

"My God!"

"No, it wasn't like that. She was kind to me. She knelt down and told me that help was coming. She was absolutely beautiful."

"But you've always described her as evil."

"And I thought she was. But I don't know who that was or what those dreams meant. Perhaps they were a warning against what eventually happened in the grove. It makes sense now. I think she tried to stop us from coming that night, when Constance got locked in the bathroom. The woman that came to me in the grove was the woman pictured in the portrait at Buxton."

He looked over at Mahernum and saw an expression of sympathetic doubt building benignly in her eyes. "I know," he said, "you think I saw what I wanted to see. Maybe I did, maybe I dreamed that visit too. But she seemed very real to me. She touched me...I remember the softness of her hand. And there was something else."

"What?"

"It was kinda strange, but before she came to me, I think she was kneeling over Brendan. She called out a name that sounded like 'Sian'."

He was certain that was the name he had heard; there would be no changing his mind on that. Mahernum knew only that he had suffered through a very traumatic experience, and thus saw no reason to raise the poor boy's blood pressure. There was a knock on the door: a nurse poked her head in to announce the end of visiting hours. Mahernum stood up in preparation to leave.

"The doctor said you should be well enough to leave here by the weekend."

"Yes."

"So, will I see you again before you leave the island?"

"Most definitely. I'd like to talk about this Cajuil story."

"*Aha*, so it's gotten your attention?" she smiled.

"It's done a lot more than that."

"Good. I'll get in touch with Sophie. And what about Constance?"

"…What about her?" he asked.

"Well, I'm sure she has a lot to say to you."

"Is that what she said?"

"More or less."

"Oh."

"So, you will talk to her?"

"If," he paused, "she wants to talk to me."

She laughed aloud and gave David a hug. "*If* she wants to talk to you, is it? Well Mr. Llewellyn, for a writer," she quipped, "you sure are tight with the spoken word."

## End

978-0-595-39202-
0-595-39202-4

Made in United States
North Haven, CT
24 November 2022

27184529R00119